ABOUT THE AUTHOR

Jeanné Olivier is a British–South African author dividing her time between Haslemere in the UK, and Mossel Bay in South Africa. *The Girl in my Dreams* is her debut novel.

Crane & Leeu Press

First published in Great Britain in 2024
by Crane & Leeu Press.

Copyright © Jeanné Olivier 2024

The right of Jeanné Olivier to be identified as the Author of the Work
has been asserted by her in accordance with the Copyright,
Designs and Patents Act 1988.

Editing: Eleanor Boyall at www.rjlocksley.com
Cover Design: Samantha Sanderson-Marshall at www.smashdesigns.co.uk
Typesetting: Laura Jones-Rivera at www.lauraflojo.com
Marketing: Vickie Boff at vickieboffconsulting@gmail.com

A CIP catalogue record for this title is available from the British Library.

eBook ISBN - 978-1-7385761-0-4
Paperback ISBN - 978-1-7385761-1-1

Published by Crane & Leeu Press, Great Britain

The Girl in my DREAMS

JEANNÉ OLIVIER

Crane & Leeu Press

To Amy, and to Riaan, always.

CHAPTER 1

M y eyelids rebelled against being pulled apart. It took a while for my brain to convince them to cooperate.

Reluctantly my pupils started to focus. I was lying on my back, in the middle of a dark road. I felt disoriented and uncomfortable. Shadows mutated in the moonlight. I screwed my eyes shut and took in a slow breath. On my second inhale, I opened my eyes and sat up. I removed my helmet and scanned the area around me.

My motorbike—or what was left of it—was lying on its side, also in the middle of the road, broken pieces scattered around it. I looked down at my legs. They were fine. I lifted my arms and twisted them up and down. Also fine.

A mangled black Mini fumed on the side of the road halfway up the muddied kerb, the driver's door open. Something felt off. The air was too thick. And what the hell was that sound? Was it humming?

Movement to my left caught my attention. Nina! The most gorgeous girl I had ever met. The girl who stole my breath and scrambled my brain every time I saw her. She was sitting on the verge. Her chin rested on her arms as she hugged her knees. I staggered over and collapsed next to her.

"Oliver," she whispered. "What happened?"

"We were in an accident." I crossed my legs and rubbed my hair around on my head before I looked at her properly. "Are you hurt?"

"I don't think so." She twisted her head to face me. I took in a sharp breath. Her soft blue eyes were glowing bright yellow.

"What…" I rubbed my thumb and forefinger in my own eyes.

"What happened?" she asked again.

"We were in an accident, Nina," I repeated softly and gestured at the mess in front of us.

"Oh." Her eyes flitted over the broken scene. "But… I was just at your gig, wasn't I?"

"Yeah…" Vague images of performing in the Guildberry tried to form in my head, but floated away without materialising.

"I think we… I…" She trailed off. A fragile expression crossed her face and an overwhelming urge to comfort her made me lean over to touch her shoulder, but my hand stopped mid-air. Blood was oozing from a cut on the side of her face. It painted a thick line all the way down to her chest.

"Nina!" I fumbled for my mobile to call for help. "Your face!"

"What?" She started scooting away from me. I dropped my phone back in my pocket and tried to cup her face to inspect it, but she shoved me away and pushed to her feet, stumbling back a couple of steps.

"I'm sorry." I put my hands in the air before getting up as well. "I want to make sure you're all right, okay?"

"I'm fine!" Her voice trembled. "Are you okay?"

"Yes! I don't know." I pulled on the ends of my hair. "I feel… strange."

"Me too." She reached for my hand and I took a step towards her.

My breathing slowed as we faced each other, but I felt sick with fear. Something was off. Way off. My lungs struggled to shift the heavy air. I still couldn't pinpoint where the hell that humming was coming from. Perhaps it was ticking, actually. I wanted to tell Nina that we really should call for help, but my words evaporated. Everything inside me centralised around an inexplicable need to comfort her. To protect her.

For a moment her glowing yellow eyes and bloody face didn't even register. My arm snaked around her waist and I closed the space between our bodies as my mouth crashed down on hers. I held the back of her head with my other hand, drawing her even closer as I devoured her mouth with a desperation I had never felt

2

before. I pulled away after a few beats and my eyes connected with Nina's.

I tried to scream, but my lungs were two solid concrete blocks. Nina's terrified eyes were still blazing yellow. Blood was still seeping from a wound on the side of her head, soaking her white top in a dark mess. Her lips turned blue. She tried to speak, but blood bubbled from her mouth. She reached out to me, but I collapsed before our fingers touched.

CHAPTER 2

I was aware of a rhythmic tick harmonising with a steady hum before my eyelids started to pull apart again. The smell of antiseptic irritated my nose and my throat was on fire. Everything hurt.

Panic threatened to overwhelm me, but my muddled brain remembered that I wasn't sixteen anymore. My heart burned at the memory. I was twenty-three now. This wasn't then. This didn't feel good. But this wasn't then.

I dragged my eyes over my surroundings. Light grey room, dimly lit. Heart monitor, ticking to my right. Oxygen monitor, humming to my left. Torso, strapped into a tight brace. Wires and tubes, protruding from around my body. Halfway down my bed, slumped over the edge, my sister Sophie, her fingers entwined with mine and her chestnut hair matted around her face.

I untangled my hand from her grip and brushed the hair from her cheek. She let out a sleepy mumble before her eyes flew open and she sprang upright.

"Oliver!" She folded herself awkwardly around my left arm and started sobbing as she buried her face in the space between my arm and my body.

"Water," I croaked, trying to pat her back. She sniffed as she sat up and wiped her eyes before she reached over for a cup of water on the bedside cabinet. She placed the straw between my lips and I sucked deeply for a few moments. "What time is it?"

"Just after four." She looked at her watch. "Sunday morning." It confused me, but she carried on before I could calculate the days in my head. "I was afraid you were never going to wake up." She started crying again and covered her face with her hands.

"What happened?" I rubbed a hand over my own face.

"You were in an accident." She pulled several tissues from a box on the cabinet as she mumbled, "Thursday night," between blowing her nose.

Thursday? Two, three days ago? What the hell? The questions tumbled through my mind, but before they could order themselves enough to come out of my mouth, a memory of Nina settled in my gut.

I was working behind the bar when she whirled through the door like some mystical damn fairy. Or something a bit more wicked, perhaps. My heart missed several beats when I realised it was her. I wasn't sure where the hell she'd come from, but it seemed like she was everywhere I bloody looked recently. It was the seventh time I'd crossed paths with her this week. This was the first time we'd come face to face, though.

She leaned over the counter to place her order, but her eyes widened and she took in a long breath. She recognised me as well.

The oxygen left my lungs when I noticed that her eyes were the same ridiculously light, almost translucent, blue as mine. I didn't know why it felt so significant. I'd obviously seen lots of people with blue eyes, but I didn't think I'd ever met anyone whose eyes were quite as pale as mine. She noticed it too and stood there staring at me without saying a word. She didn't even blink. I knew at that moment that this girl was seared into my soul.

The tiniest of grins tugged at the corner of her mouth before her lashes flicked downwards and she pushed her hair behind her ear.

I screwed my eyes shut and cleared my throat when Sophie took my hand in hers again and pulled me from the memory. "What's wrong with me?" I nodded at my body.

Sophie swiped her cheek with the back of her fingers to catch a new trickle of tears before her eyes flicked down to my legs. I immediately realised that my head was pounding, my throat was on fire, my ribs strangled my lungs every time I took a breath, but I could not feel my legs. At all.

"I'll go and tell them that you're awake." She pushed herself up, but I tried to grab her hand.

"Is it permanent?" I whispered, but she just shrugged out a heavy sigh.

"Right." I nodded, allowing an unsolicited tear to slide down my own cheek as well.

"Morning, Oliver." A nurse with a tight grey bun and a friendly smile appeared. "Welcome back, dear. See, Miss Lawrence, I told you he just needed a bit more time." She pulled a tablet from the end of my bed and waddled over to my side, checking readings on monitors. "How is your pain?" She adjusted some settings.

"My head… and my chest…" A snippet from the Guildberry played through my head again.

"Come on, Ols." Kellan slapped me on the back.

"In a minute." I sprayed the counter and wiped it down.

"Go on, Ollie. I'll do it. You need to get up early." Jack stuffed my share of the evening's tips into my hand before he started wiping the same spot I'd just cleaned.

"Thanks, Jack." I grabbed my jacket and helmet from the back.

"You need to be there for ten. The ferry leaves from Portsmouth at eight."

"Yep." I shrugged on my jacket.

"Isle of Wight is a big deal, Ollie. Don't fuck it up." He made his eyes wide as a smirk almost tugged at his cheek.

"I know." I grinned, pulled up my zip and turned around.

"Have fun." He laughed and I lifted my arm in a backward wave as I headed out to join Kellan and Charlie where they were leaning against Ian's van. I felt my pockets and cursed when I couldn't find anything. Ian joined us and handed over my cigarettes, one dangling from his lips.

"I was looking for that." I frowned.

"I borrowed them earlier when I went outside with that blonde with the nice…" He gestured at his chest. "You know, the one who used to work at

*the gym, Kel." A smirk rippled across his cheek as he looked at his brother. I
rolled my eyes. "Do you know what else I saw while I was outside with…?"
Ian gestured at his chest again, blowing smoke from the side of his mouth
and wiggling his eyebrows at me.*

"I don't know, Ian. Her arse?" I sighed.

"Naturally. But I also saw Nina getting into a right strop when she left."

*"Yeah?" My heart missed a beat. I couldn't remember ever being so
affected by a girl. She'd been on my mind all week and I couldn't keep my
eyes off her this evening. "Why?" I asked before I could stop myself, but then
told myself to at least try and maintain some dignity. They didn't need to
know the extent of my sudden and unwelcome obsession.*

*"No, never mind. I don't care," I huffed and Ian shrugged as I stepped on
my cigarette. "I'm going home." I swung my leg over my bike and put on
my helmet as they started filing into Ian's van. "See you in the morning." I
flipped my visor down.*

*"We're picking you up at six!" Kellan called from the window. Charlie
waved and Ian hooted as they drove off.*

"Dr. Harold will be here to see you shortly." The nurse forced my
attention back to the present. "The pressure will start easing soon."
She adjusted the IV again and patted my hand before she squeezed
Sophie's shoulder and hurried out of the room.

"Do you know what happened?" I turned my head back to
Sophie.

"You were on your way back to Haslemere when you crashed
into a car," she started, but the memories became clear in my mind
before she finished her sentence.

*It was just past midnight, so the traffic through Guildford was still hectic,
but the minute I hit the A3 the road cleared and I opened my throttle, flying
down the road towards Haslemere. Before I reached the Hindhead tunnel, I
swerved left into the Brook turn-off.*

*I loved that road. It was bloody magical at any time of the year. In
autumn, it was covered in a blanket of rusty leaves that fluttered up and*

lingered suspended in the air before floating down lazily whenever I sped past. In winter, the naked tree branches glistened as they poked at the bitter sky. And in spring, it felt like riding through a tunnel of daffodils.

That night, in early June, there were clear skies and the almost too-full moon that hung low above the treetops made the lush forest next to the road glow. I instantly felt happy to be alive and opened my throttle a little more, letting the sensory overload of the club leave my body.

I geared down and went around the last bend, realising too late that there was a car in front of me.

Right in front of me.

Everything started happening in slow motion. I lifted off my Ducati and heard the metal screech and glass scatter as I coasted over the car and looked down at its deformed shape. Nina levitated between the front seats and the shattered windscreen. The sound of cracking bones drilled through my ears and the air burst from my lungs as I landed on my back on the other side. I thought I heard Axl whine in the distance about not having any hopes or dreams, but the stars started going blurry and then everything went quiet.

"Soph," I whispered. "I remember. I crashed into a car on the Brook Road." Images of Nina's face moving towards the windscreen flashed through my mind again. "Nina! Nina was in the car. Is she okay?" I tried to struggle up and Sophie put her hand on top of mine, the frown deepening between her hazel eyes.

"Shh, Ollie, breathe, okay," she said and I tried to take in a breath. "I don't know, Ollie. I heard she's in a coma, but don't know anything else."

"Can you find out?" My voice was slower than it should have been. The drugs were pulling on my eyelids already.

"Okay, Ollie, shh. Just rest now, okay?" She patted my hand.

I must have fallen asleep after that because when I looked at Sophie again she had changed her clothes and brushed her hair. The room was brighter too. She put the cup of water to my mouth even before I asked. I carefully pushed up on one elbow and sucked it empty in a few gulps.

"I've told the guys you're awake." She smiled weakly and I felt an unwelcome panic stir in my gut. I couldn't let them see me like this. I couldn't face them. Thankfully a doctor entered the room and saved me from freaking out.

"Morning, Oliver." He looked to be in his early, perhaps mid-, fifties. "My name is Malcolm Harold, head of neurology." Fine lines creased his face as his green-brown eyes smiled at me. He reminded me of my dad. An unsolicited warmth settled in my chest. "Has the pressure in your head and in your lungs eased at all? How is the pain?" He shone a light in my eyes and I had to force myself not to jerk my head away.

"It's better than before." My voice came out flat.

"Are you feeling confused? Any memory loss?" He moved his fingers in front of my face so that my eyes followed them from one side to the other.

I couldn't help turning my head away. "No."

"Good, good. So"—he took in a long breath—"your limbs are intact, which is unusual for a motorcycle accident, so that's certainly positive. You do have a hairline fracture in your skull and we've had to relieve the swelling in your brain with a small incision at the base of your skull, but hopefully you should only endure these headaches for a few more days. It's important to let us know if you feel any nausea or confusion." He paused until I nodded. "You also have five cracked ribs. None of your organs are pierced, but your lungs are heavily bruised and it will make your chest feel very tight.

"Right, your back." He sighed and I held my breath. "You've sustained an incomplete burst fracture to the L4 and L5 lumbar discs in your spine."

I zoned out. I understood what "fracture" meant, but the rest meant fuck all to me. I never understood why doctors couldn't speak in plain English, or any one of the other languages I spoke.

"It means you have a broken spine, Oliver. The two lower discs are cracked in several places, but not shattered apart entirely. At the moment your legs are paralysed, but like I said, the fracture appears to be incomplete, which means the vertebrae could still be attached in some places. I'd like to send you for further MRI scans now that you're awake and the inflammation has come down a little. I'm hopeful for confirmation on our best option."

"Okay." I pursed my lips as a strained breath escaped from my nose.

"Are you happy to continue?" He lifted an eyebrow and I thought it was the most moronic question I had ever heard. What the fuck was the alternative? "Do you have any questions?" he asked and I wordlessly shook my head.

"You need to read through these forms and give your consent." He handed me the tablet from the end of my bed. "Somebody will be around to take you down to radiology shortly. Please do not eat or drink anything until we have the results. With any luck we can get you into surgery today." He strolled out of the room.

I closed my eyes for a long moment and took a few deep breaths. When I opened them again, Sophie was staring at me.

"You're going to be okay, Ollie." She squeezed my hand, probably trying to convince herself more than anything. I just about managed to tip my lips up into something that I hoped mimicked a smile.

"Ready to go, Oliver?" The nurse from earlier returned and looked at my tablet again.

"Yeah," I sighed as she started adjusting things around me.

"He's going to be a few hours, Miss Lawrence," she said to Sophie when another nurse appeared to help her push my bed out of the room. "Perhaps a good time to get something to eat? Some fresh air?"

"All right." Sophie bent down and kissed my head. "I'll be here when you get back."

"Thanks." I made another attempt to smile, but my heart was pounding in my chest again.

I spent the next two hours being scanned and X-rayed from all possible angles and I was beyond exhaustion by the end of it. Eventually they took me back to my room and pumped me full of pain-killers again. I was already falling asleep when Sophie walked in. She spoke to the nurse and I tried to listen to what they were saying, but I couldn't focus on them long enough to form any comprehension as I drifted off into oblivion.

When I woke up again Sophie was sitting in a chair across the room, next to the window, and came over when I cleared my throat with a painful croak.

"Sorry." She rubbed ice on my lips. "You can't have anything yet." She sat down next to my bed and stroked the hair from my eyes. "I've spoken to Dr. Harold about your test results, Ollie. He's quite positive that they might be able to repair the damage." She bowed her head and I frowned, not yet sure what she was saying. "The surgery sounds complicated and you're going to need some intense rehab, but there is a possibility that you will be able to walk again one day." A smile spread across her lips and I exhaled slowly.

I could feel the tears prickling in the corners of my eyes again and I covered my face with both of my hands until I heard footsteps enter the room.

"How are you feeling, Oliver?" Dr. Harold pulled up a chair and sat down next to Sophie.

I nodded that I was okay.

"Your sister explained that our investigations showed some promise? So, to prevent any further risk of movement in your discs I would like to perform a procedure called spinal fusion this afternoon. It means that we will repair the damaged discs before fusing them together in order to strengthen them. This method usually has a high success rate. Of course there are no guarantees, but in my opinion, this is your best option for hopefully making a full recovery." He gave me a small smile, but I'm not sure I reacted. "Are you happy to continue?"

Again with the idiotic questions. I nodded once.

"Good. Excellent. Here are some more consent forms to read through and agree to." He handed me the tablet. "Somebody will take you to the operating room now. Under the circumstances this is rather positive, Oliver."

He left the room when the same nurse from earlier returned to read my tablet and unplug the numerous machines around my bed.

"Ready to go?" She smiled, but I barely responded.

"I love you, Ollie," Sophie leaned over and I held her as close as I could. My own eyes burned as I felt her tears against my cheek. I knew she must be struggling as much as I was to accept yet another devastating accident.

"I love you, Soph." I squeezed her tighter, ignoring the pain. "I'll see you in a bit, okay?"

She sniffed as the nurse started rolling me out of the room. I lifted my hand in a small wave before we disappeared around the corner.

When we arrived in the operating room everybody was already prepared and waiting. The anaesthetist introduced herself and explained the procedure. She asked me to count backwards from ten and I started saying the numbers as I tried to focus on her soft brown eyes. I lost my train of thought and probably didn't even make it to seven.

CHAPTER 3

It was late afternoon and I was jogging along the Brook Road, close to where the accident had happened. I immediately realised that I was dreaming, but the shadows reached out to me and I pumped my legs even harder as I veered off the main road and into the forest. The thick air rolled through my lungs as I pushed myself to not think about anything but the euphoria of running.

Eventually I slowed down to a jog and a familiar humming started pulsing through my head. I scanned the area around me and stopped in my tracks when I noticed a splash of red in the meadow to my left. I probably should turn around and run in the opposite direction, but I walked closer. Someone sitting on a red chequered blanket turned to face me.

Nina. My breath caught when our eyes met. A smile curved her mouth and she held out her hand. I laced my fingers through hers and flopped down next to her, feeling all sense of time and reason leave me.

"I've been thinking of you," she said, her eyes flickering yellow.

"I've been thinking of you too. How are you?"

"I'm okay. How about you?"

"Yeah, me too," I stuttered, struggling to remember why I wouldn't be okay.

"Are you hungry?" She nudged some strawberries toward me, making my stomach rumble.

I reached out to take one, but my hand stopped mid-air. The plump strawberries from a second ago were now pieces of bloody flesh. My hand started shaking.

"Don't you like strawberries?"

I closed my eyes for a moment and let out a slow breath before I opened them again. The strawberries were back to normal.

"I love strawberries." I smiled before I popped one into my mouth, watching her as I threw the stem into the meadow behind her.

Her dark hair hung loose around her shoulders and her dense lashes cast faint shadows on her cheeks. She was wearing a white dress and it made her look like an angel. I reached over and pushed some loose strands of hair behind her ear. "You're beautiful," I whispered.

"So are you." She smiled, drawing lines of goosebumps on my face as she trailed her fingers across my jaw.

My arm curled around her waist and I pulled her closer, dipping my head to lean against her forehead for a moment before I kissed her. She was intoxicating. I couldn't get close enough to her. A soft sigh escaped her mouth as we breathed fierce promises into each other's souls.

"This is very intense," she whispered eventually and gestured between us with her forefinger as she searched my face with her eyes.

"Yeah." I inflated my cheeks and let out a long breath. "Intense." I reached around her to grab the bottle of water that stood next to the bowl of strawberries. I looked back up to offer it to her, but I gasped when she stared at me with glowing yellow eyes as she licked her lips. Her tongue was split and wiggled like a snake's.

I squeezed my eyes shut, hoping that she would be back to normal when I opened them again. I should have freaked out about the absurdity of it all, but I couldn't think about anything but being with her. Nothing else mattered. I hesitantly unscrewed my eyelids and exhaled slowly, watching her mouth curve into a sweet smile again. Not a trace of horror in sight.

"Oliver," she whispered as I pulled her closer again. I realised then that I was never going to be able to get enough of her. Every single breath I had left on this earth was going to be for her. She dragged her

14

hands over my arms and across my shoulders before she cupped both my cheeks. My skin burned where she touched me. I wanted to melt into her and dissolve into this world where it was only me and her.

"You overwhelm me," I whispered into her mouth before I kissed her again, but she pulled away and craned her neck to look over my shoulder. "What's the matter?"

"We have company." She giggled and I looked around to see geese gathering around our picnic blanket.

I struggled back onto my knees and tried to shoo them away, but they didn't move.

"Do you want some bread?" Nina laughed, pushing up on her elbows.

"Go away." I clapped my hands in the direction of the birds.

"Let's give them some." She pointed to a loaf of bread next to the strawberries and I broke off a piece and handed it to her. "Here you go." She sat up to offer it to them, but they started hissing and flapping their wings at her.

"Stop that!" I waved my hands toward them again, but more geese appeared, flapping and hissing at Nina. She reached out to pat one on its head, but it pecked her hand and she shrieked.

"Come on." I got to my feet and pulled her up with me. "We can get your stuff later."

"Yeah." She frowned, shooting a look at the geese. We started walking away, but the birds kept following us, pecking and flapping at Nina.

"Shoo." I tried to chase them off again, but they wouldn't leave us alone. I scooped her up into my arms and ran back down my earlier trail. We were some distance away when I saw a wooden gate to my right. It looked like it led into a walled garden. It was slightly ajar, so I kicked it open and set Nina down on the other side. I swung around to latch the gate behind me, but when I turned back to her, I crumpled to my knees.

In the middle of the garden, at a table, underneath a giant tree, sat my parents having bloody afternoon tea. With scones, and jam, and the whole damn lot. Nina was sitting with them. Her eyes were blazing yellow suns and blood was streaming from the gaping wound in her head.

"No!" I screamed, smacking my hand into the ground next to me.

"Oliver," Nina gasped, blood bubbling around her mouth. She reached out to me and I jumped to my feet, stumbling over.

"What's happening?" I screamed at my parents, who were staring at me with a perplexed expression creasing both of their faces.

"Come on, son. Wake up." My dad got up and wrapped his arms around me as I fell to my knees in front of Nina, pulling her from the chair and rocking her in my arms.

"What's going on?" I sobbed.

"Oliver, darling." My mum walked around the table and stroked my hair. "Open your eyes, my love."

The buzzing noise I'd ignored earlier vibrated through my body at a deafening volume and I struggled to focus on anything.

"No! Please!" I cried as I faded away.

CHAPTER 4

"**S**hh." Sophie's voice tried to soothe me, but my head thrashed from side to side.

"No," I whimpered, gasping for air and trying to push myself up. "No, no, no."

"Calm down, Oliver. You're all right." Dr. Harold's voice spoke next to me. "Come on. Settle down, lad." He put a hand on my arm and gently pushed me back.

I forced myself to keep still and tried to take a few deep breaths, but my lungs rebelled in my wrecked ribcage. My hands trembled as I covered my face. After a long moment of silence I could feel my heart slowing down and I removed my hands.

"There you go, Oliver. Well done." Dr. Harold smiled and Sophie visibly relaxed.

"Sorry," I mumbled.

"The anaesthetic can be disconcerting." Dr. Harold gave me a knowing nod. "Are you all right?"

"Yeah," I rasped. "Water, please?"

Sophie held the water to my lips, her own hands trembling slightly.

"Thanks." I caught her hand and held on to it.

"Better?" Dr. Harold asked, and when I nodded he continued. "Good. Right. We were able to repair the damage to your discs and the spinal fusion was successful. At the moment you have an epidural and you shouldn't experience any pain tonight. I'll come back in the morning to check on you and remove it. I'm expecting you to regain sensation in your lower back and hips at that stage and you're likely to feel quite uncomfortable, but we're usually able to manage this with intravenous pain relief.

"You'll have to wear the brace while the fusion heals. It will be, at the very least, two weeks and you'll need much rest until then. After I'm satisfied that the fusion is stable, your brace will be removed and you should be able to start going to physiotherapy." He stopped briefly and I nodded that I understood. "Let the nurses know immediately if you are feeling nauseous or if your headaches get worse. Also, I suggest that you try to eat as soon as you can and don't hesitate to ask for something to help you sleep. Let's not forget that you also still have a fractured skull and several cracked ribs, so like I said, rest is absolutely paramount."

"Thank you." I let out a long breath and he patted my arm before he left the room.

Sophie sat down next to my bed and buried her face in my shackled chest. I put my arm around her and hugged her as tight as I could manage.

"I'm okay, Soph." I patted her shoulder.

"You scared me." She looked up with tears in her eyes.

"I'm fine. I had a bad dream. I'm fine now." I smiled weakly. "Do you know how Nina is doing?"

"I asked one of the nurses, but she couldn't tell me much. They can't disclose details about other patients, Ollie." Sophie pressed her lips into a tight line. "She did say that Nina was stable though."

I knew that she wouldn't understand my concern for Nina. How could she? I was fully aware that my obsession with her wasn't normal.

"Okay." I also sighed and rubbed my hand through my hair.

"Tell me about your dream." Sophie squeezed my hand, probably trying to change the subject and not at all expecting that it wasn't just a normal dream, but actually the reason for my compulsive behaviour.

I wasn't really comfortable talking to Sophie about my feelings. Her solicitor's brain was too pragmatic to grasp the intensity of my emotions. But she was my sister, she loved me, and I'd had enough grief counselling in my life to know that I had to try and process my thoughts. So I took a deep breath and started talking. I told her about noticing Nina around town the week before, about briefly meeting her at the club that night, about the first dream after the accident, and the second dream after the surgery. I could still see every detail. I could still feel Nina's breath on my face. My body ached to be near her.

"Oh, Ollie." Sophie hugged me again after I told her everything.

"My connection to her is just so intense."

"Okay, but…" Sophie looked weary and worried and I could see that she really didn't understand at all. "The most important thing right now is to rest."

Luckily a nurse arrived with food before we could continue our conversation. Of course I had to rest, but it felt impossible to control my thoughts if I didn't know if Nina was all right. I knew that it was an overreaction, but I couldn't help it. Obviously I wanted to get better, but if I was completely honest, my reality didn't feel real. Not even close. My reality felt more like some screwed-up nightmare and these dreams felt more real than anything I had ever experienced.

Sophie helped me finish my food in silence. She mentioned the guys again, but I tensed up and she didn't say any more. My thoughts kept wandering back to Nina. Every molecule in my body was reaching out to her. I let out an exasperated sigh and tried to shift, but I was completely numb and couldn't move at all. I felt like I was going to explode with frustration. Sophie rang the bell for assistance without asking me what was wrong.

"I think we're ready for something to help him sleep." She indicated me when the nurse came in and I nodded.

"All right, love." The nurse walked out again and returned with some liquid vials, which she dispensed into my IV. "These will start working very soon."

"Thank you," I deadpanned.

"Sleep well, Oliver." She smiled and put her hand on Sophie's shoulder. "Why don't you go home tonight, Miss Lawrence?"

"No, I'll stay…" Sophie started.

"Go, please. I'll sleep better if I know that you're getting some rest too," I interrupted. "It's not like I can go anywhere." I added a little chuckle, hoping that it masked the bitterness I was feeling.

"Okay, I'm staying with the guys, so I'm only a few minutes away if you need me."

"Don't worry." I reached for her hand, but the meds must've kicked in. My words were slurred again, even to my ears, and my leaden fingers only dragged halfway across the bed.

Sophie kissed my palm before she held it to her cheek for a moment, just like Nina had in my dream. My pupils turned into two long black tunnels and I blinked slowly as I flopped my head to the side to grin drunkenly at her.

"Sleep well, Ollie." Sophie put my hand back on the bed.

"'Kay, you too, sis," I mumbled. She bent down to kiss my forehead one last time, but I must have fallen asleep before she turned around. I don't remember seeing her leave.

When I opened my eyes again the sun was streaming through the open windows. A breeze caressed my face and sent whiffs of fresh coffee and a soft, clean fragrance up my nostrils. Sophie was sitting in the chair next to the window, sipping from a takeaway cup. I watched her for a while and felt a pang of guilt about how overwhelming this must all be for her.

The past seven years had been hard, often intolerable, for both of us. Her job as a criminal defence attorney in London meant that she was always under pressure, so adding in more trauma and more worry could easily justify a dose of diazepam. Yet there she was, freshly showered and tapping away on her laptop, probably trying to catch up on work while I was still asleep.

"Morning," I said when her eyes flicked up to check on me.

"How are you feeling?"

"A bit achy, but I guess that's good."

"Yes, Dr. Harold said that you'll feel uncomfortable when the epidural wears off. I'll call the nurse for some pain relief." She put her laptop on the low coffee table in front of her.

"No, it's okay, Soph. It's not that bad. It's preferable to feeling numb."

"All right." She walked over to my bed and sat down in the chair next to me. "But let me know when it gets any worse. Did you sleep well?"

"Yeah, like a log. How about you? Did you manage to get some rest?"

"I did. I didn't realise how tired I was. I feel like a new person this morning."

"Good. You must have a lot of work to catch up on?" I pointed at the laptop on the coffee table. "I know how full-on it can get for you, Soph. Don't worry if you need to go."

"They can cope without me for a while. I want to be here."

"Thank you." I sighed, trying to push down the guilt. "What time is it?"

"Just before eight. Are you hungry?"

"Starving." My stomach let out a loud grumble and just then, right on cue, the matronly nurse came in, carrying a tray of food.

"Good morning, Oliver." She put the tray on the little wheely table and pressed a button next to my bed to raise me into a semi-sitting position. She checked my monitors and tapped on the tablet. "All your vital signs are fine. How are you feeling? Any discomfort?"

"A bit, yes, but not too bad."

"The epidural was last topped up at six. I expect it's already started to wear off again. I'll remove it after you've had your breakfast. You'll feel more pressure after that, but we'll administer pain relief."

"Thank you." I nodded as she hurried out of the room.

Sophie helped me with my breakfast. Although I was feeling increasingly uncomfortable, I was adamant about not asking for pain relief until the epidural was removed. The pain was better than not feeling at all. I hated not being able to feel my legs. It made me feel completely helpless and out of control.

"Ollie." Sophie interrupted my thoughts before they could turn darker at the prospect of my stationary future. "Kellan sent a text while you were talking to the nurse. They're downstairs." She looked at me with hopeful eyes, but I shook my head. I couldn't face the guys yet. I couldn't cope with them seeing me lying here like an invalid.

"Ollie, they're sick with worry…" She tried to reason with me, but my composure flared into panic.

"I don't want to see them! Dammit!" I smacked my hand down on the tray, which made my coffee spill all over my food and drip onto the bed.

My biggest flaw.

My temper.

Ever since my parents died I'd been a hand grenade that exploded without warning. I could feel in control one moment and ready to murder somebody the next. It was the main reason I exercised like a demon—it helped to channel my rage into something useful. Writing music was my best outlet though. It focussed my mind completely. At the moment I wasn't able to do either of those things. The fact that I was in pain—so, so much pain—and struggling to get a handle on all the trauma from the past wasn't helping either. I also really wanted a fucking smoke.

"All right." Sophie let out an exasperated breath and started wiping up the coffee. "But you can't hide from them forever."

"I know. I'm sorry," I mumbled. "I'm not ready yet. I'm sorry." I sighed again, but it sounded more like a growl. I bloody hated apologising.

My second biggest flaw.

I was pig-headed.

My mood was considerably darker after that and the atmosphere in the room shifted into a chilly silence. After my food tray was cleared away and the mess was cleaned up, the nurse came back to remove my epidural, but I hardly acknowledged her. She offered me some pain medication, but I refused. Sophie raised her eyebrows and retreated to her laptop and the seat by the window.

I lay still, staring out of the window, and wallowed in the sombre details of the time ahead. What would my life be like if I couldn't make the miraculous recovery my sister expected me to make? I tried to swallow my despair and think of a few positive things I could do with my life. I could still write, but nobody wanted to watch a musician in a wheelchair. The guys would struggle to accept it, but I'd have to leave the band. In fact, Jack would probably find an excuse to fire the band if I didn't leave. He would never admit to such vanity, but I had no misconceptions about how the music industry worked. I'd never doubted how talented we all were, but it was easier to promote us because we were young, wild and good-looking. People loved our image as much as they loved our music. It was ridiculous, but true. And, as introverted as I was, I loved performing more than anything. It made me feel like I could overcome anything. It gave my life meaning. How was I going to keep my passion for my music if I couldn't live it? Also, cycling on one of those low paraplegic bikes would never hit the same spot as running freely through the forest. And finally, what were the chances of Nina—or any other girl, for that matter—ever wanting to be with me if I was sentenced to life in a wheelchair?

I sighed deeply and tried to shift in my bed, but I couldn't get comfortable. The pain was starting to intensify and I knew that I should have asked for something, but I was too stubborn. I wasn't sure who I was trying to spite or why, but I was adamant about resisting for as long as I could. After I shifted with a grunt for the third or fourth time, Sophie got up and came back with the nurse.

"It's time for some relief, Oliver." The nurse's voice was stern. "You should not be in pain. I thought you might want to go outside for some fresh air this afternoon?" She raised her eyebrows as she changed her tactic, like you would do with a stroppy child. And, just like a stroppy child, I turned my head away to stare out of the window and barely nodded enough for her to notice, even though I did perk up a bit at the prospect of fresh air.

"Then I suggest you get some rest." She injected pink liquid into my drip. "You'll feel the pressure ease in a few minutes." She patted my arm before she left.

The stabbing at the bottom of my spine almost immediately dulled and within moments it felt like I'd been immersed in a nice warm bath. I closed my eyes without putting up a fight.

Sophie was still sitting in her spot by the window when I woke up. I felt a bit groggy, but surprisingly comfortable. There was a dull pressure at the bottom of my spine and I had a mild case of needles and pins, but it was bearable. My head and my chest were both still killing me, but I was used to it by now.

"Hey." Sophie smiled and walked over to my side.

"Hey." I yawned and rubbed my eyes. "Sorry about earlier."

"It's okay. Sorry I nagged. Would you like some lunch? They brought it in a little while ago." She pointed to a tray of food at the end of my bed.

"Thanks." I lifted onto my elbows and tried to shift back against my pillows after Sophie raised the bed. "I'm surprisingly hungry for somebody who's been lying down for five days."

"I'm sure it's good if you can eat." She wheeled my food closer. "By the way, I'm seeing the police officer who processed your incident report tomorrow."

"Thank you." I blinked a small smile as I reached for my fork. It'd be nice to know what had actually happened. Hopefully the police knew more than I could remember.

After lunch, a male nurse with bright copper hair and an even brighter smile came in and asked me if I wanted a wash. It had never even occurred to me that I hadn't had a shower or brushed my teeth since Thursday.

"Please." I nodded in disdain.

"I'll be back in a moment." He walked out again.

"I'll pop out for a coffee." Sophie also smiled and left the room.

The nurse returned moments later with another guy and some toiletries. They closed the door, drew the curtains and nonchalantly started stripping the covers back. I was outrageously nervous and humiliated, but they paid no attention to me and nattered about some club they'd gone to the night before. Every so often they asked me to lift an arm or if the water temperature was okay and after a while I started to relax a bit more. I couldn't deny that being clean was worth the embarrassment in the end.

"Thanks," I said when they opened the curtains and windows again.

"You're welcome, Oliver." The copper-haired nurse beamed and I thought that he had the happiest face I'd seen in a long time. "Would you like to go outside now?"

"Yeah." I nodded just as Sophie walked back into the room. "Could you get me some smokes, please, Soph?"

"I already did." She patted her handbag, making me smile as well. Sophie didn't smoke. She hated that I smoked. She must've felt terribly sorry for me if she'd somehow convinced herself to buy cigarettes.

"Well, let's get you out of here then." The friendly guy wheeled a weird-looking flat wheelchair contraption into the room and two more nurses followed behind him.

They transferred me into the implement and hoisted the back up until I was in a comfortable semi-sitting position. It was similar to sitting in a La-Z-Boy recliner with the legs kicked out and the back tilted halfway down.

"You'll be able to use a more conventional wheelchair next week," he explained. "We just need to be extra careful for the first few days after the surgery. I'm Stuart, by the way. I'll be in charge of your day-to-day care from now on, so just ask if you need anything."

"Thank you." I instantly liked him. He made me feel normal.

"Right, off we go."

I closed my eyes when the sun touched my face as we rolled into the light. I took a deep breath and turned my head up, feeling the tense muscles in my neck uncoil.

"That feels good," I whispered and opened my eyes again. "It's nice out here." I looked around the sizable courtyard garden. There was a large patch of healthy-looking turf with an enormous oak tree in the middle. A few wooden benches and potted plants encircled the tree trunk and a wide sandstone edge with several more wooden benches and small wrought-iron dining sets framed the lawn. It was hard to believe that this beautiful garden was at the centre of a hospital filled with broken people.

Sophie handed me a cigarette and lit it for me. The first drag gave me a rush after days of not smoking and it was good to feel the familiar thrill disengaging my head a bit. Stuart pushed me around the paved area for a while. He had a witty sense of humour and I enjoyed his company. The three of us talked about music as we sat under the oak while I had another smoke.

The pain was getting sharper again, but I didn't want to put an end to my pleasant outing, so I didn't say anything. However, I couldn't help cringing every time I tried to shift into a more comfortable position and obviously Stuart noticed. He wordlessly pushed me back inside. I peeked into some of the rooms we passed in the hallway and nearly snapped my neck off when I saw a familiar face against the pillows.

"Wait!" I called. "Nina!"

CHAPTER 5

"**N**ina!" I reached my hand towards her.

There were tubes and wires coming out from underneath the covers, just like with me when I'd woken up, but more. A thick bandage was wrapped around her head and neck. Stuart pushed me right up next to her and I saw that somebody was slumped over the other side of her bed. He looked up and stared at me with lifeless eyes. Memories from the night of the accident forced themselves into my mind again.

Nina was right on the other side of the bar counter and we stood frozen, grinning at each other like two kids on Christmas morning.

A flamboyantly groomed guy pranced in and collapsed onto his elbows next to her. "Good, you're here already. You won't believe the day I just had. I had to go all the way to…" He trailed off when he noticed that she wasn't listening to him. "Nina." He clicked his fingers in front of her face, then followed her gaze to meet mine. "Well, hello, gorgeous," he crooned. "Introduce me to your beautiful friend."

"Erm…" Nina smiled at me without saying any words.

"Oliver." I beamed, giving an idiotic little wave.

"Well, it's very, very lovely to meet you, Oliver. I'm Zach." He did a dramatic bow-roll with his hand. "And this is my little sister, Nina." Her eyes flicked down and a small smile continued to play around her mouth, but she still didn't say anything.

"Hey, erm…" I waved like an idiot. "What can I get you to drink?"

"Two beers, please." Zach laughed when she still didn't respond.

27

"Zach?" I whispered. I saw recognition flash in his eyes as he clocked my wheelchair and the state I was in.

"Oliver? I heard that it was you on the bike. I can't believe it. Can you remember what happened?"

"Yeah." I tried to clear the emotion from my throat. "I was coming around a bend and her car was suddenly right in front of me. It happened so fast." I took a deep breath. My heart was hammering again. "I woke up here on Sunday morning."

Zach nodded and his eyes got wet as he swallowed. I looked over to Nina again. My lungs contracted painfully and my breathing came out in short, scorching huffs. I'd been so consumed with my own self-pity that I'd never even acknowledged that this was all my fault. If I hadn't been so distracted I would've paid more attention and I would've seen her car. If I hadn't been going so fast I would've been able to stop in time.

"How's she doing?" I whispered, my voice barely audible. Zach shook his head and wiped at the tears that were now creeping down his cheeks.

"She has a severe concussion and she's lost a lot of blood. She's in a coma. The swelling in her brain is not going down."

It was too much. How would I be able to live with myself if she didn't wake up?

I slowly became aware of the sharp stabbing at the bottom of my spine. My head felt like my brain had swelled to twice its normal size and was trying to seep through the cracks in my broken skull. I tried to take ragged breaths, but my messed-up lungs refused to inflate.

"We have to go, Oliver." Stuart rolled me backwards.

"I'm sorry." I tried to reach for Nina's hand, but my hands were shaking and I only managed to brush her cold skin briefly.

Zach barely took note of my exit. He was still holding Nina's other hand and he was already laying his head back down on the bed next to her as Stuart pulled me out of the room.

By the time we reached my room, I was shivering uncontrollably and my brain was pounding against my battered skull. My lungs refused to let in enough air. Stuart said something about going into shock because of the pain, but I couldn't understand all his words and I couldn't really see his face. Everything sounded far off and dark spots danced in front of my eyes. Nina's pale face kept flashing through my mind until it all went dark.

When I came to my senses again, the curtains were drawn and the room was dim. Sophie was sitting next to my bed, typing on her laptop. Her hair was scraped back in a ponytail and she looked tired, but she was still wearing the navy trousers and striped top she'd had on earlier, so it must have been the same day. Or not. How would I know? I inhaled slowly and tried to assess how I was feeling. To my surprise, I discovered that I was okay. I could feel the dull sensation of needles and pins all over again and there was some pressure on my spine, but my head was a bit better and I was breathing okay.

"How are you feeling?" Sophie looked up as I let out a controlled breath.

"Okay, actually." I frowned, remembering the agony of earlier.

"Good. You should have said that you were in pain. You're not helping by avoiding pain relief."

"Okay."

"No, Oliver, Dr. Harold said that you could have damaged the fusion. It's absolutely not okay." Her voice was angry.

"I just kind of… forgot about my pain when I saw Nina. I did that to her, Soph."

"What? You're blaming yourself now?"

"Well…" I looked away.

"Ollie." She grabbed my chin and forced my head back to look at her. "It was an accident."

I blinked slowly as a tear slid down my cheek. "I won't be able to forgive myself if she doesn't wake up."

"Stop it," she pleaded.

"I was too distracted." I looked her straight in the eyes. "And I think I might have been going too fast."

"Oliver, it's impossible to know exactly what happened until we've spoken to the police."

"Okay." It was pointless arguing with Sophie anyway. "Can I have something to eat, please?" I was bloody starving again.

"Of course." She got up and came back a few minutes later with a tray of sandwiches.

When I finished my food, I asked for more painkillers and told Sophie to go home. I was looking forward to being alone, somewhere in silent oblivion.

"Could you bring a few things tomorrow?" I asked when she bent down to kiss my head.

"What do you need?"

"My speaker, the one on my bedside table, and my Kindle. My guitar, Dad's Fender in the living room, a notebook and my laptop. Please?"

"Your phone?" she asked, but I shook my head. I was surprised to hear that it had survived the accident, but I didn't want contact with the outside world.

"Sure." Her smile still looked forced. "I'll see you in the morning."

"Actually, Soph, could you bring a few of Mum's journals, please? Any would be fine."

My mum had religiously kept a journal since she was about thirteen until the day she died. We had at least a couple hundred in boxes in my music room. Sophie never looked at them—I think it was too hard for her. I didn't really read them in detail, but they brought me a great sense of comfort, and I often flicked through them.

"Of course." Sophie pecked me on my head and left.

I woke up in agony during the night. My body was covered in sweat and it felt like my organs were quivering inside my body. I pressed the call button on the side of my bed and a nurse appeared with some more pain relief. She double-checked my temperature, fluffed my pillows and tucked me back in like a child. She stayed with me until the pain eased and my body started to relax. I drifted back to the land of nothing as I mumbled a woozy thanks to her.

When I woke up the next morning my speaker was on my bedside cabinet and the bold white letters on the screen stated that it was eight twenty-two a.m. Billy Joel was singing softly about making somebody feel his love. On the other side of my bed there was a new chest of drawers with my laptop resting on top. The notebook and Kindle from my desk at home were stacked next to my laptop, and behind them my leather pen cup, filled with pencils. Next to my pencils, leaning against the wall, were three of my mum's journals. My favourite acoustic guitar was propped up in its stand against the opposite wall. The windows were open and it was another warm, cloudless day.

Sophie was sitting in her spot next to the window, tapping away on her laptop. She was showered and dressed in one of her chic Sophie outfits. How the hell did she do it? I had no idea. My sister, Superwoman. I smiled faintly as I pushed up on my elbow and tried to shift stiffly.

"Good morning." She looked up when the covers rustled.

"You're amazing." I gestured at the room and shook my head in awe.

"Oh, it's nothing. Did you sleep well?" Her mobile started ringing. She clicked her tongue as she looked at the screen. "Sorry, I have to take this." She walked out of the room and I heard her talking in her stern business voice.

Dr. Harold came in a few minutes later and checked my surgery wounds and readings. "It's all looking good, Mr. Lawrence." He put the tablet back in its docking station before he strapped my brace back on. "How is the pain this morning?"

"Okay." I tried to shift against my pillows again and cringed when the bottom of my spine stung.

"Oliver, I really cannot reiterate enough how important it is for you to get adequate rest. Adequate rest means that your pain has to be managed. I know the drugs are making you feel disconnected, but you're putting your spine under unnecessary stress."

I closed my eyes and just sighed in reply.

"If you aren't going to help us manage your pain effectively, I will sedate you until I'm satisfied that you have healed enough. It won't be ideal—I much prefer to keep track of pain levels and frequency—but if you do not cooperate I will keep you tranquilised. Am I making myself clear?"

I nodded, letting out an exasperated breath.

"Everything all right?" Sophie spoke behind Dr. Harold. Her voice sounded strained.

"Yes, fine." Dr. Harold addressed my sister. "He needs much rest, but everything is looking as good as can be expected."

"Good." Sophie gave him a tight smile.

"Right, Oliver. I'll see you again tonight. Good day, Miss Lawrence." Dr Harold swung around and left the room.

"What's the matter, Soph?" I asked and her cheeks inflated before she let out a long breath.

"I hate to ask, but I have a work emergency. I was working on a very sensitive case and I have to discuss some details with my team today, but I can't take the conference call here." She twisted her finger around in a little circle. "I've arranged a secure room at the Guildford Crown Court."

"I'll be fine, Soph." I shook my head, annoyed with her faffing.

"I don't like leaving you."

"Don't be stupid. I could do with some time on my own. I was getting a bit sick of you anyway."

"Cheeky bastard. I'll see you in a few hours." She kissed my head and grabbed her laptop and bag on the way out.

Every molecule in my body screamed to go over to Nina's room the second Sophie marched out of my door. But, since I was immobile and not able to go wherever I wanted, and since I had literally just been told off for not cooperating, I went through the day's motions without asking to be taken to her.

It was late afternoon by the time Stuart offered to take me out for my daily trip to the garden. He called for another nurse to help him transfer my hopeless bulk of a body into the La-Z-Boy wheelchair. I was six foot four and weighed a rock-solid two hundred and seventy-five pounds, but they easily manoeuvred me into the contraption.

"It's all in the skill, Oliver," Stuart explained when he saw me frown. "We use a sliding and rolling motion to move you, rather than physically trying to pick you up. So, if you get the technique right, you don't need a lot of strength, really." He wiggled his fingers and added a silly grin at the end.

On the way out I asked to stop in Nina's room. I held my breath. I didn't know what I was expecting, but I exhaled slowly when I saw her. She looked exactly like the day before—a porcelain doll. Still, pale, and, for some reason, smaller than I remembered. Fragile. Her chocolate hair fell tousled around her face and onto the pillow where it escaped from the bandages, and her dense lashes rested on transparent cheeks.

"Any change?" I whispered without looking away from Nina.

"I don't know," Stuart said quietly.

I nodded once and took Nina's hand in my own. It felt too small and too cold. It was unnatural. I covered it with my other hand and brought it up to my cheek. I wished I could make some heat seep back into her body. I wished I could make her open those pale eyes. I sat still like that for a while, my mind emptied by her presence.

I heard footsteps just before Stuart cleared his throat to get my attention. "Good afternoon," he said to whoever walked in and I straightened my ten-tonne head with effort.

"Hello," the newcomer said. "Who are you?"

"Dad, this is Oliver. He was on the motorcycle." I heard a familiar voice and tried to compose myself as Stuart turned my wheelchair around to face them. Zach was standing next to an older man in the doorway.

"Oliver, this is our dad. Jeffrey," Zach continued when I didn't react.

"Hello, Mr. Harrison," I croaked and wiped my face with the palm of my hand as I sniffed.

I thought I saw a flicker of something curious flash through his eyes as he looked me over, but then his expression softened. "Oliver." He nodded at my wheelchair. "Are your injuries serious?"

"My spine is broken," I stated bluntly. "Has there been any change with Nina?"

"No. She's unresponsive."

"I'm sorry." I was struggling to get control over my emotions.

"How do you know my daughter?"

"We met on Thursday evening at the Guildberry. I work there."

"Can you remember the accident at all?"

"I remember coming around the bend and suddenly realising there was a car right in front of me. I think I recognised Nina as I went over the car." I rubbed my hair around on my head.

"What time did you leave the club?" Jeffrey frowned.

"I'm not sure. Around midnight, I don't know."

"Marcus said they both left when I did," Zach piped up next to Jeffrey. "It was just after eleven."

Whoa! All my synapses fired at the same time. *Marcus Bentley!* I'd somehow forgotten about Marcus entirely, but he'd been there too.

"Eish, watch out for that one, Olive." Charlie raised his eyebrows when he caught me glancing in Nina's direction for the millionth time.

"No way, Ollie," Kellan warned, handing me two more glasses as Charlie rang up the order. "That's Nina Harrison."

"And?" I frowned, flicking my eyes back to her again and catching her quickly looking away as the pint I was filling overflowed. "Bugger."

"Jeffrey Harrison? Harritech?"

"IT mogul?" I asked and Kellan nodded.

"His daughter." He pointed the wine bottle he'd just taken from the fridge in Nina's direction.

"So?"

"Have you not heard their story?" He reached around for two wine glasses.

"No?"

"That"—he bobbed his head in the direction of Zach—"is her older brother, Zach, but she also had a twin sister, Grace." He paused as he handed over the wine to the girl who'd just ordered it. "We must have told you about them when we were in secondary school? We weren't best friends or anything, but Ian had a massive crush on them." He frowned and I shrugged, shaking my head. "Anyway, two summers ago, Grace died."

"Shit," I whispered.

"Yeah. Nina disappeared after that. I heard she went off to live with Zach in New York. He must be around Sophie's age."

"They came back a few weeks ago." Ian nodded. "I'm pretty sure I heard she's hooking up with Marcus Bentley, though. Best to stay away there, brother."

"Yeah, that's some weird shit," Kellan said.

"Why?" I blurted, unexpectedly irritated. "Who the fuck is Marcus Bentley?"

"Son of Chief Constable James Bentley, head of Surrey Police? Do you live under a fucking rock?" Kellan frowned at me.

"Fuck off."

"Marcus and Grace were together, Ols. They were inseparable." Ian widened his eyes as he held my gaze.

"I don't think she's your type anyway, Olive." Charlie patted my shoulder as he started assembling a tray of shots.

"And how do you know her?" I clicked my tongue.

"I don't. I've seen her getting shitfaced in here at least twice this week, though. She had to be carried out once. On Tuesday I saw her inhaling a line off that table in the corner, at lunchtime."

"Trouble, trouble, trouble," Ian sang.

"Whatever," I growled. It had nothing to do with me. "I'm going out for a smoke before we go on."

We were halfway through our second song on stage when Marcus appeared behind Nina and pecked the side of her head. She seemed disappointed for a moment, but then she smiled back up at him before she looked straight into *my eyes. I watched him squeeze her arm and it made me want to fly through the crowd and crush his fingers one by one. I didn't understand where my sudden obsession with her had come from and why I felt such a disproportionate sense of rage toward him, I just knew it made me feel unhinged to watch them together.*

I went back to work behind the bar after our last song. Nina sat with Zach and another guy in one of the small booths at the back of the club, and Marcus seemed to be deep in conversation with a different group of people at the front, near the exit. Zach and his friend got up to leave after a while. As they passed Marcus on the way out, Zach pointed to Nina and Marcus got up and walked over to her. He said something in her ear and started guiding her towards the door, but it didn't look like she wanted to go and I could see they were arguing. Eventually Nina stormed out and Marcus followed behind her.

"I thought they left together? Marcus and Nina."

Jeffrey frowned and looked at Zach, who shook his head. "He said he had an early flight the next morning, so he called a taxi."

"Oh. Have you spoken to the police? Do they know anything else?"

"I spoke to them again this morning, but there weren't any eye-witnesses, so they couldn't tell me anything more. I'll pick up the official report later, but I don't expect it to say anything."

"Okay." I scratched my chin. My heart was marching up my throat. "Do you know if they were able to calculate how fast I was going?"

"Your speedometer was stuck at forty-eight. The speed limit on that road is sixty. You were fine."

I covered my mouth with my hand and slowly blew out a breath I hadn't realised I was holding. I'd thought I was going faster, but it made sense that I'd slowed down around the bend.

"And Nina? I mean, is there any chance that she might have had too much, you know…?" I couldn't complete my question. I couldn't remember how many drinks she'd had. I hadn't kept track.

But I had to know.

"No." Jeffrey shook his head. "Her blood alcohol level was just under the legal limit."

"Who reported the accident?" I rubbed my hair around on my head.

"Nina did." His voice came out gravelly this time. "Emergency services received a silent call from her mobile. It's standard procedure to investigate all open silent calls. They tracked her phone to the scene of the accident. She must have lost consciousness before she could speak to them. The phone was still in her hand when they found her." He cleared his throat and I swallowed the lump in my own throat with difficulty.

It was deeply disturbing to think about what that must have been like for her. A toxic cocktail of my own past trauma, blended with this new anguish, combined with concern for Nina and sympathy for her family, was swirling together in my gut and threatening to overwhelm me. I closed my eyes as I took several slow, deep breaths before I looked up to Jeffrey again.

"Would it be okay if I visited her sometimes? I suppose I, um, I feel connected to her somehow…" I trailed off. I didn't know why I felt like I needed to ask her father's permission or try to explain myself, but I knew that I had to spend as much time as possible with Nina.

Jeffrey looked at me for a long moment as his expression morphed into something that I could only recognise as pity. It made me feel sick that I was the object of this man's pity. This man, whose one daughter was dead and whose other daughter was lying unconscious in the bed next to us.

"Of course, Oliver," he answered and gave my shoulder a little pat.

"We have to get a move on, Ollie," Stuart said next to me.

"It was good to meet you, Mr. Harrison." I awkwardly offered my hand as far as my broken ribs and constraints allowed me. "Well, you know, under the circumstances." I shrugged.

"Yes, you too." He carefully squeezed my hand. "Call me Jeffrey."

"Thank you." I tried to muster up a smile. "See you later, Zach."
I lifted my hand in a small wave.

"Perhaps I could pop in tonight to say hello?"

"Sure." I nodded, forcing out another smile, although this one felt a little less obliged. Even though I refused to talk to my own friends, it wouldn't be bad to see somebody other than Sophie and the hospital people. Zach seemed like a nice guy and he obviously loved Nina, so it might be good to get to know him.

When we got outside Stuart stopped underneath the oak and sat down on a bench next to my wheelchair. He handed over my smokes and I couldn't inhale my first drag deep enough.

"So, what's the story here, Ollie?" He cocked an eyebrow.

"What do you mean?" I puffed out in little circles as I moved my eyes away to stare into space. "I crashed into her car and now she's in a coma and I'm paralysed. It sucks."

"All right." He let out a soft sigh. "Although you're going to be stuck with me for a while and I can see there's more, so you might as well indulge me."

I frowned up at him, but his expression was attentive rather than nosy, so I allowed a small smile to curve my mouth. "When I met her in the club that evening it was like being struck by lightning, or something equally clichéd. I have never been affected by anybody like that. Ever. I haven't been able to get her out of my head. I feel like we're connected somehow. I don't know." I dropped my shoulders and stubbed out my cigarette in the ashtray next to the bench.

"Love at first sight?"

"Perhaps." I blinked slowly and lifted my head as I lit another smoke. "Except we never got to fall in love. I never even got to spend any time with her. We bumped into each other around town all week until we finally met that night. We talked for about two seconds at the start of the evening and then we watched each other across the club for the rest of the night. And as you know, it all ended quite abruptly when I crashed into her on that damned road." I grimaced. "I don't really know their story, but I think there is a complicated situation with Marcus Bentley as well. Like I said, it sucks."

Stuart squeezed his lips together in a funny side-pout. "All the greatest love stories seem impossible at first."

"It's a bit difficult to imagine a great love story when she's dying in there while I'm stuck over here." I tapped my wheelchair.

CHAPTER 6

"Hi." Sophie came back just after seven that evening, but I couldn't muster up enough enthusiasm to be polite. She lifted her brow at my grunted response and I could see that she struggled not to frown. She didn't usually indulge my moods. "How are you feeling?"

"Okay, thanks. How was work?" There was no point being rude to her. She didn't want me to be here either.

"Murderous." She rolled her eyes and cracked a big grin this time.

"Funny lady." I allowed my mouth to twitch up on one side. "Seriously? A murder case?"

"Yeah. I can't talk about it though."

"Sure." I dipped my head. "It must be heavy going?"

"It is. I'll have to go back tomorrow, if that's okay with you?"

"Of course." I frowned, instantly irritated with her mollycoddling again.

"I asked to be taken off the case, but it's at a crucial stage and I'll probably lose my partnership…" She trailed off.

"Stop faffing, Soph. I don't expect you to be here twenty-four seven. And I sure as fuck don't want to be responsible for you losing your job."

"I know. But I want to be here."

"I understand, but I'm all right." I squeezed her hand before pointing at my food. "Can you bring that a bit closer, please?"

While I ate my dinner, I told Sophie about meeting Nina's dad and about the police saying that no laws were broken.

"Yes, sorry, I forgot to tell you after I met with the police officer.

40

That's what he said to me too. I got the incident report today." She paused to take a bite of a sandwich she'd retrieved from a plastic bag on the floor next to her. She must've been fed up with hospital canteen food and takeaways by now. But then again, I knew she didn't eat differently in London—posh restaurant food and fancy easy meals.

"What does it say?" I asked.

"The same," she said through chewing. "The emergency number was dialled from Nina's mobile, but the call was silent and they traced the phone's location to the scene of the accident. There were no eyewitnesses and they didn't find any evidence of unlawful behaviour. They filed it as an accidental collision and that's it."

Zach came in a bit later as promised. It was good to have new company and Sophie seemed to like him too. She chatted with us for a while, but excused herself around nine. Zach and I talked about my band and a new song we'd released a few weeks earlier. It felt like I was talking about someone else's life. I itched to ask him about Nina, but I figured that he needed a break from it all and that he was purposefully asking about me. When he left an hour later I requested pain relief and slumbered off into emptiness.

The next couple of weeks passed in similar fashion. The days were blending together in a tedious sequence of bland meals, numb sleeps and sponge baths. My trips to the garden were the highlight of every day. Sophie went back to work full-time, but she visited every morning and every evening. I tried to see Nina as often as possible. It was excruciating watching her never moving, never looking any different. A girl frozen in a bed.

Her mum and dad were there most of the time. I chatted to them for a few minutes every day, but they usually popped out when I came to see her. I appreciated the gesture and cherished my private moments with her.

Zach also came to see Nina every day and he always stopped by my room on the way out. He was a genuinely nice guy and we became friends. He started telling me more about their lives and I absorbed every morsel of information he shared.

Their mum owned a coffee shop-slash-art gallery called Ingrid's in Haslemere village. I knew it well and had often gone there for brunch. Their dad, Jeffrey, was a software genius and owned Harritech, one of the biggest IT companies in the world. Grace had been into creative arts like their mum and she'd been doing a fine arts degree in photography at the University for the Creative Arts in Farnham. Nina had been doing a degree in computer science at Imperial College in London. Grace had passed away at the end of their first year. Nina had dropped out and spent the following year at their home in New York. For the past year she'd attended a computing programme at New York University. I could see that it made Zach emotional to talk about Nina and Grace. I wanted to know more, but I knew better than anyone that he had to talk about it in his own time.

Zach had gone to Juilliard, in New York City. He'd got in on a scholarship when he was eighteen and completed his bachelor of fine arts degree in dance, summa cum laude, when he was twenty-two. He had been teaching there for the past six years and had been their associate director for ballet for the past year. His eyes lit up when he talked about performing. He'd recently signed a two-year contract to teach at the Royal Ballet in London and he had workshops lined up all through summer. I thought it was very impressive, but he waved my praise away with a joke about dance not being an exact science and then moved on to talk more about their childhood.

"I was five when they were born and I was besotted with them from the start. Suddenly I wasn't alone anymore…" He trailed off for a moment before he sighed. "I adored them. We're all so different though."

"Yeah?" I smiled and he nodded.

"Yeah, totally, our personalities are opposites. I'm order. Nina's anarchy. I'm sunshine and rainbows. She's a cosmic meteor shower. A force like no other."

"And Grace?" I asked before I could stop myself.

"Grace... Grace was peace." His lips curved into a small smile. "Some days I still can't believe she's gone. It was the two-year anniversary of her death a few weeks ago and I still want to call her every day to tell her something. Usually it's something outrageous Nina said or did." He paused briefly to smile, making my own lips twitch as well. "Then I go for my phone and it hits me again. Grace is gone. Grace is gone and now Nina... I don't know." He wiped his cheek as a lone tear crept down his face. My heart ached for him. And for Nina. For their entire family. After seven years without my parents I knew that loss was the one wound that time didn't heal. I knew the force and the frequency of the wave was different for everybody, but I knew everyone was just trying to survive the same storm. I also knew that I didn't have to say anything, so I reached over and held his hand as we sat for what felt like a long time.

"Grace only went to university to please our mum." He surprised me by not changing the subject. "Mum is probably the fiercest role model any of us could have asked for. She was adamant that Grace and Nina had to be independent. She even sent them to two different colleges. Grace was a natural artist and a talented photographer. She would have done well in her degree. But the only thing she ever really wanted was to marry Marcus." He shook his head with another weak smile. "For as long as I can remember she wanted a big family with four kids, two dogs and a cat. Marcus studied medicine and Grace wanted him to be the local GP. She was going to work in the coffee shop with Mum. She had it all planned out, right down to the bloody cat's name. Marcus worshipped her and would have given her everything she wanted."

"Yeah?"

"Yeah. He's one of the junior GPs at the health centre in Haslemere now, but that's about the only thing about him that remains the same. We were never very close. We don't really relate. But we've known each other for most of our lives and we both loved Grace, so we got along. But losing her changed him. I don't know who he is now."

"And Nina?"

"Nina..." He sighed deeply and scrubbed both hands over his face. "Nina lost her mind. She stayed in bed for weeks, wailing like a wounded animal every time she woke up until she fell asleep again. I was just promoted to associate when Grace passed away, but I got a semester off and stayed back here at home with her and my parents. After a couple of months we realised that Nina wasn't getting any better. We were all struggling to be in our house. It was just so difficult to know Grace was never coming home.

"At the end of that summer I managed to convince my mum and dad that they should all come back to New York with me. Just for a while. Just so that everyone could have a change of scenery. My parents have an apartment on the Upper West Side and instead of moving into the school's house, I decided to stay with them—to help with Nina, I suppose, and just to not be alone either, I don't know. It was hard. It helped to stay together.

"Anyway, eventually Nina agreed to go to therapy and she started living again. Sort of. She will never be the same again. None of us will. But my dad somehow managed to get her into NYU. I think it was comforting to know that I could keep an eye on her. My mum and dad came back to Haslemere last autumn to renovate the house, and Nina and I stayed behind in New York until I finished my contract with Juilliard a couple of months ago. The past year was okay."

My heart ached for them all. I still didn't know how Grace had died, and I would never ask. I could only imagine what it must be like to lose a twin. A best friend. A soulmate. I even felt a pang of empathy for Marcus. How would they all carry on if Nina didn't wake up? One family couldn't possibly have to face so much loss. But I knew that that wasn't true. It really seemed that there was no fair rationing system when it came to tragedy.

The next evening Zach started asking about my family, and surprisingly, I didn't find it difficult to tell him about my childhood. It was actually quite cathartic.

"My parents were academics. My dad was a professor in music and my mum in psychology." I smiled at the memory of how intellectually scatty they both were. "They kept moving us to a new country every couple of years. They believed that learning about different cultures and speaking different languages enriched our lives more than a stable family home."

"That's interesting." Zach's lip twitched up on one side and I nodded. "Where have you lived?"

"I was born in Switzerland, but we moved to Canada just after I turned one. We stayed there until I was three." I held my hand up and raised my thumb and forefinger. "After that we were in France for two years and then Belgium for a year." I added the next two fingers and smiled as Zach nodded his head in anticipation. "When I was six we moved to Argentina for two years, and then to Germany for two years, when I was eight. That's where I met Kellan and Ian. Their dad went to uni with my dad and happened to be working on a job in Hamburg at the same time. We went to the same school and our families often got together for dinners and stuff." I wiggled my next thumb and Zach nodded. "We've been best friends ever since."

"I remember when they came back to Haslemere. They went to Grace and Nina's secondary school; they must have been eleven or twelve, I think. The girls kept talking about these two tall green-eyed German-British boys."

"Yeah." I smiled. "They told me that they remember Grace and Nina too."

"Where did you go after Germany then?" Zach gestured at the fingers I was still holding up.

"We spent a year in Portugal and then two years in the States." I uncurled the next two fingers. "After America we were in South Africa for two years, which is where I met Charlie. We went to the same school in Mossel Bay; his parents both grew up there and they lived there until Charlie was thirteen."

"Really?" Zach smiled and I nodded. "My mum's from Mossel Bay."

"What a coincidence. My mum's brother, my uncle David, also lived there for a few years before he died. It's a small community. Your mum might know them all."

"What are Charlie's parents' names? And your uncle's?"

"Charlie's parents are Eloise and Raylin Themba, and my uncle was called David Watson. He passed away before I was born though."

"I'll ask my mum." Zach nodded. "Anyway, where did you go next?"

"Oh, yeah." I remembered that I was listing countries. "After South Africa we were in Australia for a year until I was sixteen." I briefly waved all ten of my fingers before I dropped my hands back on my lap. "And that's it."

"Ten countries. What a colourful childhood."

"It really was." I nodded.

"So, did you come back to the UK for college?" Zach asked and a familiar desolation washed over me.

"My parents died shortly after we left Australia. We were in a car accident while we were on holiday back in Portugal. They both died at the scene." Along with the drunk fucker who'd crashed into us.

"I'm sorry, Ollie." Zach squeezed my arm.

"Thanks." I pressed my lips together in a small smile. "It'll be seven years next month."

"Were you hurt?"

"A couple of broken bones, a cut." I shrugged awkwardly before I lifted my T-shirt to show him the long scar that ran along the side of my ribs and curled around my waist. "A few bruises and a concussion."

Along with a helping of post-traumatic stress, a dollop of grief and a sprinkling of rage. But I didn't tell Zach, or anyone else, those details.

Nobody needed to know how I'd listened, trapped and helpless, for the longest, most excruciating two hours and seven minutes of my life as both my parents slowly lost their lives that night. I'd been fully conscious. I could still remember every second as clearly as when it had happened. It had been seven thousand, six hundred and twenty seconds from the moment we'd crashed until the moment both my parents were dead.

My mum had gone first. One of the wooden poles from the railing on the bridge got lodged through her shoulder and pinned her to her seat. She bled out in front of our eyes. It wasn't quick though. One hour and forty-four minutes from the moment of impact until her last breath. I could still see the devastation in my dad's eyes when he'd realised that she was gone. To this day, it sometimes flashed through my mind without warning and after seven years I still had to catch my breath.

My dad had been crushed between his seat and the steering wheel. He suffocated when his lungs were so full of his own blood that he couldn't breathe, twenty-three minutes after my mum died. He lived for one thousand, three hundred and eighty seconds without her.

I waited another hour and sixteen minutes—that's four thousand, five hundred and sixty seconds—until someone found us and called emergency services. And it was another nineteen minutes—one thousand, one hundred and forty seconds—until emergency services showed up. Another three thousand, one hundred and twenty seconds—that's fifty-two minutes—it took the fire brigade to cut me from the wreck and slice open my torso in the process. It was a calculated decision. It was either let me suffer through the cut or let the car drop into the river with me trapped inside. I lost consciousness when they put me into the ambulance.

Four hours and fifty-seven minutes. That's seventeen thousand, eight hundred and twenty seconds I suffered, prayed, pleaded, waited, and cried on that bridge that night. The drunk fucker who'd crashed into us died on impact. He didn't suffer for one second.

"And your sister, Sophie?" Zach pulled me back to the present.

"She wasn't in the car. We were on holiday in Portugal and she was back in London, doing her articles." I closed my eyes briefly. "She came over to get me straight away and she took care of me until I went to uni. Well"—I paused for a moment—"she's doing it again now."

47

"This must trigger some horrible trauma." He twirled his finger around the hospital room.

"A bit." I nodded. He didn't have to know that it just about killed me sometimes. I'd had moments the past couple of weeks where it devastated me so much that I couldn't see a way forward. It would overcome me without any notice or reason and I would have to use all my energy to force myself to not think about anything that wasn't happening in that exact moment.

It's a tried-and-tested method. See something—usually the pigeon that sat on the rail that ran across the bottom of my hospital window, or sometimes it was just the rail, covered in pigeon shit. Hear something—always the music that was playing from my speaker. Feel something—usually the fabric of my T-shirt rubbing against my skin as I breathed in and out. Smell something—usually the nicotine that permanently lingered on my fingers. Breathe in through my nose, hold for eight seconds, breathe out through my mouth. Five times. Carry on with my day, pleased that I hadn't yet lost my mind completely.

"What does 'Non omnis moriar' mean?" Zach quoted the Latin words tattooed along the scar on my ribs, changing the subject slightly.

"It means 'I shall not wholly die.'" I rubbed my finger over the words underneath my T-shirt.

"That's cool. Do you have any other tattoos?"

"Yeah, a few." My chest, shoulders and back were covered entirely. It was actually three different designs, but they connected and blended together to look like one painting. My right shoulder, biceps and chest were covered in a sketch I'd made of the cliff in Sintra, the forest and the bridge over the river, where I'd lost my parents. My back had a world map and compass design. My left shoulder and biceps had daisies weaved between the opening notes to Bach's Prelude in C Major, from *The Well-Tempered Clavier*. It was my dad's favourite piece of music and my mum's favourite flower. I also had the Christian fish symbol on my left foot to remind me to look up whenever I fell down. And the decorated words along the scar on my ribs.

I'd designed them all myself. They were dark and intricate and I'd spent days, or a couple of times even weeks, at a time on my friend Jürgen's table in Berlin. I would show up there, sometimes unannounced, and he'd close his parlour for as long as he needed. We'd live off cigarettes and coffee as something along the lines of Rammstein, or Einaudi, or occasionally even Taylor Swift, blared through the speakers at a volume that made you feel the music deep inside every organ in your body, while he transformed me into a work of art.

"Come on then. Show them off." Zach smiled.

"Some other time, my friend." I had talked enough for one day and I wasn't ready to explain my ink.

I just couldn't shift the sorrow from my soul that evening. It was suddenly too much. I missed my parents. I wanted to walk. I wanted Nina to be okay. I wanted to stop being in pain. Some moments, like that one, it felt like every single part of my body was hurting. I just wanted everything to be normal.

I excused myself and told Zach that I wasn't feeling well.

I flicked through my mum's journals for what felt like hours. They were from her early twenties. It was a couple of years after she'd met my dad, and she was nearly finished with her first degree in psychology at the University of Surrey. Her best friend was someone called MH and they were interested in human neurological functions. I also got the impression they were dabbling in drugs. The thought made me release an unsolicited smile. My mum had always had a wild streak. I wondered what my dad thought about that. Like me, he'd been very much not into drugs.

My heart ached at the visions of what my parents had been like when they were my age. I wondered what they would have thought about my dreams about Nina. I wished I could ask them.

Eventually I couldn't keep ignoring the fact that I was becoming increasingly uncomfortable, so I asked for some pain relief and succumbed to the darkness.

That was the first night I dreamed again after my surgery.

CHAPTER 7

I was strolling on narrow cobblestoned lanes. Tall whitewashed houses with bright blue window frames lined the streets. The sun tumbled down on me and I could smell the ocean.

I immediately knew that I was in Ericeira. It was one of my favourite places in Portugal. Fond memories of our very last holiday in Portugal when I was sixteen, that fateful holiday my parents died, clung to every building and every face I passed. I slowly made my way down to the beach and stopped at the South Beach Taverna for a drink.

"Bom dia, Claudia." I beamed at the girl who worked behind the bar. I'd spent my days surfing with her and her brothers that summer. "Como você está?"

"Ben olá, Oliver." Her dark eyes twinkled. I'd forgotten how sweet she was. We'd had one of those innocent, hormone-driven romances back then. "Grande obrigado. How are you?" She treated me to a shy smile.

"Yes, great, thanks." I smiled as well. I was great here in my dream, where I could wander through the quaint streets of this town, and where I could sit at this taverna to watch the sunbeams twirl around the vast turquoise Atlantic. In the real world, not so much.

"Limonada?" She made the best fresh lemonade in town and I used to drink gallons of the stuff.

"Oh, yes, please."

She handed over a jug of cold lemonade and a tall sugar-rimmed glass filled with ice cubes and mint.

"Muito obrigado." I tipped the glass towards her.

I turned away from the counter to find a table on the seafront, but I found my favourite pair of pale blue eyes staring back at me instead. A lazy smile curled all the way around Nina's lips and reached her eyes in a way that made her entire face radiate. My heart did a few somersaults. The lines were already blurring and I knew I was going to forget my harsh reality very soon, but I didn't care. Hell, I was looking forward to it. My whole being was craving this dream with Nina.

"Hey," I breathed as I put the lemonade on her table and sat down next to her before I stroked my thumb across her cheek.

"I've missed you." She leaned her face into my hand and closed her eyes.

I moved my thumb over her lips and pulled her closer to me. I kissed her slowly. She tasted of sunshine and sweet lemons. "Me too," I whispered.

She opened her eyes and they flickered yellow for an instant, but I ignored it. I refused to let my nagging reality spoil this dreamtime with Nina. If I could forget that this was a dream, it would be even better.

She pulled away and looked at my face. The dimple in her left cheek winked as a smile rippled over her face again. It made me want to kiss her again, but I restrained myself and topped up her lemonade instead. I filled my own glass and leaned back in my chair. I lit two cigarettes and handed one to Nina before I took a drag of my own as I let my eyes drift over her.

She was wearing light blue jeans and a white tank top. Her dark hair tumbled over her shoulders, stray strands flicking in the breeze.

"What?" Her smile turned suspicious.

"You're lovely." I laced the fingers of my other hand through hers.

"You're pretty nice too." Her smile broadened again before she turned her head and looked out towards the ocean. "Where are we?" Her eyes narrowed as if it had only just occurred to her that we were somewhere foreign.

"In Portugal. Ericeira." My heartbeat picked up slightly.

"Why are we here?" She dragged on her cigarette.

"I'm not sure, Nina."

"I like it here."

"Me too." I sighed. She was confused. I should have tried to explain, but I was too selfish. I wanted to have this time with her.

"Are you going to leave me again?" Her voice was timid.

"I don't want to." I pinched her chin and lifted her gaze back to mine. "I don't want to leave you."

"But you're still going to."

"Yes," I admitted.

She blinked and a lone tear escaped, painting a line on her cheek. I wiped it away with my finger and leaned in to kiss the corner of her eye. She tilted her head up and pressed her soft lips against mine. I pulled her onto my lap and stroked her hair as she rested her head on my shoulder and we stayed like that for a long time until she eventually hopped off.

"Let's walk on the beach." She held out her hand.

I let her pull me up, but I pulled her back to me and clamped my arms around her. "I'll go anywhere with you," I whispered into her hair and she hummed against my chest, sending shivers through my body.

We took off our shoes and I pushed them under our table with my foot.

"Por favor, podemos deixar nossas coisas, Claudia?" I called over to Claudia, asking her to look after our stuff while we took a walk. "Nós estamos indo para uma caminhada." I hung Nina's bag on her chair and left my cigarettes on the table.

"Claro, Oliver." Claudia waved us off with a smile.

"Obrigado!" I waved back.

I wrapped one arm around Nina's shoulders and steered her onto the soft white sand. I didn't have a watch, but the sun was already painting the sky with pink and gold strokes, so I guessed we probably only had another hour of light left on the beach.

"Where did you learn to speak Portuguese?" Nina interrupted my calculations.

"Here, in Portugal. We moved a lot when I was a child." I twirled a lock of her hair through my fingers.

"Do you speak any other languages?"

"Well, English and Portuguese." I smiled. "And French. And German. And Spanish. A little Afrikaans and a tiny bit of Xhosa," I finished, wiggling my eyebrows.

"Wow, that's impressive." She laughed. "You're full of surprises."

"And you're gorgeous."

I hugged her closer and as our eyes found each other's again something blossomed between us. She felt it too, because the same longing was written all over her face. I pulled her closer and she wrapped her arms around my waist before she let one hand drift up under my T-shirt, setting my skin on fire. She dragged her other hand slowly up my arm and tangled her fingers into my hair as she pulled my head down to her lips. I kissed her deeply and hungrily and as she moaned into my mouth liquid fire burned through my veins and turned my bones to jelly.

"Oliver," she breathed and I became aware of our exposed position on the beach. I forced my mouth away from her lips.

"Come with me," I whispered into her ear.

She followed me into a secluded cove I'd discovered the last time I was here with my parents. It was hidden away behind some giant rocks at the front, and the cliffs sheltered it from the back. It was completely hidden from the beach and you could only access it at low tide through a gap in the rocks. It felt like a secret paradise. The shallow water that lapped through the rocks was crystal clear and the white sand was somehow finer and softer than the main beach. Green moss covered the rocks at the front, and the cliff was sprinkled with purple wildflowers.

I sat down on the cool sand and pulled Nina towards me. She kneeled next to me and wrapped her arms around my shoulders, cradling my head against her chest. I curled my arms around her waist and held her against me for a moment before I trailed my hands up her arms and held her face to look into her blazing yellow eyes. It should have frightened me, but I just wanted to be close to her.

I moved my hands into her hair and kissed her with every splinter of emotion I had ever felt. All my pain, grief, fear, joy, love, excitement, anger and all the sharpest fragments of utter madness, it all melted into desperation. I could feel the same urgency rolling off her as well, and it brought me back to my senses. I lifted my mouth and kissed her eyes and then her cheeks as I tried to slow things down. It didn't matter how much I wanted her, this wasn't the right time or place. This wasn't real.

"What's wrong?" she whispered as she felt my reluctance.

"Not here." I continued to kiss her face.

"Don't you want me?"

"Nina, I want you more than I can explain, but not here."

"Oliver," she whispered, pulling my face up to look into her eyes. "We don't have time. I can feel it." Her eyes were flicking between bright yellow and pale blue and I realised her body was shivering. "I don't want you to go. I'm scared." Tears started forming on her dark lashes.

"Nina, I can't explain it, but everything will be all right. I promise. Trust me, okay?" I wrapped my arms around her and she blinked. I didn't know why I'd said that. What did I know? There was no reason for her to trust me. I had no idea what was going on with either of us. But I knew I had to try and make her feel better. I had to trust that everything would be okay.

"Okay." Tears streamed down her cheeks as she nodded. She hid her head in my chest and I screwed my eyelids tightly shut, hugging her even closer.

When I opened my eyes, I was crouched into myself, hugging my legs against my chest, and Nina was gone. This time, she was the one who'd left me. Although it wasn't as traumatic as the dreams where I'd left her, and although I hadn't forgotten that I was dreaming this time, her disappearance still left me bereft. I wanted to stay curled up in my little paradise forever, but I was getting cold and the tide was coming in. It was time to wake up and get back to my mundane hell. I leaned my head on my knees and took a few deep breaths before I pulled myself up and dragged my heavy feet back to Claudia's taverna.

My dad was sitting at the little table I'd shared with Nina earlier. All Nina's belongings were gone. My heart compressed and I swallowed the emotion away with effort.

"Hey, Dad." I slumped down next to him.

"Ollie." He squeezed my shoulder. "All right, son?"

"I don't know." I shrugged with a heavy sigh.

"You have to stay focussed, Oliver. Things are not what they seem."

"How?" I snapped, but I knew he wouldn't answer. I raked my hands through my hair and let out a frustrated groan. "Everything's so messed up." I dropped my head on my arms on the table in front of us.

"You're stronger than you think."

"I don't think so, Dad," I whispered as I turned my head toward him.

"You are, my boy." He touched my cheek.

I clasped my fingers around his hand on my cheek and silently held on to him for as long as I could.

"It's time to wake up." He finally stood after he watched me for a long time.

"I miss you so much." I scraped my own chair backwards and unfolded my limbs before I enveloped myself in the warmth of his chest as he hugged me close.

CHAPTER 8

The room was grey with the haziness of dawn when I woke up. An antiseptic smell assaulted my nostrils while the comforting scent of my dad still lingered at the edges of my mind. My brain was thumping against my skull and I felt like I wanted to crawl out of my own skin, but I wasn't sure if it was actual pain or just heartache. The white numbers on my clock screamed that it was only just gone four twenty-three a.m. and there was no way I was going to stay awake to try and figure it all out. I requested some pain relief and allowed my heavy eyelids to take me back into the darkness.

"Good morning." Sophie's voice intruded into my state of oblivion all too soon. I groaned and turned my head away. "Hey, sleepy." She sounded way too lively, and I wished I could still throw stuff at her like I used to do when I was a teenager. "Come on, darling. It's half past eight."

I yanked my head back to the other side again and opened one eye to glare at her, which only made her laugh.

"Gosh, Ollie." She smiled warily and I started pinpointing objects within my reach to chuck at her.

"What do you want?"

"Are you not feeling well?" She looked at me through narrowed eyes and felt my forehead like you would with a bloody toddler who had the sniffles.

"No, Sophie. I'm not feeling well, actually." I swiped her hand away. "I'm stuck in this bed like a fucking imbecile. I can't even take myself for a piss when I feel like it. So no, I'm not feeling well. Not well at fucking all."

"Did you have a bad dream?" She ignored my rant and asked another condescending question that just happened to be spot-fucking-on.

I growled something inaudible and enhanced it with a dramatic hate stare.

"What is it?" She sat down on the chair next to my bed, but I ignored her and turned on the music player.

Joey Ramone was singing about Sheena, who didn't want to go surfing with the kids from school, and I mumbled along as I tried to tune Sophie out. I wondered if Sheena ever did make it as a punk rocker in New York.

"Ollie!" Sophie interrupted my Ramones mysteries and turned the music down.

"Why do you care? It's not like you can do anything." I turned the music up again and tapped my fingers along to the beat. I bloody loved the Ramones.

"Oliver!" she snapped.

My mother always said that she smugly thought all the so-called teenage moodiness passed Sophie by completely. Sophie was just born mature and level-headed. But then I'd turned thirteen and my mother had realised that I got enough moods for both of us and then some. The thought unintentionally cheered me up and I half-heartedly allowed a grin to twitch at the corner of my mouth.

"Sorry." I sighed and reached over to turn the music down again.

"All right. What's going on?"

"I feel this huge sense of loss, Soph," I blurted out after a long moment of silence. "I was flicking through Mum's journals last night and I wish I could speak to her. And to Dad. I had another dream about Nina when I fell asleep and I saw Dad at the end. I just wanted to crawl into his lap and stay there."

"Ollie, I can't even imagine how difficult this must be for you, but you have to stay positive. You have to work hard to get your life back."

My blood was starting to boil again. I knew she meant well, but I wanted to grab her by the shoulders and shake her until she really understood how I felt. "Don't you think I know that? Don't you think I want to get out of this motherfucking bed more than any-thing?" As I paused to catch my breath, I realised that I didn't want to fight with Sophie. "Why did you wake me anyway?"

She closed her eyes for a moment before she took a deep breath. "The boys are—"

I held up my hand to stop her before she could finish. "Absolutely not."

"Oliver! They're downstairs and they're not going to leave until you see them." She was trying to stay calm, but I could see that she was losing her temper too.

"I said no." I turned the music up again.

The song had changed to Skunk Anansie, 'Hedonism', and my mind pondered on the guys. My best friends. My bandmates. My brothers.

"Ollie," she tried again, but I raised my finger to silence her.

"All right. I'll see them after breakfast." I closed my eyes and pinched the bridge of my nose. I knew they weren't going to stop trying, so I might as well get it over with.

I tried to drag my breakfast out as long as possible, but eventually I had to finish my food before it was inedible. Sophie had to leave for work and I knew that there was nothing I could do to delay their impending visit any longer, so I told her to send them up on her way out. I couldn't remember the last time I'd been so nervous. I knew that they only wanted to be there for me, but I didn't know how to cope with it.

Guns N' Roses were singing 'Don't you cry' on my speaker and my fingers itched to play along. "Can you hand me my guitar, please?" I asked the nurse after Sophie left.

I'd not tried to play since the accident. I tested my stiff fingers, strumming the familiar chords. It felt great and by the time the chorus started for the second time, I was in my element. I quietly sang along and halfway through the third verse I looked up when three other voices joined in.

I hadn't noticed them coming in. I met their gazes one by one without breaking a note. They sat down on my bed and we finished the lyrics together. They waited for me to play through the extended guitar solo near the end until the music stopped. I put my hand over the strings to silence the guitar and closed my eyes, trying to fight back the tears that were threatening to spill over again.

I'd always been a moody fucker, but the past few weeks had turned me into a weeping little bitch. I shook my head and opened my eyes again. The guys closed in and locked their arms in a circle around me. I hung my head.

"I'm sorry," I whispered eventually and lifted my eyes to look into their faces again. I expected to see pity and despair, but I only saw relief. However, Kellan started frowning and I knew what was coming.

"What the actual fuck, Oliver? It's been three weeks. We've been worried bloody sick. You don't even have enough decency to give us a call?" He pulled my mobile from his jacket pocket and tossed it in my direction. It bounced off my chest and landed in my lap. "What are you anyway, some fuckwit, refusing to have your phone? Do you think you're the only one who's going through a hard time? How would you feel if it was one of us who nearly fucking died and then blanked you for three weeks? You're a self-absorbed bastard, do you know that?" He threw his hands in the air and glared down at me.

"Enough, Kel." Ian stepped closer to Kellan and squeezed his shoulder, but Kellan pushed his hand away and told him to piss off.

"It's all right, Ian. He's right." I locked gazes with Kellan. "I am sorry."

"Why didn't you want to see us?" Charlie asked from behind Kellan and Ian.

"I don't know." I shook my head. "It seems stupid now. I'm messed up." Kellan's scowl softened. "I didn't want you to give me a pep talk. Or, worse, pity me."

"Yeah, well"—Kellan shrugged—"we're here now, so get over it. And keep your fucking phone on."

"Yes, you're okay and that's all that matters." Ian nodded, visibly relieved that Kellan hadn't kicked my arse right out of the hospital bed.

"Thank you. And I really am sorry. I mean it." I lifted my eyebrows, silently adding that I would not apologise again and that Kellan should drop it.

Kellan smiled briefly and nodded, but he kept staring at me through narrowed eyes. He knew me well. Very well.

"No worries, Olive." Charlie grinned and instantly lifted the mood. He possessed an internal happiness and childlike inability to hold a grudge. He also had an honest aversion to any form of confrontation. It was one of the things that had pulled me in when I first met him. "Where do we go for a smoke in this joint?" He produced a crumpled-up packet of fags from his jeans pocket.

"In the garden." I pointed at the window with my thumb. "You guys go ahead. I'll ask Stuart to bring me out." I rang the bell.

"Sure." Ian started moving towards the door. "Come on, Charlton."

"Take my guitar." I looked at Kellan. "We can play while you're here."

"I'm waiting with you."

"I'll take it." Charlie picked it up and walked out of the door.

I nodded, feeling nervous about Kellan watching me being put into my pram, but I could see that there was no way I would be able to get him to leave with the other two, and if I was completely honest, I wasn't really expecting him to anyway.

"You okay, Ols?" He leaned his face into mine as soon as Ian and Charlie left the room. "I mean here." He tapped my heart with his middle and forefinger.

Like I said, Kellan knew me well. There was a time after my parents died when I'd just fallen apart. Frequently and violently. I was angry, and aggressive, and I sought out trouble wherever I could.

Charlie and Ian had mostly kept a wide berth, but Kellan had had to get me out of trouble more than a few times, and if he hadn't literally beaten me back to my senses, I would have ended up in jail.

"No," I admitted with a sigh. "But I will be."

"Are you sure?" He kept his deep green eyes fixed on me.

"Not really. I'll let you know when I need to be straightened out though." I produced a lopsided grin, which made him nod in satisfaction.

"Don't worry. I'll be watching." He straightened up.

"You called, Ollie?" Stuart came into the room and started walking towards my bed, but stopped in his tracks and openly gawked at Kellan. "Didn't I just see you go out?"

The effect Kellan and Ian had on people never stopped amusing me, and Stuart obviously wasn't immune to their tall-dark-and-devilish-in-duplicate charm either.

"My brother." Kellan smirked.

"Oh. Okay. Wow." Stuart's eyes widened before he pulled himself together again. "What can I do for you, Ollie?"

"Could I go outside for a bit, please?"

"Yes, of course." He got the wheelchair from the corner.

I'd got upgraded from the La-Z-Boy contraption to a normal wheelchair earlier in the week, and I also only needed one person to assist me getting into it, so I was silently thankful that I wasn't quite as pathetic as before. I knew that I was being dramatic and that Kellan wasn't the one who was uncomfortable with my helplessness, but I was still glad he never got to see me like that.

We stayed outside for an hour, smoking and singing. We even managed to draw a bit of a hospital crowd, and when everybody clapped after we played our last song, my face cracked a genuine smile for the first time in weeks.

CHAPTER 9

After the guys left, I had a nap and ate my lunch before I went for my first physio session. I didn't know what to expect, but even though it was physically more challenging than I'd thought, I did start feeling flickerings of optimism to get my own life back.

I asked the nurse who pushed me back from the treatment centre to leave me in Nina's room for a while. I expected Zach or her parents to be there, but unfortunately Marcus Bentley was standing next to her bed and he cocked up my day entirely.

"Marcus." I grimaced as the nurse left the room.

"Oliver." He nodded politely and instantly got on my nerves. "How are you?"

"Really well, actually," I answered snottily.

"That's good." He smiled, sincerely and without any malice, and for some reason it made me want to rip his head off.

He was standing on the other side of Nina's bed with his hands in his pockets, appraising me with a curious look on his face. It took all my strength not to tell him to piss off. I held his eyes for a moment and started stroking my thumb across Nina's hand, at which point he released a breath.

"Do you have a problem?" I enunciated the words.

"No. I am intrigued by your interest in Nina though, especially since she's the reason you're here."

All the hair on my body stood up. "What? What are you talking about?"

"Nina was drunk that night," he said and I could almost hear the oxygen leave my body.

"I will kill you," I snarled as my self-control slipped, but he just kept looking at me with raised eyebrows. My brain felt like it was exploding. I hated him. I wanted to hurt him. I wanted to tear him apart piece by piece. But I knew he wasn't lying. He was right. It had been at the back of my mind since I woke up, but I'd refused to accept it. I'd refused to remember.

"Her blood tests?" Fury detonated in my stomach.

"I don't know. There must have been a mistake."

"How?" My voice sounded too slow now. Raw. Like a savage's.

"I don't know, Ollie."

"Why did you let her drive?" I clenched and unclenched my jaw as I tried to force oxygen into my lungs.

"I didn't. I called her a taxi."

"Why the fuck did she drive?"

"I don't know." He shook his head. "She was being difficult. My taxi arrived before hers. She was making a scene. I had to get to the airport. I left. I'm sorry."

"Fuck," I growled, my brain throbbing behind my eyes.

"I didn't realise she would get hurt. I expected her to wait for her taxi. I never would have left her if I knew."

"Why are you telling me?" Things were starting to go out of focus. I couldn't process the words he was saying.

"I feel responsible."

I couldn't respond. My body was shaking as I gripped the arm-rests on my wheelchair. My knuckles turned white with the pressure. I had a million inconsistencies running through my brain, but I couldn't put the letters in the right order. I couldn't tell my mouth to form the words. It was all too messed up. I couldn't cope with it.

"I'm sorry, Oliver." He rocked back on his heels and left the room without a further glance at me. I sat, numbly staring at Nina.

I wanted to break something. I wanted to be sick—I could feel it churning in my stomach. I wanted to scream, and shout, and lose my shit. But I didn't do any of that. I silently dropped my head on my arms on Nina's bed. I knew Marcus Bentley was right. I knew

Nina had been drinking too much that night. I knew this was all her fault. I had known it all along. I'd just refused to admit it. I couldn't. I don't know how long I stayed like that beside her. Time stood still.

"Ollie?" Zach spoke next to me and I lifted my head. "What's the matter?"

I just shook my head. I couldn't answer him.

"You know?" He ran his hands through his hair and pulled up a chair next to me.

"*You* knew?" My voice was hoarse.

"Yes." He closed his eyes and massaged the side of his head. "When her bloods came back clear I knew there must have been a mistake."

"Why didn't you say anything?" I frowned, struggling to control my voice.

"Why do you think? We've all suffered enough." His eyes were apologetic, but I knew he was more sorry that I had found out. And even in my unhinged state, I couldn't blame him. "How did you find out?"

"Marcus told me."

"Why?"

I just shrugged. Who cared why? Or how the blood tests got it wrong? I pressed my thumb and my forefinger into my eyes and tried to take a deep breath, but my heart was marching up my throat and my breath came out in short puffs. I had to get out of her room. I had to get away from her.

"I can't be here," I choked.

Zach nodded once before he got up and pushed me back towards my room. He paused at the nurses' station and told them that I wasn't feeling well.

"Do you need pain relief?" the nurse asked as she helped me into bed and I nodded with closed eyes.

"I'm sorry, Ollie," Zach said next to me and touched my shoulder, but I ignored him.

I spiralled into my drug-induced black hole and stayed there for as long as I possibly could.

When Sophie came in at dinnertime she asked if I was okay, but I just said that I was tired from having the guys over and going to physio earlier that day. Was it really the same day? I mechanically ate my dinner and requested drugs to help me sleep. I didn't know if she stayed with me after I fell asleep and I didn't care. I just wanted to have silence. I just wanted nothing.

A few times during the night I felt myself almost touching the edges of a dream. I saw glimpses of Nina's face and I heard shards of her voice, but I forced myself to wake up and not give in to the dream. I ended up lying awake, contemplating my fate for hours. By the time the first sliver of morning started peeking through my window I had convinced myself that I had to pull myself together and get my life back.

I'd had to sit through enough cognitive behavioural therapy in my life to know what I had to do to move forward. I was going to put all my energy into my recovery so that I could get up and walk out of this motherfucking hospital as soon as bloody possible. And, when I wasn't busy with physio, I was going to write new songs for the band. I was going to get the guys to come and rehearse with me every single day. But, most importantly, I was going to stay the hell away from Nina. In this hospital, and in my dreams. I was going to force my brain to focus on the positive things. Productive things. Things I did have some control over. Because, if I allowed myself to drown in the swamp of shit that was brewing just beneath the surface, it was likely that I would never come back up again.

I kept my new, ambitious attitude up for a couple more weeks, and it pleased everybody around me. Dr. Harold and Sophie thought that I had finally taken a turn for the better and they encouraged me to stay focussed. I worked my ass off in physio and with every session I could feel myself getting stronger and regaining more and more control over my arms, torso and hips. My legs were still useless, but it was quite amazing to learn how to manage my body without them. It made me increasingly determined to keep going. I started regaining some feeling, almost like needles and pins, in my left foot. Dr. Harold said that although some sensation in paralysed limbs can almost always be expected, he was still hopeful that I would eventually make a full recovery.

The guys came every day, sometimes more than once a day. They were a huge distraction and it was cool to have them around. Kellan spent noticeably more time with me than the others.

"I'm onto you, you know." He put his guitar in the corner and kicked his legs up on the side of my bed as he leaned back in his chair and clamped his hands behind his head.

"I know." I sighed and put my laptop on the bedside table. It was late one afternoon and we were working on a new song I'd started writing earlier that week. "Let's go out for a smoke." I pointed at my wheelchair. Kellan called for Stuart to help me transfer into it and then pushed me outside to sit under the oak.

"So, what's with the new attitude?" He blew smoke from the side of his mouth.

"It's the only way I can cope at the moment," I admitted, dragging on my own cigarette.

"Although you're not really coping, are you?" He cocked an eyebrow and flicked into the ashtray next to him.

"I guess not." I shrugged. "It's better than drowning in my own shit, which is what I really want to do. So give me a break."

He stayed silent for a bit, chewing on his lip. "You're just treading water in it now and I'm thinking it's not going to be pretty when you go down."

"Yeah, I know." I stubbed out my cigarette.

"Look, Ols, I can only imagine how difficult this must be." He gestured at my wheelchair. "I really can, so don't think I'm trying to take away from the enormity of your situation. I just don't think it's the only reason you're so messed up though, and I expect that Nina, or your thoughts about Nina, has something to do with it." He poked his thumb in the direction of the hospital building.

I hadn't really talked about Nina with the guys, and I wasn't sure

I wanted to, so I looked down and picked at an invisible thread on my sweats.

"I'll take your silence as a yes then. Sophie told me that you've been having these weird dreams about her and that you feel connected to her in some way. And I remember how you looked at her that night. But I've noticed that Zach hasn't been around the past couple of weeks. You've not been to see her either, and the more I think about it, the more I suspect it's because you have some internal battle going on in your head about who's to blame for the accident."

"Close," I mocked bitterly, "but not quite. And yes, I'm having a hard time dealing with it. I absolutely do have a battle going on in my head. And yes, again, I know it's going to be a disaster when I go down, but like I said, I don't know how else to cope! So I'm going to keep treading for as long as I can!"

"Well, I don't think you're treading nearly as well as you think you are."

"I don't give a fuck what you think," I sneered. "You don't know shit."

"Explain it to me then, Ols. Why are you conflicted?" He softened his gaze as he held mine, and for some reason his pity, or consoling, or whatever he was doing, pushed my temper to boiling point.

"Because, you insolent arsehole, Marcus Bentley told me two weeks ago that Nina was blind fucking drunk that night! She wasn't supposed to drive at all. The hospital fucked up the blood tests somehow!" Kellan's pupils dilated and I paused as he digested the information. "So, I'm using every fucking ounce of dignity I have to try and keep it together. I know her family has been through a lot. I know they don't deserve more trauma. But can you even begin to comprehend how it's destroying me that my life has once again been ripped apart by a drunk fucker who will, once again, never suffer the consequences! I'm right back on that fucking bridge, Kel! All alone. The same terrified kid waiting for someone to come and save him!" A raw sob tore through my chest. "Argh!" I roared into the air, overcome with anger. And grief. And pain.

I pushed my thumb and forefinger into my eyes and took many deep breaths. Eventually, the rage left my body and I removed my fingers from my eyes before rubbing my hair around and around on my head. Kellan watched me, a frown knotting his dark brows together. After a few moments, he reached out and took one of my hands into both of his before he leaned in.

"I get it, Ollie. It's so unbelievably, impossibly cruel. On so many levels. And yes, I will never, for as long as I live, understand why you've had to suffer through so much. I don't think anyone will, because it is utterly fucking diabolical. But she's been unconscious in that bed for the past four—or is it five?—weeks as well. And yes, her family is also suffering. They are also going through hell. As unfair as it might be, and as much as this is her fault, she did not paralyse you on purpose and then skip off into the sunset. And you know better than anyone that your hatred is going to destroy you."

I shook my head and dropped my eyes.

"None of us will ever fully understand what you're going through, Ols." He held the back of my neck and forced my eyes back to him. "But you have to keep fighting for yourself, brother. We're all here for you. We'll always be here. You'll never be alone again. But you have to fight as well. You have to deal with this anger. You have to let go of this hatred. Or you will drown." He shook my head a little. "You. Are. Not! What happened to you, Oliver Lawrence. You are love, and passion, and talent, and determination, and fucking magic!"

He rested his forehead against mine as I wept silently. Eventually I lifted my gaze and he kept his eyes locked on mine until I finally sighed, wiped my face with my hand and nodded an end to the conversation.

I saw Zach sitting next to Nina's bed when we went past her room and I tried to look away before he noticed me, but our eyes met and he lifted his hand with a small smile. I nodded back at him. I hadn't spoken to him since the week before and I felt bad, but he was too close to Nina.

"Can I come in for a moment?" He popped his head around my door a few minutes later.

"Hey, Zach. Sure." I gestured at the chair next to my bed.

"I know you're upset, and angry, and I understand why, but I wanted to let you know that Nina's not doing well, Ollie." He sucked in his lower lip before letting out a deep sigh.

I just stared at him. What could I possibly say?

"Her heart is failing. They told us she doesn't have much time left." His voice broke.

"I'm sorry," I finally choked some words out.

"Me too, Ollie." He scrubbed his hands over his face. "And if Nina was awake, she would tell you that she was sorry too."

He looked bloody awful. Completely and utterly defeated. I should have been more devastated. But I was numb.

"Anyway." He got up. "I wanted to tell you." He stuffed his hands into his pockets.

"Thank you." I stared up at him. "And I really am sorry. I mean it."

"I know." He squeezed my arm before he put his hand back in his pocket and left the room with hunched shoulders.

CHAPTER 10

When Sophie turned up the next day, I could see that she was feeling as shit as I was. "Hey." She smiled, but it didn't quite reach her eyes.

It was unusual for her to look down, but I knew how she was feeling. The anniversary of our parents' deaths was coming up and no matter how hard I'd tried to prepare myself in the past, it never got any easier. I could imagine how hard it must have been for her as well. She always tried to be the brave one. The pragmatic problem-solver. The sane one, always taking care of me. But she was also only human.

I felt an unexpected wave of admiration and gratitude wash over me as I looked into her eyes. I could almost hear her brain straining under the pressure of trying to keep it all together and yet she never complained. Not once.

"Hey." I smiled and reached for her hand.

"Okay?" She sat down next to me and took a sip from her take-away coffee, swearing when she scalded her lip.

"Yeah, fine." I waved my other hand dismissively. "You?"

"All right. This is always going to be a difficult week. We just have to get through it. Next week will be better."

"Do you want to talk about them for a bit?" Sometimes it helped to talk about my parents and remember them together, especially when we were this sad. I guess it made us feel connected to them and reminded us that we were once a happy family, that there were so many happy times. So many happy memories.

"Not today. Thanks though." She put her coffee down and leaned into me for a tight hug. "It all just feels like a bit much at the moment, you know?"

"Yeah." I held her against my chest and kissed the top of her head.

She only stayed for another fifteen minutes before she left, promising to be back that evening. Just like every day. The same monotonous routine. It made me sick.

At some point that day Charlie came in for a visit and his uninhibited joy instantly cheered me up. He actually, for real, skipped into my room and made one of the nurses burst into a fit of giggles when he grabbed her hand, twirled her around, kissed her on the cheek and spun her out of the room before coming back in and plopping down on the end of my bed.

"Howzit, Olive?" He nonchalantly pulled Ian's drumsticks from the afro-man-bun affair he had going on on top of his head and tapped them on my legs. Ian had a fit every time Charlie played his drums and I bet Charlie had taken the sticks right after Ian told him to get off.

Charlie might have been the best on the piano, but he wasn't nearly as bad on the drums as Ian tried to make out. In fact, Charlie was talented enough to play any instrument in any band. Music simply flowed from every part of him. His family was a blend of Afrikaans and Xhosa cultures and Charlie believed his African heritage made him feel rhythm on a different level than the rest of us. Wherever his unrestrained talent came from, I was just glad to have it in our band.

"Hey, Charlton." I smiled. "How are you?"

"Lekker, Olive, lekker." He pushed the drumsticks back into his hair, criss-crossed through the afro-man-bun thing, like two sophisticated Chinese hair sticks. It should have looked ridiculous, but on Charlie it was just cool.

He was the most fashionable out of the four of us by about a million miles. He made everything look unpretentious. I was brutal. Too big, too temperamental and much too contemplative. I lived in old jeans, faded T-shirts and biker boots. Kellan and Ian were well-presented demons. Kellan was more restrained than Ian, but still devilish. Tall, charming, and very mischievous. They wore branded jeans, witty T-shirts and posh trainers.

Charlie was elegant and masculine in exactly the right measures. He had the lightest green-brown eyes you'd ever come across and his dad's brown complexion and African hair. He dressed in outrageous outfits that made him look like he came straight off the Vivienne Westwood runway. The only reason I even knew who the hell Vivienne Westwood was was because Charlie had actually walked her runway at the London and Paris Fashion Weeks for the past three years. People openly stared and commented on how beautiful he was wherever he went. There was just no other way to describe him; he was the most beautiful and enchanting person in every room.

He picked up my guitar and started playing the intro to 'Beautiful Day' and it made me smile some more. "What are you up to today?" I asked.

"Nah, Olive, niks, brother, nothing, nada. It's Charlie day today." He smoothed into Bruno Mars's 'Lazy Song'. He bobbed his head along and made up his own words as he carried on and I was thoroughly amused by the time he finished. "What about you? Exciting plans?" He continued strumming some generic chords.

"Yeah, terribly exciting." I snorted. "I have physio later, then a nap, followed by a highly appetising tea of steamed chicken and veg, perhaps an early evening trip to the garden, before finally finishing the day with a relaxing sponge bath and only slightly uncomfortable catheter change." I wiggled my eyebrows.

"Haibo." Charlie chuckled as he transitioned into another Bruno Mars song, 'Count on Me'. He jumped up on the last bit and twirled around before he curtsied.

"Bravo, Charlton!" I clapped. "You're the bomb, brother."

"Any time, Olive, any time." He did a little bow and roll with his hand. "You know you're my favourite." He winked before he hugged me tight, kissed my cheek with a smack, and put my guitar to the side.

"Thanks." I laughed, but then realised with a shock that I had just spent the past ten minutes feeling happy.

That was one of the most unsettling things about grief. People thought that you spent every moment in a deep, dark depression, and in some ways that would almost be easier. But grief didn't work like that at all. Some normal things still entertained me just as much as they would have done before, like Charlie.

We'd started at the Academy of Contemporary Music in Guildford on the same day. Kellan and Ian had gone there too, but I'd had to take a year off because of the accident and my parents' deaths, so they were ahead of us. Charlie was a year younger and we ended up in the same year and some days he was the only reason I had enough courage to get up and go to my lessons.

Even when we were kids, when I first met him back in Mossel Bay, I'd gravitated to him. He had this brilliant effervescence that made me want to be around him all the time. We'd clicked within the first five minutes of meeting, and a couple years later when we reconnected, even though I was monumentally messed up because of the loss of my parents and the trauma of the accident, Charlie still made me laugh just as spontaneously as before. I would almost feel normal. Almost. But then reality would smack me in the face with a force that made me lose my breath, and I would feel worse than before, because now I also felt guilty for laughing and forgetting about my loss for a moment. Then Charlie would remind me that I still deserved to laugh and have fun.

The process was utterly exhausting, but it was one of the few things that made me feel like life was worth living. And this morning, just like then, Charlie made me forget—he made me feel like I had something to live for, like I could achieve anything. Being around Charlie made me happy; and, perhaps more importantly, Charlie also made me feel like it made him happy to be around me. Charlie breathed life.

He stayed with me until Stuart came in to take me to physio. He promised to be back later that evening and then flounced off to fasci-

nate the rest of Guildford. Stuart helped me transfer into my wheelchair and made small talk on the way to the gym, but I was distracted
and nodded along. As we rolled past Nina's room I noticed her parents, Zach, and Dr. Harold gathered around her bed. Ice slithered all
the way down my spine and I looked up at Stuart with a frown.

"It's not good, Oliver." He shook his head. "One of the nurses
called the family to be with her last night."

I closed my eyes and nodded, exhaling slowly.

She was dying.

"Do you want to go in?" Stuart asked, but I shook my head. I
shouldn't be there. Nina was dying. It had nothing to do with me.

Everything became fuzzy and it felt like I was stuck between reality and the dreamworld. Images of Nina flashed through my mind.
The first time I'd laid eyes on her crossing the road in Haslemere.
The first time we'd spoken at the club. The first time I'd kissed her
in those dark woods, in my dream. The way her eyes crinkled at the
sides when she smiled. The way her skin felt under my hands. The
faint scent of wild flowers that surrounded her. I gripped the sides of
my wheelchair tightly and tried to breathe. It was too much.

I have to do something.

What?

"Do you want to go back to your room, Ollie?" I felt Stuart's
hand on my shoulder.

"No." The word came out gravelly and I cleared my throat.

I didn't really register when Stuart left me in the gym. I went
through the motions like a robot. The physiotherapist kept telling
me to focus, but it was Nina who consumed me completely.

My body was in the gym. My mind floated around in a mirrored room and everywhere I looked Nina was staring back at me.
Most of the images were memories of moments we'd shared in
the dreamworld, but I caught a glimpse of an image I had not seen
before. I knew it wasn't from my dreams.

I was sitting in my wheelchair and Nina was curled up in my lap.
I had one arm wrapped around her waist and I ran my other hand

through her hair. She had a thick scar, which ran all the way from her temple along the side of her face and across her throat. It ended just above her collarbone. She tipped her head back with a smile and I kissed a trail from the corner of her eye to the bottom of the scar. She looked back up at me and whispered that she loved me. I closed my eyes in contentment and hugged her closer to me.

It was an image of the future.

The real future.

Our future.

I had to do something.

I had to get out of there.

"Oliver, be careful!" The physio's voice ripped through my ears.

It was too late.

I had already made my decision.

My hands slipped from the H-bars I was holding on to.

My useless legs buckled underneath me and I fell on my arse with a thump before my head bounced back up and then smacked against the floor.

All the air left my lungs.

I heard the physio scream for help and I knew that it was bad.

As it should be.

"Keep still, Ollie." She bent her head down next to mine on the floor. "Stay very still."

I tried to nod, but I don't know if I did.

I had no idea what the hell was going on, but for the first time, it felt like it was as it was meant to be. It shouldn't have made sense, but somehow it did. I felt at peace. Nothing else mattered.

CHAPTER 11

I woke up with a terrible feeling of déjà vu. Heart monitor beeping on one side. Lung monitor whizzing on the other side. My sister slumped over the edge of my bed, clutching my hand. My brain battling to break through my skull, my throat catching fire with every breath, and my torso strapped into a tight brace.

"Soph," I whispered, squeezing her hand as she lifted her head and opened her eyes with effort. "What happened?"

"You had an accident yesterday." She rubbed one eye with her free hand, smearing make-up across her cheek. "In the gym, remember?"

I shook my head and tried to clear my throat.

Sophie let go of my hand and passed me a glass of water. I forced my head up and took a few sips while I willed my thoughts to take order. I leaned my head back against the headboard and pinched the bridge of my nose.

"Ollie." Sophie sighed. "You cracked one of the fused discs."

The moment she said the word 'cracked', I remembered.

Stuart pushed me past Nina's room and I was overwhelmed when I realised she was going to die.

"Dr. Harold said the injury was too delicate to attempt another surgery." Sophie started crying. "But the disc..." Her voice drifted off as I replayed the previous day in my head.

I wasn't concentrating in the gym. I saw a vision of my future with Nina. I slipped off the H-bars. I decided to fall. I chose to fall. To be with Nina.

"There was a lot of pressure on your coccyx, which they had to relieve with a small lumbar procedure. They kept you sedated to manage the pain and to keep you still," Sophie droned on, oblivious to my recall of events.

I nodded, but I found it difficult to focus. I wanted to know what had happened to Nina. Was she still alive? I couldn't ask Sophie, though. It would tip her over the edge. I could see that she was not okay. I closed my eyes with a sigh.

"Soph," I whispered eventually. "It's all right. Everything will be okay."

Confusion pulled on her tired eyes. "Ollie." A heavy breath forced its way through her lips.

"It'll be okay," I said again, but trailed off when Dr. Harold and Stuart walked into the room. Sophie's phone started ringing and she moved away to answer it.

Stuart looked at all the readings on the hardware that was plugged into me and discussed it with Dr. Harold, who nodded and made satisfied noises. Dr. Harold read through my notes while Stuart disconnected the machines and raised my bed.

Dr. Harold launched straight into his explanation on the extent of my injury. He clarified that it was a hairline crack, rather than a break, and he reassured me that it was much more stable than the first injury. Which was all positive. However, I now had some lacerated nerves and it was too unpredictable to attempt another surgery, which could have muscular implications as well. Further nerve and muscular damage could cause complications with my pelvis and hips, which had been unaffected until now. Given that the new injury was stable, there was a possibility that it might heal enough to attempt another surgery, or even that I might eventually get some control back in my legs without surgery, but it was too early to know and the only thing I could do now was rest. I had to wear the brace again for a week. And then start physio again.

He looked tired and fed up as well. He had been pleased with my progress and I could see that it pained him that I was almost back to square one. Sophie came back into the room and stood next to Stuart.

"I understand," I said eventually, keeping my eyes down.

"I'm sorry, Oliver," Dr. Harold said with a sigh and Stuart just squeezed my hand before he slumped out of the room ahead of Dr. Harold.

Dr. Harold followed him, but he stopped at the door and looked back. "Don't lose hope, lad." He nodded with a faint smile and I allowed my own mouth to briefly turn up at the corners too.

"What happened, Ollie?" Sophie sank into the chair next to my bed.

"I'm not sure." I took her hand in both of mine. "I'm sorry."

"Don't apologise." She started crying again and leaned her head on the bed. "It was an accident."

"I don't..." I stroked her hair and kissed her hand. "I don't know. I don't think I was supposed to get better."

"Ollie, don't say that."

"Sorry." I wiped her cheek with my thumb. "I need to sort out my head."

She sniffed again. "That was Kellan on the phone. He'll be up in a minute." She fished around in her bag for a tissue and wiped her nose.

"Why don't you go home for a while, Soph?"

"Are you sure? I can stay."

"Go and get some rest. Kellan's here now."

"All right." She tried to smile, but she looked devastated. "I love you." She kissed my head as she got up to leave.

"Love you too, Soph."

"Whoa." Kellan nearly bumped into Sophie as he walked in. "Hey," he said softly and touched the ends of her hair before he kissed her on the cheek.

"Hi." She moved into his arms for a lingering hug. I cringed inwardly and turned my mouth down. It was too weird not to notice. But it was the very least of my problems and I didn't dwell on it. Kellan kissed the side of her head again and she turned around to smile faintly at me once more before she walked off.

Kellan gave me an awkward sideways hug and patted my shoulder before he sat down on the chair next to my bed. He turned on the speaker and Imagine Dragons started singing their song about demons. It poked holes through my soul. Kellan slumped back, resting his ankle on his knee and linking his fingers on his lap, appraising me for a moment before he spoke. "So, you went under."

"Yeah." I sighed, pursing my lips together. "I went under."

"What happened?" He scratched his cheek.

"I messed up in the gym." I tried to shrug. "I damaged the fused discs."

"Why?"

"Nina's dying, Kel," I choked the words out. "She's probably already... I don't know." The memory of the day before overwhelmed me again and I took a few deep breaths to try and get my thoughts in order.

Kellan stared at me for a long time and I opened my mouth to try and explain again, but he held up his hand to silence me. "We'll talk about it later," he said and I nodded. I didn't know how to explain it anyway. It would just make me sound like more of a lunatic than I already was. I tried to focus on the song that was filling the silence instead.

"She woke up last night. I just spoke to Zach downstairs. She's going to be all right." He leaned forward and watched me closely. I covered my face with both hands and let out one of the breaths I had been holding for weeks. "I'll get Stuart." Kellan unfolded his long limbs. "You should go and see her."

"Thank you." I grabbed his arm and held his gaze.

"Always, Ols." He smiled, turning up the music as he walked out of the door, and Imagine Dragons roared even louder.

We rolled to Nina's room in silence and I was certain that they could hear my heart marching up my throat as we got closer. I covered my mouth with my hand when I saw her. She was propped

79

up against the headboard and her dark hair spilled onto the white pillows. She still looked fragile, but her cheeks were pink and her eyes sparkled.

I nodded at Stuart to push me inside.

CHAPTER 12

"**O**liver Lawrence." She smiled, making her dimple wink.

"Nina Harrison." My mouth smiled of its own accord. There was no way I could rationalise the feelings I had about this girl. On one level, I felt closer to her than I'd ever felt to anybody in my entire life. It was like I was compelled to be with her. I was consumed by her. But, on another level, I didn't know her at all and she had wrecked me completely. I resented the fact that she could just sit there and make her dimple wink as if she hadn't ruined my life. Opposing emotions swirled through my gut and, just as I was about to be sick all over myself, I managed to ask, "How are you feeling?"

"Okay." She nodded. "And you?"

"All right." I couldn't help openly staring at her.

"I can't believe it." She shook her head.

"I know." It really was surreal. My fingers wanted to reach over and take her hand, but my brain couldn't bear the thought of touching her.

"It's so weird."

"Weird?"

"Zach told me we met at the club that night, and I remember seeing you around town before. But I feel like I... know you... and now you're sitting here and... it's hard to explain." She let out another strained breath.

"I understand. I feel the same." We got lost in each other's eyes again. "We obviously had a great *impact* on each other." I pressed my lips together, not really knowing why I was trying to be funny. It felt like I was having an out-of-body experience. My mind and my mouth weren't co-ordinating.

"Yes, clearly." She snorted. "Do you remember that night?"

"Yeah. You?"

"Not really. I'm struggling to piece it all together." She tucked some hair behind her ear. I nodded as I remembered those first moments after I'd woken up and how confused I'd been. She must've felt disoriented after missing so much time.

"Will you tell me about it?" She interrupted my thoughts.

"Okay." I inflated my cheeks and blew out a slow stream of air. I didn't want to tell her everything. I didn't know yet if I was ever going to tell her that she'd been drunk. But I started talking. "I was working behind the bar at the Guildberry when you came in." I paused when her eyes widened. A soft expression crossed her face and my heart had the audacity to skip a beat.

"You were working behind the bar and our eyes met," she blurted out and a slow smile curved her gorgeous mouth. For some inexplicable reason I was thrilled that she remembered that moment. It made me feel unhinged that I was so desperate for her to like me. I almost called for someone to take me back to my room. I couldn't cope with all the rival emotions her presence summoned up inside me.

"I kept seeing you around town and I wanted to speak to you every time," she carried on before I could say anything. "I don't know. Sorry." She caught herself and shook her head. "Go on." A warm glow spread from her cheeks across the rest of her face and she flicked her eyes down.

I couldn't stop my lips from tipping up. "We looked at each other across the bar and"—I took a deep breath—"and I was happy to finally meet you." I winked and she waved her hand with a shy smile. *What the actual fuck is wrong with me? Why am I flirting with this girl?* But, even as I berated myself, I knew I wasn't going to stop. I didn't know how I was going to live with myself, but I did know that I wanted to get to know Nina. I wanted to be with Nina. "We only talked briefly, and then you hung out with Zach and his friend for the rest of the night and I didn't get to speak to you again."

"Yeah." She smiled broadly, making my heart do another few unpermitted somersaults. "You performed with your band. Lawless, right?" She tucked her hair behind her ear again and flinched as her hand rubbed against a scar on the side of her face. Unmistakably the cut I'd seen in my dreams. "I was so surprised when Jack called you on stage with the band. I thought that it was just Kellan and Ian and the other guy."

"I'm with the band," I quoted a T-shirt I'd seen somewhere. I was like a giddy bloody teenager with a celebrity crush. My head knew that this was the girl who'd crippled me. This was the girl who'd wrecked my life. I resented her with a force that scared me. But another part—probably some delusional, desperate part of my fucked-up heart—didn't give a shit about any of that. I just wanted to make her smile.

"I really liked you," she blurted out, and her cheeks instantly coloured once more. "Shit." She shook her head and touched her glowing cheek.

"I really liked you too." I made a conscious decision in that moment to stop overthinking. To stop judging every reaction and every emotion I felt when I was with her. To just give myself the space and permission to allow my feelings to develop naturally.

"Yeah?" She smiled.

"Yeah. I'm pretty sure I still like you," I whispered. She bit her lower lip as she searched my face and it made my body temperature rise by about a million degrees. "Anyway, Jack called the last round when we finished on stage and everybody left a little while after that."

"Me too?" Her eyebrows furrowed and I nodded.

I tried to be as vague as possible as I told her about the accident. She had her head tilted to the side as she listened to my recollection of events. The accident was still so clear in my mind, yet it also felt like it had happened centuries ago. Nina twirled a lock of long hair through her fingers as she tried to remember those final moments, but I could see that it wasn't coming to her.

"Are your injuries serious? Sorry, obviously it's serious, but I mean is it permanent?"

I couldn't help smiling at her. I loved how she stumbled over her words. It created the impression that she was honest and innocent. It made me feel off-kilter.

Stuart spared me from having to explain the depressing details of my injuries by clearing his throat behind me. "Ollie, time to go."

"Will you come back later?" Nina asked.

"I'll try." I reached over to brush my thumb over her hand, shuddering at my own vulnerability.

It was nearly five when I asked Stuart to take me to see Nina again. I tried to just go with my gut, without analysing my thoughts or intentions, but my stomach was twisted in knots the whole time.

"Ollie, Stuart." Jeffrey nodded as he came out of Nina's room just when Stuart pushed me inside. He seemed so happy that it made my heart expand in my chest.

"Hello." I smiled. "I would ask how you were, but I already know."

"Grateful, Oliver, just grateful." He gleamed in Nina's direction.

Ingrid, Nina's mum, was still sitting with Nina and holding her hand, but she also stood when she noticed me. "We'll be back in a bit." She kissed Nina's head before she came over to give my shoulder a squeeze as they walked off.

I was glad they didn't notice that I was demoted to the brace and specialised wheelchair again. I didn't want to tell them that I'd got hurt again and I didn't want Nina to know that I'd been doing better before she woke up.

"Hey," Nina whispered after Stuart settled me next to her bed.

"Hey," I breathed as I curled my fingers around her hand. I did it without thinking, but she linked her fingers through mine and a small smile curved around her lips, so I didn't pull away like my brain told me to.

"How was your afternoon?"

"It was fine. Yours?"

"Good." She bobbed her head up and down. "It's good to see my parents and my brother. What about your family? Are you close?"

I was a bit taken aback by her question, but then remembered that she didn't know me at all. Of course she didn't know that my parents were dead.

"We were very close." I nodded, swallowing down the lump in my throat. It never stopped hurting. It was particularly hard with the anniversary looming just a few hours away. But I wanted Nina to know me. I wanted to be honest. Or as honest as I could be. "My mum and dad died a few years ago. It's just me and my sister, Sophie." I smiled, trying to hide my melancholy. "And the guys; they're my family too."

"I'm sorry, Ollie." She sighed heavily.

"It's okay." I rubbed my thumb over her hand.

"We don't have to talk about it," she whispered and grasped my hand a little tighter. It was a small thing, but it made me feel closer to her. People often thought it was okay to ask what happened and I always wished I had the guts to ask them why they wanted to know. Over the years I'd learned to politely deflect the intrusive questions, but it was still a trigger for me even when I didn't show it. To be with someone who understood loss enough to respect those boundaries was a sad, but profound moment.

"My sister died two years ago." She swallowed heavily. "We're twins. Some days I get so scared that I'll forget the things that made her Grace. That's her name, Grace. Sometimes I feel like we're blending into the same person in my mind. I don't know. It was the first thing I remembered when I woke up yesterday. Grace is gone."

I lifted her hand to my mouth and placed a kiss on the back. She blinked a few times as she came out of her trance and shook her head.

"I'm sorry." She wiped her cheek and seemed surprised to find it damp.

Our words dried up after that, but I sat with her until she started falling asleep. I realised that I didn't feel uncomfortable or upset. It felt like I was meant to be there, like I would never want to be anywhere else. It puzzled me to feel such an overpowering commitment to her, but I somehow knew that it was unconditional and unchangeable.

Nina was categorically linked to my heart and it excited me and scared me shitless in equal measure. When I'd had that vision of our future the day before, the truth had slammed into me with a force. I couldn't even try to fight it. I'd just instantly known that we needed each other to be alive. I'd been convinced that I had to be paralysed in order to save her life.

I didn't know how I felt it so strongly. I didn't know how it was possible. But I knew with every fibre in my being that our lives were connected in a way that made her get weaker as I got stronger. The more I focussed on myself, the more I resented her, the more she suffered and the emptier I became. I didn't want to live in a world where she didn't exist. It was insane, but I had to choose to save myself—to motivate myself with hatred and resentment—or to save her and damn myself to this sedentary hell. I knew now that I would choose her every time. But what if she wouldn't have chosen this life with me? Would she still be interested in me if she knew that my future was so restricted?

I groaned and pressed my lips against her hand. She smiled sleepily, opening her eyes and meeting mine with so much tenderness that it took my breath away. I stroked the hair away from her face and trailed my fingertip along the length of her scar.

When I lifted my head, I looked straight into Sophie's eyes. She was standing right there in Nina's doorway. I kept my eyes locked on her as different emotions swept over her face. She walked over to me and pushed me to my room in silence. She left, came back with a nurse and continued to stare at me until they settled me back in bed.

"What's going on, Oliver?" I could hear the strain in her voice.

"It's hard to explain, Soph."

"Try." She looked angry. I didn't know what to say to her. I didn't want to lie to her, but she would never understand what I felt for Nina. "Oliver!"

I sighed and tried to explain the dreams again, the vision from the day before, my connection with Nina, but I knew I sounded delusional. Sophie kept frowning at me, not trying to hide her exasperation.

"Soph, I know how crazy it sounds, but I had to fall. I had to save Nina."

She inhaled deeply and covered her mouth with her hand. We kept our eyes on each other as realisation dawned on her face. She didn't understand my choice, but she accepted that I believed there was a choice. And she clearly thought I was insane.

I grimaced and closed my eyes with a sigh. It was gutting to see the pain on her face. How could she ever understand what I'd done? A few tears rolled down her cheek and she wiped them away. She kept staring at me for long seconds before she forced her lips together and nodded. She wordlessly turned around and left.

I wished my parents were there. My dad would have done something to show me a different perspective, to distract me and keep my mind from going down this spiral. My mum would have had something profound to say to calm me down. I rummaged around my mum's journals for some comfort. Some salvation. A sliver of peace.

I wondered if she would have understood me. Normally my dad was the one who got me—we were so similar—but my mum was a psychologist, after all. She was the most open-minded person I'd ever known. Perhaps she would have been able to make some sense of what I was going through? Of course I didn't expect any real answers, but somehow God took pity on me and my eye caught the last entry in a journal from 1990 I was flicking through:

I definitely smoked too much this evening. (Johnny's not impressed. I'll have to make it up to him.) Anyway, I cannot help but wonder if there might be a way for humans to link with each other subconsciously. What if there is one subconscious network? Perhaps similar to a body? Trillions of cells, each with their own intelligence and purpose, but no specific separation. What if individuals do not exist in isolation from others?

My mum had been twenty-one in 1990, so in her third year of psychology. I immediately went through the other two journals, but the one was from 1989 and the other from 1986. I paged back through the journal from 1990, to the place where I'd read about her interest in neurological functions, but it was all about how we could influence our own subconscious minds with repetitive behaviour and it focussed heavily on creating a healthy self-esteem. That last entry from the 1990 journal was the only entry about linking with other people.

I spent the night searching the Internet for information, but it was all much too wacky even for me. I wanted to phone Sophie to tell her about it and ask her to find the next journal, but I knew it would just upset her even more. I was more alone and more confused than ever before.

CHAPTER 13

It felt like someone was sitting on my chest the next day. I hated this day. I couldn't believe we had somehow survived seven whole years without my parents.

Every year it made me feel like I was a lost boy, a boy trapped in a crushed car on a wooden bridge in a desolate forest. This year felt worse than ever. This year an iron fist clamped down on my heart and squeezed the last remaining shreds of life from my body.

When I spotted the vacant chair by the window, disappointment ground through my chest. I knew Sophie was confused. I knew she was battling with her own overwhelm. But I couldn't believe she would leave me alone. How had we got to a point where she would rather be on her own on this day? I couldn't stop the tears that crawled down my cheeks. I allowed myself to cry, silently, uncontrollably, inconsolably, until Stuart came in.

"Oliver," he said softly next to me. "Can I do anything?"

"No." I wiped my nose on my hand. "It's the anniversary of my parents' deaths."

"Oh, Ollie." Stuart sat down. "Do you want to be on your own?" he asked when I covered my face with my hands.

"Please stay," I whispered, before I crumpled into my hands again and mutely gulped down mouthfuls of uneven air.

He stayed with me, without saying another word, until I gathered myself again and started breathing more easily. "Thank you."

"Of course." He squeezed my arm.

When I went outside later, my heart already made demands to be near Nina again, but I wasn't sure I would be able to cope with seeing her when I was feeling so raw. However, when we rolled past her room my melancholy bloomed into irritation when I saw Marcus Bentley sitting next to Nina's bed. I scowled at them like the petulant child I was and my dark mood settled in my stomach.

"Okay, Ollie?" Stuart gently took the lighter from my hand. I had been flicking the flame on and off.

"I don't know. Sophie…" I trailed off and cleared my throat, realising I didn't want to discuss my sister. "I don't like Marcus Bentley," I blurted out and gestured towards the hospital entrance.

"Ah." Stuart nodded and waited for me to say more, but I just took the last drag of my cigarette and put it out in silence instead. "Anyway." He handed back my lighter when I pulled another fag from the packet. "Shall we go back inside after this one? It's a bit too hot for my complexion out here this morning."

"Okay." I exhaled a stream of smoke as I looked around the sweltering garden. "Can I stop in Nina's room?" My jealousy, or irritation, or whatever, got the better of me.

"Not for long, Ollie. We still need to be careful while you wear the brace. It's only for a few more days."

"I know." I let out another long, sombre breath and stubbed out my half-smoked cigarette.

Nina was sitting up in her bed smiling at something on the television when Stuart pushed me into her room.

"Morning." I smiled weakly and felt some of the darkness leave my body.

"I'll pick you up in five minutes," Stuart said as he parked me next to her bed.

"*Friends,* eh?" I said.

"Huh?" Her dark eyebrows twitched and I flicked my eyes up to the television where *Friends* was playing. "Yeah. I've watched every episode at least a hundred times."

90

"Me too."

She started talking about one of her favourite *Friends* moments and I wanted to hold her hand and smile along, but I couldn't shake Marcus Bentley from my mind. I let out a groan as I rubbed my hair around on my head without hearing what she was saying.

"Are you okay?" she interrupted herself.

"Oh." I half-smiled sheepishly. "I saw Marcus in your room this morning and... I don't know."

"I called him yesterday." She nodded, instantly pissing me off. Today was never going to be a good day for self-control, but I surprised even myself with the intensity of my emotions.

"So, what's going on then?" I snarled before I could stop myself. "I mean... Sorry." I sighed, closing my eyes for a moment. "Is there anything between you two?" I softened my voice. "There were rumours."

"No." She slowly shook her head. "Things were complicated with us for a while, but we've always just been friends, if that. I asked him to come; he was the last person who saw me before I left that night."

"Oh." I picked up her hand without thinking. "Sorry. You shouldn't have to explain yourself." I finally allowed myself to relax a bit. Even though I still felt unhinged, being near Nina made me feel different, a bit less broken somehow. I placed a kiss on the back of her fingers as I searched her face. She bit down on her bottom lip and kept her eyes locked on mine. I could feel my muscles uncoil a little as we sat there making silent promises to each other. Eventually I nodded and we both knew that an unspoken alliance had formed between us and that we had moved on to something more. Something sincere. Something faithful. Just the two of us. Just like that.

The guys came in later and it coloured a piece of my black, empty heart. I knew they wouldn't leave me on my own all day, but I was surprised by the sense of relief I felt when they finally showed up.

"Your folks would be proud, brother." Kellan patted my cheek and held me close for a moment.

"Thank you," I whispered and wiped my hand across my face.

I was more grateful for them than I could ever explain. They made the emptiness a bit smaller, a bit less dark. Their presence, their love and their brotherhood were sometimes the only things that kept me going. Them and Sophie. Always Sophie. Except this time.

We all went outside and found Nina and her family under the oak. Charlie, Ian and Zach entertained Nina by doing an a capella harmony of 'Wrecking Ball'. Zach's voice was surprisingly good and he slotted in nicely with the boys. Kellan was chatting to Ingrid and Jeffrey, who both sent fond glances Nina's way every time she laughed. The sun was low in the cloudless sky and my chest felt warm as I watched everyone. I just wished Sophie was there. We were supposed to be together. We should always be together on this day.

"I had a nice time, thank you." I strained to produce a small smile when I went back to my room after a little while. "I wish Sophie was here."

"She needs time, Ols." Kellan patted my hand. "She doesn't understand what's going on with you."

"I know." I sighed. "She shouldn't be alone today."

"She's not."

At some point later that night I woke up to Nina sitting next to my bed, holding my hand and watching *Friends* on mute. "It's better with the sound on, you know."

"I didn't want to wake you." She reached over and stroked my cheek. "You looked so peaceful."

My heart rejoiced at her touch and I leaned my face into her hand. "That's because I was dreaming about this girl."

"Oh, yeah?"

"Yeah. When she smiles her eyes sparkle like white diamonds and light up her entire face."

"She sounds ridiculous."

"Totally outrageous." I linked my fingers through hers and stroked the top of her hand with my thumb. "Aren't you tired?" I looked at the clock and it was nearly midnight.

"I couldn't sleep. I thought I'd come and sit with you. Is that okay?"

"Of course. Everything all right? Are you supposed to be walking by yourself?"

"I'm fine." She waved her hand and I caught a flash of stubbornness in her eyes. It made me smile again. "It feels weird that I've missed so much time, and I really wish I could remember more about that night."

"Yeah, I get that. But you're all right and that's all that matters." I was a hypocrite, but apart from probably crushing her, it would make no difference to the situation if Nina remembered what happened that night.

"I guess so." She shrugged. "Are you okay? Today? I know I don't… I guess I don't really know you, but you seem sad?"

"It's the anniversary of my parents' deaths."

"I'm sorry." She put her head down on my bed and held my hand against her face.

After a long while of sitting quietly like that, I brushed my fingers into her hair and said, "Come up here and turn the sound on."

"Are you sure? I don't want to hurt you."

"I'm strapped in so tightly, I don't think you could even if you tried." I rapped my knuckles on my brace.

She crawled onto my bed and settled carefully in the crook of my arm, but she bumped against my shoulder as she wiggled to get comfortable. "Sorry." She winced.

"No, I'm okay." I pressed my lips against her forehead and when she locked eyes with me, I knew that we had moved on to something more again. I bent my head and my heart felt like it was suspended in my chest for several long moments. I searched her face and every cell in my body reacted to her closeness. Her allure, her warmth, her all-consuming presence surrounded me and as I brushed my mouth over her soft, full lips all my nerve endings fused and set my body on fire.

She tasted like heaven, and sin, and every other decadent flavour in between. I growled low in my chest and deepened our kiss, tangling my tongue with hers. She hummed into my mouth and I knew we were past the point of no return.

"I don't think I'll ever get enough of you," I whispered after a few long beats and my heart bloomed as she smiled up at me and nestled her head into my neck.

We watched *Friends*, snuggled together like that, until we both drifted off to sleep.

When I woke up again the television was still playing and my arm was still draped around Nina's shoulders. The clock said it was past one. I looked down at her head where it was resting on my chest and I stroked the hair away from her face. She must have been uncomfortable staying so still, trying not to hurt me, but she let out a soft sigh and the small smile that played around her lips caused my own mouth to curve upwards as well. I kept running my fingers through her velvety hair as I drifted off again. But one eye snapped open when a nurse appeared next to us and clicked her tongue.

"There you are, Miss Harrison." She sounded a bit exasperated.

"Nina," I whispered against her hair.

"Mmm?" Nina smiled.

"I think you have to go, sweetheart." I also smiled, but dropped it when the nurse gave me a stern look.

"You can't sleep here, Miss Harrison. And you should not put your back under unnecessary pressure, Mr. Lawrence. And you definitely should not be walking by yourself, Miss Harrison. I'll get a wheelchair." The nurse huffed as she hurried out of the room.

"Oh, dear." Nina peeled her eyes open and giggled sleepily as she struggled to sit up. She looked adorable. "I guess I'll see you later." She carefully untangled herself from my arm and got into the wheelchair when the nurse came back.

"Bye." I grabbed her hand and brought it to my lips before the nurse tutted again and pushed her out of the room.

CHAPTER 14

Zach came into my room with Nina's arm hooked through one elbow and a tray of takeaway coffee in his other hand, just as I finished my breakfast.

"Morning." I smiled, happy to see her again so soon. "No wheelchair?"

"Nope." She shook her head as she sat down next to my bed. "I had to promise to take it slow though." She rolled her eyes before looking up at Zach and holding out her hand for a cup of coffee. She wrapped both hands around the cup and a soft moan escaped her lips when she took the first sip.

I couldn't stop the grin that spread across my face and I reached out to squeeze her leg. She caught my hand and kept it on her knee as she took another sip. It made me feel a bit giddy.

"You're delightful." Zach laughed and handed me a cup from the tray.

"Thanks." I tipped it towards him. I was about to ask who the fourth cup was for, but he handed it to Stuart before I could start speaking.

"Thank you." Stuart accepted it with a smile of his own and he and Zach exchanged a heated look. I winked at Nina when her lips also twitched in amusement.

The nurse who was in charge of Nina's care came in and they talked for a few minutes, but I was thoroughly entertained by the sparks flying between Zach and Stuart, so I was only half listening to the conversation.

"You're delightful." I smirked at Zach after Stuart left the room with Nina's nurse.

"I know." Zach beamed and Nina snorted, choking on her coffee.

"Are we in trouble for bunking up?" I asked after she recovered.

"Not really." She waved her hand dismissively. "The nurse actually just came to say that I had to see Dr. Harold later. They need to do some follow-up scans of my head and chest. I might be able to go home if the results come back okay."

"That's great."

"Yeah." Nina pinched her lips into a little pout. "I'll miss you though."

"I'll be out before you know it. I also have to go for some X-rays today, so fingers crossed." I moved my torso from side to side in my brace and assessed my body. I was hardly feeling any tenderness in my back. The day before it had felt like my spine was going to explode at any minute—I'd had constant stabbing pains pulsing through my arse bones—but I was feeling all right today. A bit achy, but not much more than I would after a heavy workout. It made me feel hope and dread in equal measure.

After Zach took Nina back to her room and Stuart came back to help me get ready for my X-rays, I couldn't stop the growing wave of dread from overpowering the hope that had been there earlier. It was all great when Nina could curl up in the crook of my arm to watch *Friends* and then go to her room to get ready while Stuart facilitated me in everything I needed to do. It was all okay while we were both patients in this hospital. But how did I really expect this to go out in the real world? What kind of relationship could I offer anyone while I was stuck in this damned wheelchair? What did it matter that I wasn't in excruciating pain if I still couldn't move? A groan escaped me before I could force it back down.

"It'll be okay, Ollie." Stuart patted my arm before he dragged my wheelchair closer and called for someone to help him transfer me into it.

"I wish I could agree with you." I sighed, allowing a deep sense of melancholy to overtake my mood.

Just how was it going to be okay when even the simplest things like walking hand in hand with her would be impossible? How was I going to take her out on a date? How was I going to sweep her into my arms, carry her to my bed and love her in the way I wanted to while I was stuck in this godforsaken chair? It made my stomach churn. The whole performance of going for X-rays was just making me feel worse too. As they settled me back in my bed I almost vomited with the harsh realisation of exactly how helpless I really was. The level of vulnerability and dependence I was going to have to accept made my head spin.

"Hi." Sophie miraculously appeared and saved me from the darkest depths of my mind.

"Hey." I held her close for a long moment when she leaned into me for a hug.

An uncomfortable silence stretched between us. What was I supposed to do? Should I say sorry? But where would I start? Should I pretend that everything was normal? Should I just try to explain? "Look, Soph," I started.

"Ollie, I know…" she said at the same time. "Sorry, you go first."

"Okay, thanks." I pressed my lips together. "I know you're angry that I fell and got hurt on purpose and I know you don't understand why." I suddenly felt overwhelmed and I swallowed loudly. "And I'm so sorry for disappointing you."

"No, Ollie, stop. Actually, can I go first?" she asked and I nodded. "Please, don't ever say that again. You could never disappoint me, but you are right that I don't understand why you would let yourself get hurt. And when I saw you with Nina the other night it really shocked me. When you tried to explain your feelings for her it made me very uncomfortable. I felt a level of resentment for Nina that scared me. I don't understand the intensity of your emotions, or this connection you think you have with her." She closed her eyes briefly. "I'm not programmed the way you are. It's the sole purpose of my existence to prove the logical explanation for everything. You're operating on a level that doesn't even exist to me."

"That doesn't mean it's not real," I started protesting. She made it sound like I was living in a fantasy world. But, then again, could I blame her? Perhaps that was exactly what I was doing?

"Wait, let me finish, please. I don't understand what's going on in your head at the moment, but when I saw you with Nina the other night, all the deep feelings and special connections you've been talking about were very evident. There's no way I can logically explain it, but I also can't deny it."

"What are you saying?"

"I don't have any comprehension of your commitment to Nina, and I certainly don't understand why you would choose this." Her tone wobbled as she gestured at my legs, but she swallowed, blinked slowly and then carried on with a steady voice. "But I accept how real your bond is. It's clear that you want, or even think that you need, to be with her more than anything. And, whatever your reasons might be"—she took a slow breath and cleared her throat—"I will always support whatever, or whoever, makes you happy."

I stared at her for a long time. She believed in me, despite the fact that my reality was completely removed from her frame of reference. If more people had a shred of the emotional maturity my sister had, the world would be a much, much more tolerant place. How could I ever explain what her acceptance meant to me?

"I don't know what to say, Soph." I rubbed my hand across my eyes and inflated my cheeks before I blew out a slow stream of air. "Thank you."

"I love you and I'm so proud of you." She wrapped both of her hands around mine. "I'm sorry that I made you feel like I was disappointed in you. Please know that could never happen. And I'm sorry I wasn't here. I needed time to sort out my head."

"Honestly, Soph, I don't know where I would be without you."

She started to say something else when Stuart came in with my breakfast.

"Dr. Harold will be around shortly. He's going to discuss your options going forward. Regarding physio and taking care of yourself"—he poured some coffee into my cup—"have a think about any questions you might want to ask while he's here." He bobbed his head and gave Sophie a pointed look before he left the room.

I tried to nod in agreement, but I started to freak out again. The thought of being a paraplegic outside of this hospital made me feel sick.

"Ollie?" Sophie smiled and I moved my eyes to meet hers. "I hope you don't mind, but I've been gathering information, and I've started making arrangements for your life to run as smoothly as possible when you get discharged." She got up and walked over to retrieve her laptop from the table by the window. "I've found quite a few suitable cars," she said and I nodded with what was probably a bewildered look on my face.

She spent the next ten minutes explaining how these cars were adapted to cater for paraplegics, before she moved on to list the minor modifications that needed to be done around my bungalow.

I kept staring at her, dumbfounded by my sister's ability to take control of a situation. I had not even started thinking about any of these practical arrangements that needed to be taken care of. I'd been too busy wallowing in the grim reality of facing the outside world from a wheelchair. A gratified smile crept across her face before she dropped the final bombshell.

"And last, but by no means least, I would like to present you with the best part of my master plan." She got up again and walked out of the door before returning a moment later with Stuart in tow.

"What?" I frowned up at them as they both stood grinning at me.

"Here he is." Sophie gestured at Stuart, who lifted his hands above his shoulders.

"I'm the best part of Sophie's plan." Stuart twirled around and bowed in a peculiar fashion. They were both clearly very excited and I really wanted to vibe with them, but I had no idea what they were on about.

"I'm sorry, but what?" I mustered up a little twitch on the side of my mouth that could hopefully pass as a smile.

"Ollie." Sophie rolled her eyes. "Stuart is going to be your full-time carer."

I rubbed my hair around my head as I let the information sink in. "Really?"

"It was one of the easiest decisions I've had to make in a long time." He bobbed his head.

"Why?" Why would Stuart want to babysit me, if he could have a proper job here at the hospital?

"Because I've been thinking about moving into individual reha-bilitation for a while now. And also because you're going to pay me quite well." His smile didn't falter.

"So, what do you think?" Sophie clapped her hands together.

"I think you're both bloody fantastic." I laughed, only slightly hysterical. There really wasn't anybody I would rather have taking care of me.

Shortly after Sophie and Stuart's big revelation, Dr. Harold came in to discuss my stationary future. I basically needed twenty-four-hour care. Extensive occupational therapy. Long-term physiother-apy. Constant check-ups and monitoring. My brace could come off the next day. Physio and occupational therapies would then be escalated from the following week onwards, and if it all went well, I would hopefully go home at the end of the week after that. That would bring my time in hospital to a total of eight weeks since the night of the accident, five of which Nina had spent in a coma. Apparently Stuart was trained in neurotrauma recovery and was capable of assisting me with my physio and adjustment to being a paraplegic. *Clever Stuart.*

I listened as Dr. Harold outlined the grim path forward. I nodded at the appropriate intervals, but I struggled to accept it all. I was riding an enormous emotional roller coaster, even by my standards. How was it possible that the notion of Stuart taking care of me made me feel so thankful one moment when all I could think of the next moment was the fact that my life was over? I didn't think that I could do it. I hated being dependent on other people. Hell, sometimes I didn't even want to be around other people. How was I going to cope with having to rely on somebody to do everything for me? How was I going to function if I needed to have somebody with me twenty-four hours a day?

"I realise it's a lot to digest, Oliver," Dr. Harold interrupted my internal struggle. "Just take it one day at a time." I knew it was the best advice. Exactly what my dad would have said. But it was overwhelming. "You're in excellent hands with Stuart."

I sighed heavily. I was a fighter by nature, but I'd only ever had to fight for my own survival. Now I had gone against every instinct I possessed to fight my own deep desire to thrive in order to save Nina.

I blew out a long breath and dragged my hand through my tousled hair. The thought of Nina's beautiful face replaced the haphazard images of self-pity and chaos. I thought of the vision I'd had that day when I fell in rehab, the day I'd thought she was dying. It had been a vision of happiness. A vision of hope. I could feel my face burning with shame. Who was I to value my legs more than Nina's life?

What if individuals do not exist in isolation from others? My mum's words scrolled through my mind again.

There had never been any guarantee that I was ever going to walk again. It had always been just hope. Speculation. The likelihood of recovery had been better than it was now, but it had never been guaranteed. How dared I feel sorry for myself? And besides, I knew I would never have been able to forgive myself if Nina had died.

"Yeah. One day at a time," I finally said to Dr. Harold, who was patiently waiting for me to put my thoughts in order.

"You're stronger than you think, Oliver." He smiled as he left the room, but I didn't respond. I wasn't so sure. I was suddenly exhausted.

CHAPTER 15

I was fiddling around with my guitar a while later when Nina's beautiful, smiling face popped around my door frame. My mouth automatically formed a smile and I wondered when she was going to stop having that effect on me. Probably never. I put my guitar to the side and held my hand out to her.

She crawled into the crook of my arm and lifted her head to give me a swift kiss. I cupped the back of her head and moved my mouth over hers as I stroked the tender spot underneath her ear with my thumb.

"Mmm," she hummed against me and a strained groan escaped my chest. I pulled her flush against my body. She melted into my arms and pushed her fingers through my hair as our mouths moved over each other's greedily.

"You're going to get me in trouble," I murmured into her hair as I tried to adjust myself awkwardly under the covers.

"I'd like that." She grinned.

"Me too." I kissed the top of her head, and she sighed deeply. "You okay?"

"I don't want to leave you," she whispered against my throat and for a second my heart stopped. Vivid images of the horrific separations we'd gone through in my dreams forced themselves into my brain and I had to shake my head to put them out of my mind. This was the real world and she just meant that she was going home.

I felt the briefest pang of something unpleasant. Fear? Melancholy? Envy? I decided to settle for uncertainty. We were moving into another new phase, that was all.

"You don't want to be stuck in here any more." I pinched her chin and tilted her face towards me.

"I know, but I don't want to be away from you." She sounded vulnerable and I realised once again that she needed me as much as I needed her.

"I know." I kissed both her cheeks and rested my forehead against hers, trailing my thumb over her scar. "I'll probably go home next week too."

"I'm sorry I'm so needy." Her voice wobbled. "I'm feeling weird about going back to normal life."

"You can be needy for me any day. I can't think of anything that makes me happier at the moment." I smiled down at her. "And I totally get that you're feeling weird about getting back to life. I've been worried about it too."

"You have?"

"Of course. It's going to be a big adjustment." I inhaled slowly, knowing that I had to be honest about my fears. But not only that, I also had to give her a chance to walk away. "A part of me feels like I should let you go so that you can be free to live your life, to find somebody else." I swallowed hard. "Somebody with fewer complications."

"What the hell, Ollie?" She jolted up next to me so that our eyes were nearly level with each other. "What does that mean? Fewer complications?" She searched my face.

"I'm probably never going to get any better and I don't want you to be burdened with me while you can be free and live a normal life." I sighed heavily.

"Stop." Her eyes filled with tears. "I want to be with you. I thought you felt the same?"

I pulled her into my arms again. "Please don't cry. Of course I feel the same. You know I do. But I have to be fair to you too."

"Then don't say things like that. I have never felt more free than the past few days. With you."

"Nina." I held her face with both hands and wiped her tears away with my thumbs. "I feel the same."

The rest of the week passed fairly easily and I rarely had a moment without Nina. Sometimes Zach or Jeffrey and Ingrid would join her, but most of the time she was on her own by my side. Sophie and the guys also kept coming and going and they seemed to accept, or even welcome, Nina's determined presence.

Looking back, I realised that my constant stream of company was probably organised by Kellan in an attempt to help me keep my shit together, and it worked brilliantly. Not only did those days serve as a foundation for my sister and the guys to bond with Nina and her family, it was also when Nina and I really got to know each other. We spent endless hours talking and with every conversation I became more enchanted by her. By the end of the week it felt like I had known her my whole life. It was strange to be so connected to another person and my soul felt uncharacteristically peaceful.

Like Dr. Harold expected, my brace was removed the day after Nina was discharged. It was liberating to be less confined, to breathe more freely. Between trips to the gym, the physio, and visits from Nina and everybody else, the week flew by without time to dig around in my own brain. So much so that I almost couldn't believe it when the very last Friday afternoon, after too many weeks in hospital, finally arrived.

"You seem uncertain, Oliver." Dr. Harold handed me the signed discharge form. "Would you rather stay?"

"Hell no." I shook my head. "It's just overwhelming."

"You're going to be fine." He offered his hand. "Good luck, lad."

"Thank you for everything." I shook his hand before adding my other hand as well and holding on a moment longer.

Sophie had rented one of those wheelchair-accessible vans and I couldn't stop myself from pulling a face when I saw it parked outside the hospital entrance.

"Don't be a brat. You can look for something else when you can drive yourself." She rolled her eyes.

I obviously wasn't going to complain about the ugly van. But, as much as I was uninterested in fashion, or gadgets, or most forms of consumerism, I did like cars. And I was indeed going to buy a nice car and have it converted to be paraplegic-friendly as soon as I could drive.

They loaded me into the ugly van with ease and we drove the twenty minutes to my bungalow in relative silence. It was unsettling to be outside the hospital boundaries for the first time in so many weeks. Everything still looked the same, yet everything was completely different. We stayed on the motorway all the way to Haslemere and I was glad we didn't have to drive past the spot where the accident took place.

I wasn't ready to go back there.

CHAPTER 16

My room was much darker and quieter than the hospital and it took a moment to get my bearings the next morning. I stretched my arms at my sides and took a deep breath. It was great to be in my own space, to have the familiar smell of my stuff in the air.

I sat up with a smile and reached for my mobile on the bedside table. Sophie had had a smart system installed in the bungalow. From an app on my phone, I could do things like open the blinds, adjust the temperature, turn on the lights and control the television and speakers. It also had a function to buzz Stuart if I needed him. I briefly considered tapping it to ask for coffee, but I opened the blind and turned on the music. I selected an Amos Lee album and sat back against the headboard, digesting the view over the woodlands as I listened to Amos reminisce about drinking coffee on a night train.

My time in the hospital had almost made me forget how much I loved this bungalow. Even though we'd lived abroad most of our lives, my dad had always had this property in Haslemere and it was the only consistent home we'd had as a family. I'd lived with Sophie in London for the first few years after my parents died, but we'd still come down to stay on weekends. I think it made us feel closer to them.

When I went to uni, I'd stayed with Kellan, Ian, and Charlie for a while, but eventually I'd renovated the bungalow and moved in permanently. I would've hated leaving it to move somewhere with more accessibility. I wasn't materialistic and my advantages were sometimes lost on me, but I always appreciated that I didn't have to worry about money. Especially in that moment. We were never super wealthy—nothing like Nina's family, anyway—but we'd always had a privileged life and we had enough to be comfortable. Sophie'd got the flat in London and I'd got this bungalow, so I was very grateful to my parents.

Just then the door opened and I ticked off two more things to be thankful for: the beautiful girl who walked in and the mug of steaming coffee in her hand.

"Good morning." Nina smiled.

"It certainly is." I grinned, taking a sip of coffee before setting it down and pulling her towards me.

"I think it's about to get even better." She swung her leg over and straddled my hips. I stroked my fingers up her arms before I touched her face and kissed her deeply. She tasted delicious. Like mint, and coffee, and seduction.

My need for her spiked and I sat up, away from the headboard. I kissed a trail from the top of her scar, down the side of her face and across her throat. She moaned as I sucked on the space where her neck joined her shoulder and I knew it was going to leave a dark hickey. The idea of seeing my mark on her skin made the blood pulse through my veins. I soothed the spot with a slow lick before I continued to kiss a path over her shoulder as I pulled the strap of her vest down. She stroked her hands under my T-shirt and up my back. My skin burned where she touched me. I wanted to feel her fire everywhere. I pulled my T-shirt over my head with one hand before stripping her vest off.

"Okay?" I murmured.

"You're beautiful," she whispered, trailing her fingertips over my tattoos.

I'd forgotten that she'd not seen me without a top yet. Not in the real world. I looked down at her unblemished skin, pressed against the meandering motifs on mine. "You're perfect."

"I can't get close enough to you," she breathed, grinding her hips against mine.

107

"Me neither." I fumbled with the waistband on her shorts. They had to come off.

A very faraway, very faint voice at the back of my mind tried to remind me that I wasn't supposed to have sex yet. Stuart had had 'the talk' with me the day before, and he'd explained that unless I was looking for a disturbing situation that involved all sorts of bodily excretions, I had to be diligent about doing my toileting routines every time, before and after I had sex.

Motherfucker! The obscenity of it all detonated in my brain. I locked my arms around Nina's waist and dropped my head against her chest with a heavy sigh.

"Argh," I groaned against her shoulder. "I shouldn't…" I trailed off.

"It's okay. Whenever you're ready." She laced her fingers behind my neck.

"I'm more than ready. But it's not that straightforward for me any more. I need to do certain things." I cleared my throat and closed my eyes in shame. "You know. Before I can…" I dropped my head again, my arms falling limply to my side.

"Oliver." Nina raked her fingers through my hair, tilting my face up. "Please don't be weird about this." She kissed me deeply. "If I had taken a moment to think about the logistics, I would have realised that we might need to do a bit of planning and I wouldn't have flung myself at you." Her cheeks flushed pink and she rested her forehead against mine. She was trying to make me feel better, but it only embarrassed me more. Who else needed to schedule having a piss before having sex?

I clenched my jaw hard, feeling the muscles twitch. Nina hugged my head against her chest and I drew in a long breath, trying to contain the rage bubbling inside me. What I really wanted was for her to get out of my room before I punched my fist into the nearest hard surface, but her fingertips raked through my hair, over and over, and it kept me grounded enough to keep some self-control.

"Oliver," she whispered, planting warm kisses on my head. "Don't be upset."

I forced my broken, useless body to hold on to the scrap of dignity I still possessed and I somehow managed to keep it together. I curled my arms around her waist again and exhaled slowly.

"It's going to be okay," she said against my cheek and I lifted my gaze to meet hers.

Her lips met mine and she kissed me with an intensity that made my fury dissolve. I knotted one hand into her hair and tightened the other arm around her waist, holding on to her for dear life.

"Thank you," I whispered against her sweet lips.

"It's going to be okay," she repeated, stroking her hands down my arms and pursing her lips together in a small smile that made her dimple wink.

"You're amazing." I touched the dimple with my thumb.

"Only because that's the way you make me feel." She laced her hand through my fingers and kissed my palm, her eyes crinkling at the corners.

"I promise to make you feel even more amazing very soon." I winked cockily, making her laugh, the sound vibrating through my body.

"I can't wait." She kissed me one last time and put her top back on before handing me my T-shirt and hopping off. "I'm gonna take a shower in the other bathroom," she called over her shoulder as she walked towards the door.

I slumped back against the headboard with a groan and flung my arm across my face. "Fuck," I muttered under my breath, just as Stuart walked through the door.

"What's the matter?"

"Bollocks," I grunted, moving my hand so that my thumb and forefinger were sticking in my eyes. Then I burst out laughing. Hysterically.

A small frown was pulling on Stuart's eyebrows, but he waited for me to elaborate.

Eventually my laughing calmed down enough for me to explain, "I just got really excited with Nina." I pointed at the door she had just disappeared through. "But I had to stop because I realised I've not had my obligatory piss yet. And now I have this massive boner"—I lifted the duvet to show Stuart—"but I'm not sure whether it's because I'm horny, or because I really, really have to pee."

I tried to contain another outburst of hysterics, but when I saw the grin Stuart was hiding behind his hand, it set me straight off again. We laughed until I was struggling to catch my breath and Stuart was snorting in a rather unflattering way.

"Gosh, Ollie, I'm surprised you didn't pass out." He shook his head after we'd calmed down.

"I know, right?" I lifted the duvet again, frowning at the monstrosity that was trying to escape my boxers.

"Let's get you to the loo at once." He helped me into my wheelchair and pushed me into the en suite.

After Stuart did the tedious catheterising, which thankfully took care of Mr. Elephantine, he helped me to have a shower and a shave and I came out feeling like a million quid, albeit worked up still. But Stuart emphasised again that there was no reason why I couldn't put my friskiness to good use if I stuck to a toileting routine. In fact, he encouraged me to challenge myself to do whatever I needed to do in order to be happy, even if that meant that I had to go to the loo before I had sex. I solemnly vowed that I would at least try to make the best of the situation.

We went through to the kitchen and a smile immediately pulled at the corner of my mouth. Brandi Carlile was blaring at top volume and Nina had her head thrown back as she sang along into the spatula. Just before the song finished she twirled around, lost her balance and swore horribly, before she laughed at herself and spotted us behind her. She gestured at us to sing along to the last few words.

"'Oh, yeah, well, it's true that I was made for you,'" Stuart and I joined in, beaming at each other. When the song finished, she pulled on the sides of the flowery dress-shorts-thing she was wearing and curtsied before she came over to me.

"Well, hello again." She planted a kiss on my mouth. "Food's nearly ready." She sashayed away from me again. "Are you hungry?"

"Ravenous." I winked at her and a slight blush coloured her cheeks before she dropped the spatula and swore like a trooper once again.

"I'll set the table on the patio, it's lovely out there this morning," Stuart piped up behind me.

"Perhaps we can go for a walk or something later?"

"Sure." I nodded. "What do you think, Stuart? We could invite Zach?"

"Sounds good." He shrugged, but I didn't miss the way his eyes lit up at the mention of Zach's name.

We were still sitting on the patio after breakfast when the doorbell rang. Stuart jumped up and pushed past Nina to answer it. "Oooh." She wiggled her eyebrows, making me laugh again. "Do you want to go into town for a bit?" she asked before she lit a cigarette and handed me the pack.

"No." I shook my head, putting one between my lips, as I looked out across the fields leading up to the forest. Even though the band wasn't big enough for us to be famous yet, there were plenty of music lovers in the area who might recognise me from festivals or gigs. I just couldn't face the pitying looks and awkward attention. "I'm not ready," I finally admitted, blowing out smoke. "Is there anywhere less crowded we can go?"

"What about Wisley Gardens?" Stuart suggested as he walked back out onto the patio with Zach on his heels. "Lots of flat walking grounds and a nice cafeteria."

"Won't it be a bit crowded on a day like today though?"

"Young families or pensioners. No one who will pay you any attention."

"Okay." It didn't sound great, but it was better than sitting in the house all day.

"Shall I invite Sophie and the guys along?" Nina offered and I nodded.

We spent an hour walking around the gardens before having coffee and sandwiches at the cafe. It was fine, but honestly, I was so preoccupied with thoughts of being with Nina, nothing else really registered. My attraction to her had been strong from that first moment I'd seen her, but it had become increasingly intense over the past couple of weeks, and it had been off the charts since I'd come home the night before.

Charlie jumped up and pulled me from my daydream. "Check you later, Olive." He kissed me on the cheek. "I need to stop in to see Jack quickly. I'll get some pizza on the way back," he said to Kellan.

"Pick up some beer too. Do you need anything?" Kellan asked Sophie and she shook her head. "Ian, go with Charlton. Soph, come with me." He squeezed her hand and clapped me on the back as he passed me. "See you tomorrow, Ols."

"Where's your car?" I asked Sophie as she walked over to hug me.

"At the house," she said.

"How long are you going to stay with them?" I narrowed my eyes.

"I've moved in for now, Ollie."

"Mmm." My frown deepened. I knew she'd been staying there temporarily to be close to me, but I didn't realise that she had properly moved in. Although there was probably no way she would go back to live in her flat up in London, not for a long time. I knew she would have preferred to live with me, but she knew the sliver of independence I had left was important, and besides, now that Stuart was living there, I didn't have enough room. Unless she moved into the third bedroom, but it was my music room and she would never even consider that. The guys had a spare room with an en suite, so I supposed it was just practical to live with them instead of renting somewhere else. However, Sophie and Kellan had been peculiarly close the past few weeks, and it was getting on my nerves.

"Ready to go?" Nina smoothed the frown between my eyebrows with her thumb and planted a kiss on the spot. I nodded with a smile and kissed her fingers.

"I want to go out for a bit, if that's okay?" Stuart said as he helped me settle in bed when we got home.

"Sure." I bobbed my head.

"I'll only be down the road. Buzz me if you need me. Otherwise, I'll be back in two hours."

"I'll be fine." I waved him away.

"See you later." He turned around to leave.

"Actually, could you light some candles? I think I've got some in the bottom drawer." I pointed to my chest of drawers.

Sophie had given me a few jars of sandalwood the year before and I remember thinking that it was a bit useless at the time, but I had to admit that it added a nice touch.

"Very romantic." He smiled. "Have a good night, Ollie."

"Thanks." I beamed. "You too."

After he left me, I quickly compiled a romantic playlist and I was sitting back listening to London Grammar's version of 'Wicked Game' when the door opened.

CHAPTER 17

I stopped breathing and my heart rate spiked as Nina walked towards me. She'd had a shower. Her skin was flushed and her hair was damp and tangled. She was wearing a pair of black boxer shorts and a tight black vest. When she sat down on the bed her scent engulfed me and I closed my eyes, inhaling slowly.

"Hey," she whispered, stroking my cheek.

"Hey." I turned my face into her hand and kissed her palm as I sat up a bit.

"Are you okay?" A slight frown formed between her pale eyes.

"I'm so much better than okay." I stroked my thumb over her eyebrow and along her scar.

"You were quiet today." She searched my face.

"I couldn't stop thinking about you." I pushed my hand into her hair. "Touching you." I pulled her head down. "Kissing you." My lips met her mouth with a lazy kiss.

"Me neither." She sighed, tangling her fingers in my hair and deepening our kiss. "This is lovely." She eventually pulled away and gestured around the room.

My lip curled up on one side. I was pleased that she liked the candles and stuff, but also not really able to care about anything other than what was about to happen. I pulled her back to my mouth.

"We don't have to do this if you're not ready." She lifted her head and held my gaze.

"I'm so very ready, Nina." I pinched her chin and bent my head down to her lips.

We scooted down and I rolled on my side, leaning on my elbow and cupping her face with my other hand as I drew circles on her cheek with my thumb. My lips landed fluttery kisses on her eyelids, across her cheeks and down her throat before lingering on her lips as I slowly started peeling her clothes off.

"You're beautiful," I whispered, stroking her face and kissing her when her shorts joined her vest somewhere on the floor.

She moaned and nudged my T-shirt up my back. I pulled it over my head with my free hand while she started pushing my boxers down.

"Lie back," she whispered, getting on her knees and pulling off my underwear as I reclined. I briefly felt embarrassed about not being able to kick my own pants off, but it disappeared completely when I noticed the fire in her eyes.

"Nina." I crashed my mouth against hers before I flipped us over and covered her soft body with mine. "I've never wanted anyone as much as I want you," I groaned against her skin. "I am so in love with you." My voice came out thick with the passion of telling her for the first time. I shifted on top of her, resting my elbows on either side of her head and kissing her urgently as I tried to convey the depth of my feelings for her.

"I love you too, Ollie." She wrapped her legs around my waist and gasped into my mouth as we melted together.

"Are you okay?" I stilled for a moment.

"I'm so much better than okay." She copied my words from earlier and started moving underneath me. We discovered each other's bodies leisurely and deliberately, keeping our eyes locked the entire time, until we fell over the edge together.

"It's never been like this for me," she said afterwards, trailing her fingertips over the tattoo that ran along the scar on my ribs, lathering my skin in goosebumps.

"Me neither." I caught her fingers and brought them to my mouth.

I'd been with enough girls to know how much I loved sex; I'd just never been able to find anyone I wanted to commit to, and I'd never had a girlfriend. I did realise at some point that I wanted to be in a relationship, so for the past couple of years I hadn't whored around as much as I used to. But now, with Nina, it felt like everything had just clicked into place. It felt like my world started and ended with her.

"What are you doing to me?" I brushed my lips over her knuckles.

"Hopefully it's almost as incredible as whatever you're doing to me." She smiled against my chest.

"Infinitely more so. Honestly, Nina, you overwhelm me in the most extraordinary way." I kissed her nose.

"You certainly know how to use your words, Mr. Lawrence. And your hands. And your mouth." She blushed.

"Is that so?" I grinned, pulling her on top of me.

"Yes." She swung her leg over and straddled my hips as she knotted her fingers in my hair. I clutched the soft flesh on her hips tightly and made her groan as I buried myself in her again.

"Bloody hell." I licked a trail back to her mouth after we both cried out in ecstasy a second time. She grinned and lay down in my arms again.

We stayed quiet like that for a while. I kept looking down at her. Her beautiful face. Her pale eyes, framed by those dark, heavy lashes. Her soft skin. Her wild hair. Her gorgeous, luscious curves. Everything about her turned me on.

"Have you been with many girls?" She broke the silence eventually as she traced a finger along the tattoo lines on my chest.

"Yeah."

"Yeah? How many?"

Even though the questions sounded like jealous ones, her tone was nothing but lazy curiosity, so I answered easily. "I'm not sure. Many. Fifty? Sixty?" I made a quick calculation in my head. "Probably more."

"Bit of a slut." She tickled my ribs.

"Yeah." I grabbed her hand and bit her forefinger lightly before kissing it and putting it back on my chest. "I was out of control after my parents died. It carried on for a few years, but I eventually calmed down. It's been a while since I've been with someone." I tried to recall the last girl I'd been with and realised that it had been before spring. "Not for about six or seven months actually."

"Why?" Her fingertip drew a path around the motif on my shoulder.

"I don't know. I wanted more. Aimless screwing around wasn't really enough any more, most of the time." My lip twitched briefly on one side.

"Did you want to have more with me?" Her fingers played along the dents in my abs.

"What do you think?" I pinched her chin and tilted her head.

"I know you do now, but what about that night at the club, before the accident?"

"Hell, Nina, you took my breath away when you strolled through the door. It was like some big epiphany or something."

"I just wonder if we still would've ended up together if the accident hadn't happened." She frowned.

"I have no doubt about that. I would have found a way to make you mine." The pad of my thumb brushed slowly across her lips. "You caught my eye so many times that week. I kept looking out for you everywhere in town. And I couldn't bear the thought of Marcus touching you that night at the club." Even now, with her lying naked in my arms, I still didn't like thinking about it.

It also triggered a sudden surge of panic about our whole situation. The accident. The dreams. Our connection. Marcus's revelation about Nina causing the accident. Something felt off about him. I had to start digging and stop being so passive.

"What we had was never…" She shook her head and trailed off for a moment. "The only love we ever shared was for Grace."

I didn't really know what that meant, so I didn't comment. She traced her finger around the lines on my chest again. "He's not a bad guy, but whatever we had was not healthy."

"Did you sleep together?" I asked, immediately regretting it, but still desperate to know.

"Yeah," she whispered and when she lifted her head I could see tears brimming her eyes.

"It's okay." I pulled her tighter against me, pressing my lips against her forehead. "It's okay," I repeated.

"No." She shook her head as a soft sob escaped her. "Grace loved him so much." She buried her head in my neck again and I stroked my hand up and down her back. "I lost my mind after she died, and so did Marcus; it was fucked up. I hate myself for it."

"Shh." I continued to rub her back. "Grace would have understood. Grief is so messy, Nina. You shouldn't feel any guilt."

"That's all I feel, Ollie. Guilt and shame. And even though I despise myself, and even though I knew exactly how much he hated what we did, we carried on doing it. I can even understand why he would want to fuck me. I look exactly like her. But what type of psycho sleeps with her dead sister's boyfriend?"

"Nina," I whispered and clamped my arms even tighter around her, squeezing our bodies together so that we touched from our noses all the way down to our toes. I hated the fact that she'd slept with Marcus. It made my skin crawl. I could feel the muscles ticking in my jaw, but I took several deep breaths and held her until she started talking again.

"I think I just wanted to feel like somebody wanted me, even if it was just the pieces that looked like her. I just wanted to be a part of something that used to make her happy. I don't know, it made me feel like fragments of her were still here." She sighed and I ran my fingers up and down her back as I struggled to control my own emotions.

"Yeah, I get that. That's why I went off the rails when my parents died. I wanted to feel wanted." Her relationship with Marcus bothered me. A lot. I couldn't stand the thought of them sleeping together. It made me want to rip his dick off. But I understood, one hundred percent, without any confusion, why she had kept going back to him while she felt so lost.

"I never told you that I dreamt about you while I was in hospital," she said after we lay in silence for a while.

"You did?" My body stiffened and I pulled away to look at her face.

"Yeah. I can't remember much, but every now and again I get a glimpse of a memory from a dream." Her fingers played over the lines on my chest again.

"Like what?" I tilted her chin up to look at me. What if we shared the same dreams? It couldn't be. Could it? She opened her mouth to talk, but a knock on my bedroom door interrupted her.

"What?" I barked at the door and Nina frowned, noticing my fluster for the first time.

"I'm home, Ollie," Stuart's voice announced from the other side. "Can I come in?"

"Give us a minute," I called, reaching for Nina's top and pulling it over her head.

She found my boxers and shimmied them up my legs. "Thanks." I grinned as I tugged them over my bum. "Where are your shorts?"

"I don't know." She giggled, scanning the messy bed. She located them and bent over as she reached behind the bedside table, giving me a glorious look at her arse and instantly making all my concerns evaporate.

"Nice view." I reached over and squeezed her bottom before pushing my fingers between her legs.

"You're despicable." She squirmed against my hand before she stepped away and pulled up her shorts.

"You have no idea." I adjusted myself in my boxers and yanked her back to me for an amorous kiss.

"Oh, I think that I do." She hopped off the bed again and threw my T-shirt at me before fluffing the pillows and shaking out the duvet around me. "I have to go to the bathroom. I'll be right back." She wiggled her eyebrows, making me laugh.

"Sorry, Ollie." Stuart walked in as she left. "You need to go to the toilet. Especially if you've..." He gestured at the bed.

"Thanks." I pursed my lips together in a small smile.

"How did it go?" he asked as we took care of business.

"Eh?" I frowned.

"Medically. How did it go physically? Did anything go wrong?"

"Oh." My lip twitched up on one side. "It was fine." I couldn't stop the grin that spread across the rest of my face. "Pretty fantastic, actually." I ran my hand through my dishevelled mop.

"Good for you." Stuart patted me on the shoulder as he pushed me back into the room and helped me into bed.

I heard Nina talk to somebody in the hallway and cocked my head to have a better listen. Zach's unmistakable laugh jingled on the other side of the door. "So." I arched an eyebrow at Stuart. "You and Zach?"

"Yeah. Is that okay?"

"Of course." I beamed. "He's great."

CHAPTER 18

I got up early the next morning and went to sit outside on the living room patio. I lit a cigarette as I stared out over the fields. The air was still hazy with the remnants of dawn, but I could already see that it was going to be another sweltering day. It must have been the longest summer in a decade. I'd never experienced weather like this in Britain before.

"It's going to be another scorcher." Stuart placed my coffee in front of me before he sat down next to me.

"I was just thinking the same thing." I stubbed out my cigarette and picked up my coffee. A lone runner came jogging up the footpath and disappeared into the woods. The image instantly made me depressed. I wasn't sure if it was because I felt sorry for myself for not being able to run anymore, or if I felt sorry for the poor bugger who was jogging at five-thirty on a Sunday morning. "Could you hand me a guitar, please?"

Stuart retrieved an acoustic that used to belong to my dad. Another one of my favourites. I tuned it before I allowed my fingers to pick the strings randomly until a little melody started forming.

"Would you mind getting a pencil and a notebook, please?" I asked, unexpectedly excited about the harmony that was emerging. "I've got some stuff in the top drawer." I pointed to the sideboard in the living room and Stuart got up.

"Here you go."

"Thanks." I jotted down the chords on a clean page.

"I'll go and have a shower, if you're all right on your own?"

"Sure." I waved and put the pencil in my mouth, bending over my guitar again.

When Stuart returned, I had already finished the intro and verse part of the song. I started working on the chorus and the music just seemed to ooze from my fingers.

"That sounds good, Ollie," he said, placing a fresh cup of coffee and a plate of hot pastries in front of me, making my stomach rumble in response.

"Thank you." I took a sip of coffee before I shoved a croissant in my mouth.

"You make it look so easy." He sat down next to me.

"Sometimes it is." I inhaled another croissant before lighting a new cigarette. "When it flows effortlessly like that." I pinched my cigarette between my lips and played the tune from the beginning again.

I grinned as a familiar thrill swirled in my gut. I just knew that it was going to be a good song. The intro started with a slow, intricate picking melody and then worked into an impressive chord sequence for the verses. I wanted to keep the chorus powerful, but decided to slow it down again, giving it a captivating edge.

Stuart sat quietly reading a novel as I worked, almost like I was possessed, for the next I don't even know how long. Finally, I put my guitar down against the side of my chair and sat back with a huge grin as I stretched my arms above my head. "There." I rolled my neck and reached for another croissant. "All done."

"Let's hear it."

"Okay." I swallowed down the pastry and rotated my shoulders before I picked up the guitar again. "Actually, would you mind recording it, please?"

"Sure." Stuart pulled his mobile phone from his pocket and turned on the voice recorder.

"New tune. No lyrics. Take one," I said into the microphone before playing the whole thing. I nodded at Stuart to stop recording after I'd finished and the guitar down again.

"That's just lovely, Ollie."

"Thanks." I grinned, taking another cigarette from my packet.

"Do you always compose the melody before you write the lyrics?"

He looked at the scribbly pieces of paper in front of me.

"No." I put the lighter down on the table. "Sometimes I write the lyrics first, almost like a poem, and the melody will come later. Other times, I do them together. You know. Do a few chords, write a few words." I shrugged. "It all depends on my mood, or the inspiration, I guess."

"You're very talented."

"Thank you. It's all I've ever known though. It comes naturally."

"You're going to be a star one day soon."

"We'll see. Let's record it again." I leaned over to erase and scribble some more on the paper. "I want to hear what it sounds like if I swap this Gadd9 for a B minor here." I tapped the paper.

Stuart fiddled with his phone. "Whenever you're ready." He placed it on the table in front of him.

I nodded, sitting up a bit straighter. "New song, take two," I said and played the revised version. "Mmm." I rubbed my chin with my forefinger. "I'm not sure which one I prefer. What do you think?"

"Don't ask me." He laughed. "They both sound good."

"Mmm." I chewed on my cheek. "Can I listen to it again, please?" Stuart hit play and I listened intently to the first version. "All right. Next one." I nodded after it ended, leaning forward to concentrate on the chord change in the second version. "I'm not sure," I mumbled to myself, linking my fingers behind my head.

"They sound pretty similar to me." He shrugged.

"I like the B minor more." Nina's voice spoke behind me and my head snapped around. She was leaning against the door frame. "I think it has more range." Her bare feet crossed at the ankles and her hair cascaded messily over her shoulders. I stared at her stupidly for far too long before I responded.

"Yeah, you're right." My heart did a little dance and then galloped towards my throat. *Is she ever going to have a less dramatic effect on me?* I doubted it.

"It's beautiful, Ollie." She pushed away from the door and walked over to me.

"Thank you. Did I wake you?" I craned my neck to look at the giant outdoor clock on the side of the house.

"No. Did you just compose the whole thing?" She bent down to kiss me.

"Yeah." I shrugged and pulled her into my lap. "Did you sleep well?" I nuzzled her neck as she sat down with her back against my chest.

"Very." She turned her head to meet my lips again.

"Right." Stuart scraped his chair as he got up. "Would you like some coffee, Nina?"

"Yes, please. I'll give you a hand." Nina tried to get up, but I locked my arms around her waist.

"No, no, you stay here and keep Ollie company." Stuart laughed. "I'm sure he'll appreciate it more."

"For sure." I grazed my teeth along her jaw and she giggled, squirming in my lap, instantly reminding my body how much it worshipped her. I tangled my fingers into her hair and brought her head down to my lips again.

"Why did you get up so early?" Nina eventually whispered against my mouth.

"I don't know." I stroked circles on her cheek with my thumb before I continued kissing her.

"Ahem." Stuart cleared his throat. "Coffee," he chimed, setting two cups in front of us and disappearing into the kitchen again.

Nina grinned before she took a sip. "Ahh," she sighed and my heart did another somersault.

"What do you want to do today?" I reached around her and took two cigarettes from my packet, lighting them both before giving one to her.

She inhaled lazily. "My mum just called to invite the three of us to lunch. Would you like to go?"

"Yeah. It would be nice to spend more time with them. You haven't really been at home since you've come out of hospital. I feel a bit guilty actually."

124

"Don't worry about it. They understand. I want to be with you."
She pecked my cheek.

"I want to be with you too." I curled my arm around her waist.
"And on top of you"—I nibbled on her ear—"and so on," I whispered, making her shiver.

She turned her mouth to meet my lips and tangled her fingers in
my hair as I ran my free hand up her thigh and kissed her like my
life depended on it. I was just pushing my hand under her vest when
a phone started ringing inside.

"What are we like?" She smiled against my lips.

"I know." I laughed, kissing her nose and adjusting her clothes.
"That's probably Sophie."

"Do you want to invite them along to lunch too?"

"Nah." I shook my head. "Let's just spend the day with your folks."
I smiled as Stuart came out with my mobile in his hand.

"Hi." Sophie sounded unusually chirpy. "How are you?"

"Yeah, good, you?" I frowned.

"Very well, thank you. What are you up to today?"

"We're going over to Nina's for lunch."

"That's nice," she said, and then giggled. In the twenty-three years
I'd been alive, I had never heard my sister giggle. I thought I heard
Kellan's voice in the background, but then it went quiet for a moment.

"You okay, Soph?"

"Yes, yes, fine." She coughed. "Do you want to meet us in Guildford for coffee later?"

"No." I shook my head. "I'm not ready for Guildford."

"Sure." She cleared her throat. "We could come to you, bring a
cake or something?"

"Thanks, but let's give it a miss today," I said, combing my fingers
through Nina's hair. I fully intended to bring her back and ravish
her completely after lunch. There would be no time for cake.

"Great," Sophie squeaked, before clearing her throat again. "I
mean, okay, enjoy your lunch. I'll pop in tomorrow, okay. Bye-bye,"
she babbled.

"Yeah, okay, bye." I frowned, ending the call.

"Everything okay?" Nina cocked an eyebrow.

"I don't know. She giggled." I narrowed my eyes, rubbing my jaw and mulling it over. "Son of a bitch!"

"What?" Nina jolted on my lap.

"Kellan's shagging my sister!" I clasped my hand over my mouth. "Have you noticed how weird they've been?"

"I don't know." Nina chewed her lip.

"For fuck's sake," I groaned.

"Are you upset?" She frowned, searching my face.

"Honestly, my brain doesn't want to process it. The image of Kellan and my sister"—I waved my hand around—"makes me throw up in my mouth."

"Ollie." Nina shook her head with a smile.

"My sister! My best friend! She's five years older than him!"

"So?"

"She was standing up in a courtroom when Kellan and I were still jerking off to pictures of Megan Fox," I huffed. Nina burst out laughing, but I was fucked off to say the least. "It's stupid." I rubbed my hair around my head again. "Kellan is the biggest man whore who ever walked the planet and I don't want him to screw around with my sister. It's wrong."

"She's a grown woman, Ollie." Nina patted my cheek. "Besides, I think it's more than just messing around. They seem close."

"Mmm." I scratched my jaw with jerky movements.

"They're adults." She tangled her fingers into my hair. "Leave them alone."

I growled before lifting my mouth to her smiling lips, but she disengaged and hopped off, settling in the chair next to me as Stuart came out with omelettes and orange juice.

"This looks yummy, Stu!" She clapped her hands together. "You're the best."

"Did you know about Sophie and Kellan?" I launched at him without acknowledging the breakfast. He held my gaze for a few seconds before his mouth quirked up.

"I've noticed."

"How long?"

"I don't know."

"I'm going to kill him."

"Ollie." Stuart looked pointedly at me. "Kellan adores her."

"We'll see." I picked up my knife and fork. "Thanks for breakfast." I cut through my omelette. Ham and mushroom. My favourite. I shovelled a forkful into my mouth. My stomach rumbled in appreciation. "It's great," I mumbled through chewing.

It was past eleven when we finally left the house and as Stuart turned on his blinker to turn into the high street, I asked him to take a detour to the Brook Road, where the accident had happened.

"Have you been back?" I peered sideways at Nina when we were almost there.

"I've driven past a few times."

"You haven't stopped?"

"No, I've slowed down." She sighed. "It feels weird. I'm not sure where it happened anyway."

"Over here." I pointed to my left. "Can you pull over?" I asked Stuart and he pulled onto the kerb, almost exactly where it happened. "Can I get out, please?" I asked, my voice strangely quiet.

Stuart rolled me out onto the side of the road and Nina got out after me. I wrapped my arms around her waist when she climbed into my lap.

"It does feel weird," I whispered and she nodded.

"So, this is the spot of impact." Stuart looked around, kicking at the ground.

"Yeah." A shiver ran down my spine as the memory of that moment when I'd spotted Nina's Mini in front of me manifested itself in my mind.

"You're remembering?" Nina held the side of my face and I nodded. "I wish I could remember too."

"I'm glad you don't."

"Why?" Her eyebrows knitted together.

"Because it's not a pleasant memory to have playing through my mind." I sighed, shaking my head again, trying to clear it. "The images get warped and I have no way to know which memories are real and which are just my imagination. It's better that you don't remember at all. Anyway"—I blinked a few times—"there's nothing here. I don't know why I wanted to come. Let's go." I patted Nina's leg and she hopped off, narrowing her eyes at me, but not saying anything.

We circled back towards her house again, both of us silent and probably feeling strange. A million questions about what had really happened that night raced through my mind again. I really wanted to speak to Marcus Bentley, but I couldn't risk Nina ever finding out that she had been drunk and that I knew about it. It would be the end of us.

I knew I should just try and move on, but it was impossible to let it go knowing that it had altered my life beyond recognition. Would I still have taken that turn-off if I knew how it was going to break me? No way. But what if it was the only way for Nina and I to get together? No, I didn't believe that. I'd wanted her from the first moment I saw her. I would have pursued her anyway. But how did it all relate to this connection we had? It reminded me of the entry in my mum's journal and I made a mental note to look at the next journal. Perhaps she had come across something similar.

"Would you still have gone to the Guildberry that night, if you knew?" Nina echoed my thoughts, making my skin crawl.

"Of course not." My voice came out harsher than I intended.

"Even if it meant that we wouldn't have met?" She bit her bottom lip.

"We were bound to meet at some point, Nina. At the club, or your mum's shop, or somewhere in town. I would have fallen in love with you no matter when, or where, we met." I softened my tone, taking her hand. "I was already infatuated with you before we even said hello to each other. Do you remember how many times we bumped into each other that week before the accident? You took my breath away every time."

"I guess so. I just can't help feeling that the accident brought us together." She searched my face. "Do you know what I mean?"

"I do. But"—I smiled, trying to put her mind at ease, but feeling guilty about all the secrets I was hiding—"the accident happened for whatever reason. I am with you because I want to be with you, because I love you." I kissed the side of her mouth.

CHAPTER 19

W
e turned into a winding country lane before turning right into a narrow private track that stopped in front of two huge wrought-iron gates. 'Lake View' was engraved on a plaque against the fence. Nina said the security code and the gates opened when Stuart punched them in. We drove slowly down the long drive and I tried not to gape at the manicured gardens or the huge house that stood on the other side of the lake. Obviously I'd known that Nina's family was very successful, but this was something else.

"Wow." Stuart whistled. "Beautiful."

"Thanks." Nina smiled.

"How long have you lived here?" Stuart asked as he parked in front of the house.

"My parents bought it when Mum was pregnant with Zach. Mum wanted to create a haven for our family." Nina's smile turned proud before a glimmer of sadness flashed through her eyes. "It didn't feel the same after Grace died. Her absence was everywhere. I went crazy. Eventually we all moved to New York with Zach. Mum and Dad came back last summer and renovated the entire place. Zach and I only came back a few months ago. It feels like a different house, a different life. But not so tragic most of the time. We're almost happy here again, in our own way."

"I understand." I squeezed her hand before bringing her fingers to my mouth for a soft kiss.

"Anyway." She took a deep breath. "Mum and Dad honoured Grace beautifully in the new house, while still creating a personalised space for the four of us. Zach hasn't lived with us for a few years, but he's not left my side since Grace died. I don't know what I would have done without him." Her eyes briefly connected with Stuart's in the rearview mirror and I saw him nod with a small smile.

I could see why Ingrid called it their haven. Even though it was only a mile from Haslemere, it was secluded and private. From the outside, the house was modern with clean lines and panoramic windows that faced the lake and pristine landscape.

Stuart pushed me over the gravel towards the front door where Jeffrey was waiting, pleased to see us all. He kissed the side of Nina's head and led the way to the kitchen where Ingrid was getting lunch ready.

"Hey." Zach came into the kitchen and gave Nina a one-armed hug. "Hi, Ollie." He squeezed my shoulder before he leaned over to peck Stuart on the cheek.

"Come on." Jeffrey put his hands on Zach and Stuart's shoulders. "We're sitting outside."

Nina and I followed them through the vast living room. Artistic pictures of the family—of Grace and Nina, of all five of them together and of everyone individually—covered the wall behind a large sectional sofa. All the pictures were printed in black and white, with only flecks of colour here and there: a red umbrella, green leaves on the trees, orange flames of the fire, yellow beach towels, a blue cottage roof, pink flowers, a purple dress. There was something in colour in each photo. They were all blocked, with wide white borders and thin black frames, and spaced evenly to cover the entire wall. There were hundreds of photos, but it still somehow looked minimalist. It was breathtaking.

We passed a prominent white stone fireplace in the middle of the room and a glass-fronted dining room on our right. Folding patio doors opened one wall of the living room onto a tiled terrace, with an infinity pool to the left and the lake to the front. I don't think I've ever been in a house with so much glass and open space.

"You have a beautiful home." I gestured around me.

"It's a great space, isn't it?" Jeffrey smiled and I could see he really thought the space was great and not that he was great for having it. I liked that about him, his unassuming modesty. "Everybody happy with a beer?" Jeffrey walked off to a bar area on the right side of the living room and everyone but me agreed.

"Ollie doesn't drink, Dad," Zach chirped while I was still contemplating whether I should ask for something else or just nurse the bloody beer.

"Coke okay, Ollie?" Jeffrey asked.

"Thank you." I smiled.

"You don't drink?" Nina frowned.

It had occurred to me—the day before, actually—that I'd not told Nina that I didn't drink. It wasn't that I was trying to hide it from her. Not really. Perhaps a bit. But it was really just that, even with all the hours of talking we'd done, the conversation had never required me to mention it. I nodded and pursed my lips together in a small smile, hoping that she could see that I was uncomfortable.

"Why?" she asked.

"I've just never developed a taste for it." I shrugged, starting to feel unsettled. I didn't like talking about it. I didn't want to explain that I was totally screwed in the head because of the way my parents died. I couldn't express my mental block against alcohol without getting emotional. It was not a discussion I wanted to have in front of her family.

"But you work in a club? Behind the bar?"

"I know. I'm funny like that." I tried to lift the mood, but she didn't even smile.

"You don't mind if other people drink?"

"Not really."

"Have you ever been drunk?" She fired the next question.

"No."

"Have you ever had a drink?"

"No. Don't worry about it." I reached over to hold her hand. "It's not important," I lied.

"I can't believe that Zach knew about this, but I didn't." She pursed her lips.

"I happened to tell him about it before you woke up. It's just not come up between us yet." I brought her fingers to my lips. "It's not a big deal," I lied again.

"Okay." She squeezed my hand, but I could see that the conversation wasn't over. I didn't quite understand what her problem was, though.

Stuart started telling Jeffrey about how he decided to get into nursing when Nina piped up next to me again.

"So, does it bother you that I drink?"

"Not really," I lied, once a-bloody-gain, and patted her hand before I leaned closer to Stuart to listen to what he was saying, but Nina wasn't satisfied yet.

"What if I got drunk? Would that bother you?"

I frowned, letting out a slow breath. Stuart stopped talking and also frowned. Even her father looked a bit surprised.

"Nina." I gave her a tight smile. "Can you let it go for now, please?"

She scrunched her face. "Would it bother you?"

I held her gaze, hoping that she would back off, but she wasn't having any of it and I rubbed my hair around my head. "Yes. Yes, it would bother me if you got drunk."

We stared at each other for another long moment and I struggled to read her face. I couldn't understand why she seemed so upset and why she was creating tension.

"Are you saying that I'm not allowed to drink anymore?"

"I'm not saying that." I didn't want them all to think that I was some dogmatic moron, but I wouldn't be able to hide my aversion to alcohol, so I had to try and explain a bit. "I don't feel comfortable when people get drunk. It makes me nervous."

"I don't see the problem, Nina," Jeffrey intervened with a stern edge to his voice.

"I just don't think there's something wrong with having a bit of fun every now and again," she snapped.

133

"Nobody is saying that there is anything wrong with having fun, but there also shouldn't be a problem if someone feels uncomfortable with your version of fun." Jeffrey looked pointedly at her.

"Whatever." Nina waved her hand dismissively. "Everybody just needs to chill out."

"Well, there's a phrase I haven't heard in a few years." Jeffrey chuckled, lifting the mood.

"Yes, take a chill pill, old man." Nina laughed, instantly relaxing me.

"I'm the master of chill." Jeffrey wiggled his eyebrows as he stood up. "And you know it." He walked into the house, pinching Nina's cheek as he passed her.

"No, you're a grumpy old man"—she stuck her tongue out at his back—"and you are a broody control freak." She kissed my cheek.

"Mmm." I caught her chin between my thumb and forefinger. "Be careful." I pulled her face closer, making her turn her head so that her hair fell in a thick veil around us, shielding us from Zach and Stuart. "This broody control freak might like to punish moody fairies," I whispered against her mouth, making her smile. I wasn't into anything kinky, but I couldn't deny the fact that I was indeed broody and controlling at times. Just not in a creepy way. I smirked at myself and cupped the back of Nina's head, pulling her down to me for a hard kiss.

Zach cleared his throat dramatically and Stuart snorted in that unflattering way of his. I heard their chairs scrape back and their footsteps disappear into the house.

"I think we're making the boys uncomfortable." Nina giggled as she pulled away a little.

"Then they shouldn't watch." I nipped her bottom lip between my teeth before soothing it with my tongue.

"Are you trying to drive me crazy?" she asked, her voice breathy.

"Most certainly," I whispered against her mouth, pushing my hands into her hair before laying a long, hot kiss on her throat. She shivered, a sprinkling of goosebumps instantly covering her chest and arms. "Like I said"—I flicked my tongue over the spot again—"I might like to punish moody fairies."

"Let's go," she moaned softly.

"Actually"—I patted her bottom as she hopped off—"I would like another Coke, please."

"What?"

"I'm feeling quite thirsty. Please, may I have another Coke?" I tried to look sincere, but struggled to keep the wolfish smirk off my face.

"No," she whispered. "You don't play fair."

"I've told you before that I don't." I grabbed the waistband of her shorts and pulled her down on my lap again. "Just think how much sweeter it will be tonight, if you've been waiting for it all day," I whispered, rubbing my stubbled chin along her jawline.

We heard the others making their way outside again. She turned in my lap and ran her hand over my crotch. "Two can play this game," she whispered in my ear before squeezing lightly. "Another Coke, Ollie?" she sneered as she walked off to the bar.

"Argh," I groaned, shaking my head with a defeated smile. I shifted in my chair and strategically placed my hands in my lap as I glowered at her. "Game on." I saluted her and she burst out laughing.

"Anybody else want another drink?" Nina asked as the others filed back onto the terrace, carrying plates of nibbles. Everybody called out their orders and Nina walked back and forth a few times to deliver their drinks. She was swaying her hips more than she usually would and she kept making eye contact with me, her eyes smouldering as she chewed on her bottom lip suggestively.

"Hello, Earth to Ollie?" Stuart's voice interrupted my inappropriate thoughts and I felt my face heat up a bit.

"Sorry." I shook my head, rubbing my glowing cheek. Nina winked at me, her lip slowly curling up on one side. Fuck, she was sexy. There was no way I was going to last the day. "What were you saying?"

"Ingrid was asking about your rehabilitation programme and I said that our main focus is to get you to transfer yourself in and out of your wheelchair as soon as possible."

"Yeah, definitely. I'd also like to get a car as soon as possible."

"Don't you like the van?" Jeffrey asked.

"No, not really. It's fine for now, but it's a rental and I'm a bit of a petrolhead. I'd like to have something nicer. Or even something more normal, I guess."

"That makes sense. I also like cars. It's my guilty pleasure."

"Oh, yeah?" I arched an eyebrow. "What do you drive?"

"Well, Ingrid got me a Vanquish for my birthday this year, so it's definitely my favourite at the moment." He looked like an excited child.

"Nice." I beamed. "My dad was also a massive Aston fan. I inherited one from him, actually."

"So why do you want to buy another car if you already have one?" Nina asked.

"It's kind of special."

"Special? Like sentimental?"

"Yes. Very sentimental, but it's also a classic. I would never have it converted to suit my needs," I explained.

"What is it?" Jeffrey shifted forward in his chair.

"1960 DB4 GT Zagato."

Jeffrey whistled. "Lovely."

"So, my teetotalling petrolhead classic-car-owner boyfriend, how many more secrets are you keeping?" She cocked an eyebrow.

"Ha. It's a secret." I winked, not feeling entirely comfortable. I was all too aware of the secrets I was keeping and would have to keep forever.

We talked a bit more about which car I was thinking of getting and what my physio and exercise programme entailed. It was good being with them. They seemed genuinely interested in my future and I loved the feeling of inclusion it brought me.

We had barbecued chicken, garlic bread and various salads for lunch and we all ate way too much. After dessert Nina pushed me around the garden and told me more about their childhood. I realised again, like I had when Zach and I talked about it in hospital, that even though their family had been through hell and even though the loss of Grace was written all over each of their faces, they were still a family unit. I couldn't help the twinge of self-pity I felt for the loss of my own family. I knew Sophie and I had each other. I guessed it just felt different when only the kids stayed behind. We had no roots. No grown-ups to turn to. No one to give us advice, or comfort us, the way only parents could.

"You okay?" Nina noticed the unexpected sadness that swept over me.

"Yeah." I forced a smile. "I like your folks. I know I have Sophie and the guys…"

"And me. You have me too." She climbed onto my lap and took my face in her hands.

"I know." I pushed my hand into her hair and brought her mouth down to mine.

CHAPTER 28

When we arrived home Stuart helped me to get settled and I wondered how long it was going to be until we all lived independent lives again. Normal lives, where we didn't have to consider two or three other people before making any plans. Lives where Stuart didn't have to help me get undressed before I wanted to be with my girlfriend. Or clean me up afterwards.

"I'll be back in two hours. Call me if you need anything. Zach and I are just popping down to the café around the corner." Stuart pushed my wheelchair into its spot behind the desk and I nodded. "Actually, Ollie"—he turned back to me—"we didn't talk about this when we had our talk the other day, but I just wanted to make sure that you and Nina were being safe."

"Gee whiz, Mum." I laughed.

"Sorry. The risks are still the same."

"Yeah, thanks, but don't worry. We had that talk in the hospital, way before we even did anything." I waved my hand and Stuart lifted his eyebrows. "Neither of us has been with anybody since then, so I think it's safe to assume that we're both clean."

"Yes, I know, but I mean, the risk of getting pregnant is still the same."

"She's on birth control, Stu. Don't worry, okay? We're being responsible. I promise."

"Okay. Good."

"Now go and charm Zach." I waved him out of the room, eager to be left alone.

Nina came in a few minutes after he left. She was still wearing the soft white shirt she'd had on earlier, but she was missing her bra, denim shorts and sandals. She looked like an indecent angel as she padded over to the bed and lay down next to me. I wrapped my arm around her shoulders and ran my fingers through her hair.

"Are you sleepy?"

"No." I let her hair fall through my fingers. "Are you?" I asked and she shook her head.

I bent my head down and kissed her softly, feeling her body respond to mine. She moaned as I twisted her hair around my hand and pulled a little, deepening our kiss. My tongue stroked slowly through her mouth and I pushed her down on the mattress, rolling on my side to kiss her throat as I tangled my fingers in her hair again.

"I ache for you. I want you so much. All of the time." I scraped my teeth across her neck before I sat up and pulled her on top of me.

She closed her eyes and moaned again as she wrapped her legs around my waist, making me groan low in my throat as I tore her underwear off, letting the pieces of flimsy lace flutter through the air. Her buttons popped off one by one and scattered on the floor as I slowly ripped her shirt open. I pulled away, letting my gaze travel over her body. She opened those molten pools of lucent blue and treated me to an unhurried smile as I pushed into her. My hands roamed over every soft curve and contour, leisurely discovering all her secret places, until she fell apart and I knew that I had never seen anything more beautiful in my life. We held each other's gaze as I shattered as well.

I placed a soft kiss on her shoulder before I rolled on my side again. She slid into the crook of my arm and her skin rubbed against mine all the way down until our eyes were level with each other's. We lay there staring at each other for a long time, our limbs entangled and our bodies moulded together so closely that I could feel her heartbeat against mine.

"What are your plans for the week?" I asked after a while.

"I guess I should start showing up for my Harritech internship at some point."

"Hey, you have to try to get back to some kind of normal. I have to go to physio and to the gym anyway. That is, if you want me to get strong enough to do all sorts of wicked things to this luscious, wonderful, fantastical body." I let my hand wander over her hips and around her waist and she hummed happily.

"I know." She sighed. "I'd rather be with you though."

I kissed her nose. "I won't let you give up your future because of me."

"It can wait, Ollie. My dad would be happy to put it on hold."

"Would you be happy with that? I'm sure you've told me how much you were looking forward to it." I skimmed my thumb over her eyebrow, trying to iron out her frown, before running it over her scar. "Does it still hurt?" I asked when she didn't respond.

"No, it tickles." She squirmed and I licked a line from the bottom to the top and back down again, nibbling on her ear as she wriggled and tried to get away from me. "No, Ollie, stop." She laughed and pushed my shoulders, but I caught her hands and held them above her head as I gnawed on all the sensitive spots around her neck. She was writhing around by the time I finally let go and fell on my back as I laughed.

"I'm going to get you for that."

"Is that so?" I wiped my eyes as she pushed up on her elbow, arching her eyebrow and playfully walking her fingers down my torso. "I'm not ticklish, so good luck," I laughed, but she found what she was looking for and my breath caught in my throat when she lowered her mouth to me.

"Ah!" I curled my fingers around her shoulder. "Nina," I ground out, feeling my stomach muscles ripple as I forced myself not to fuck her mouth like the savage I was.

I threaded my fingers into her hair and pulled her up. She crawled over my body, straddling me, and I kissed her hungrily as she slammed down on me. I closed my eyes, feeling like an untamed animal. I wanted to be rough and relentless, but I opened my eyes again and when they connected with hers something clenched in my soul. The wild fire in me calmed to a deep smoulder.

140

"I'm not going to be able to walk tomorrow." She fell down next to me.

"Good." I caressed my hand over her shoulder and down her arm.

"Could you get any hotter?"

"I could try." I wiggled my eyebrows arrogantly.

"I'll hold you to that." She kissed me swiftly before getting off the bed. She reached into the laundry basket and retrieved one of my T-shirts. "But I really have to go to the loo now." She wrinkled her nose and crossed her legs. She dropped the T-shirt over her head and it fell to the top of her thighs, not quite covering her bottom.

"Yeah, me too." I'd probably overdone it slightly. "Could you hand me my phone, please? I need to give Stuart a call." I pointed to where it was still in my backpack on the back of my wheelchair. I shifted uncomfortably, suddenly very aware of the pressure in my bladder.

"Sure." She smiled, bending down to kiss me. "I can help you though."

"No." I shook my head with too much emphasis.

"Why not?"

"Nina." I frowned, instantly annoyed. "Definitely not. There's no way I would ever let you help me with that."

"Don't you trust me?"

"It's not about you. It's embarrassing and undignified and I don't want you to see me like that."

"Ollie…"

"I do not want to talk about this, Nina. Can you just give me my phone, please?" I held out my hand.

She drew in a sharp breath, shocked by my sudden mood swing. I didn't know why I was being horrible to her. She hadn't done anything wrong, but I couldn't help myself. The caged beast inside me was rearing up, trying to break out. She handed me the phone and stared at me, chewing on her lip.

"You okay, Ollie?" Stuart answered on the first ring. "I'm just walking up the drive now."

"I'm fine. I just need the toilet." I felt my face heat under Nina's gaze. I hated that she was standing there listening to me as I asked Stuart to come home to take me for a wee like a toddler.

"I'll be there in thirty seconds," Stuart said, ending the call.

I saw Nina's eyes widen at the exact same moment I felt the warm wetness spread under my arse and up my back. It was too late. I had just pissed myself in front of my brand-new girlfriend. I closed my eyes and inhaled slowly.

"Oliver," Nina whispered.

"Please," I grunted, pointing at the door.

"Ollie, no." She shook her head, touching my cheek, but I shoved her hand away and turned my face to the other side.

"Please," I ground out, gesturing at the door again, my body shaking with humiliation. She stood frozen in place and I lost it. I threw my phone across the room, shattering it against the opposite wall. "Get out!" I thundered, just as Stuart opened the door.

She turned around and pushed past him out of the room.

"Fuck!" I shouted, dropping my head in my hands. "Motherfucking fuck!" I balled my fists and slammed them into the mattress.

"It's okay." Stuart touched my arm and pulled the covers off. I glared at him as I yanked my arm away, but he didn't react. He helped me to have a shower and get dressed without saying a word. He opened the sliding door in my bedroom and pushed me out onto the little patio, disappearing briefly to bring me my cigarettes and a cup of coffee. He squeezed my shoulder and left me again. I heard him moving around the room, changing the bedding and clearing up.

I'm sure it didn't take him long, but I'd smoked two cigarettes by the time he returned. He pulled up a chair next to me and we sat in silence for a while. After I smoked one more, I finally felt a bit of control coming back to me.

"I'm sorry," I said.

"It's okay."

"I'm still sorry for being such a dick." I cleared my throat. I fucking hated all the apologies I felt obliged to issue recently. It was the fucking icing on top of the shit cake.

"Don't worry about it. I'm sorry that you have to go through this. It will get easier."

"When?" I felt pathetic.

"As soon as you can get yourself in and out of your wheelchair you can start taking yourself to the toilet."

"How long will that take?"

"Everybody's different, but I expect a couple of weeks, if you work hard."

"How long will it take to get more control over my bladder?" I lit another cigarette and inhaled it almost in one drag.

"I don't know, Ollie. Some people never regain full control, but with an incomplete injury like yours the chances of recovery are better. You'll just have to keep going at it with physio. I can't say that this will never happen again, because it most probably will, but you'll learn to read your body's signals better and if you stick to a strict toileting routine these incidents should be minimal."

"Yeah, I get it." I couldn't stop a small smile from creeping around my lips. "So, having a two-hour sex marathon probably doesn't count as sticking to a strict toileting routine?"

"No." Stuart shook his head, also smiling. "You should go to the toilet every time after you have sex, or at least after the second... session... if it happens in a short amount of time."

"Okay." I stubbed out my cigarette. "Is Nina still here?"

"She's out back with Zach."

"I'm so embarrassed. I was such an arsehole."

"It's going to be okay." He got up and I silently looked out across the dark fields.

I turned my head when I heard her coming into the bedroom. Her steps faltered when she saw me watching her, but our eyes locked and she straightened her shoulders and walked the last few feet with her head up. She'd had a shower too. Her hair was still wet and she was wearing a clean vest and shorts. I could see that she had been crying though. Her eyes were red and her chest was blotchy. I felt like a piece of shit.

"Hey." She sat on my lap and I curled my arms around her, inhaling her clean scent. "I'm sorry." She caressed my face.

I shook my head, running my fingers through her hair. "You didn't do anything wrong. I'm the one who's sorry." I remembered the shock that had flashed over her face when I lost it. "I was out of line. It won't happen again. I'll keep it together."

"No, Ollie. I don't want you to keep it together. I don't want you to hold back around me." She stroked her thumbs over my cheeks. "I want all of you. Not just the nice and easy bits. I want everything."

"Nina." I dropped my head against her chest. "I don't want you to be my caretaker."

"I know that, and that's not what I meant. I don't want you to be embarrassed and freak out when something goes wrong." She threaded her fingers into my hair, making me look up at her. "I'm not embarrassed about any of this, Ollie." I felt my face burn and I tried to look away, but she held my head and forced me to keep eye contact with her.

"Did Zach ever tell you how Grace died?" she asked when I didn't say anything.

"No." I shook my head and automatically tightened my arms around her.

"She got meningitis. We don't know how, she just became very ill, very suddenly. She was fine in the morning. Started feeling off around lunch. Nothing much, said she had a headache. She had a seizure just before two. By the time they got her to hospital at twenty past two she already had brain damage." Nina started crying and buried her head in my neck.

"It's okay, my love." I rubbed her back. "You don't have to talk about it."

"I want you to know." She wiped her face. "They kept her sedated until the next day, and when she woke up she had lost hearing in her left ear, her vision was almost gone, her mind wasn't quite the same and she kept having seizures. So many seizures. Five days she lived like that. On the sixth day, she didn't wake up again. They kept her on life support for two more days, but she had almost zero brain function by then. We agreed to let her go on day eight. Eight days it took Grace to go from my beautiful, smart and kind sister to a shell of a girl."

"Nina." I held her as close to me as I could. She sobbed silently for a few minutes, but then she took a deep breath and carried on, remarkably calm and collected.

"For those eight days, I stayed with her every second of every day. Mum and Dad were there too, obviously, and Zach most of the time. But I was there through everything. For every catheter change, for every seizure. Everything. I cleaned her up every time she had to be changed. All I kept thinking was that I wanted her to be as comfortable as possible, and that's what I want for you too." She lifted her eyes to meet mine.

"I understand." I framed her face with my hands and kissed her cheeks and then her mouth. "I really do. I admire and love you for it, but…" I hid the rest of my sentence in another kiss.

I didn't think it was the same at all. I understood that she wanted to take care of her sister. That she wasn't embarrassed for her sister. But it was her sister. Her twin. Not her new boyfriend.

"Ollie, if the situation was reversed and I was the one who was paralysed, would you have been embarrassed, or weird, about anything I had to go through? Even now, in these early days of our relationship?"

"No." I shook my head. "No, I wouldn't have been."

"Exactly. I can understand how vulnerable you must feel and I get that it makes you angry, but it hurts me when you shut me out. I need you to trust me. I need to know that you trust me enough to let me be here with you. Through all the hard parts too." She held my gaze.

"I'll try." I closed my eyes and clamped my arms around her waist.

CHAPTER 21

I had a GP check-up the following day and imagine my exasperation when the bloody GP was Marcus fucking Bentley.

"Oliver." He nodded when Stuart left me in his examination
room.

"Why are you here?"

"I work here. I'm the junior GP."

"Where's Dr. Camberley? She's my registered GP."

"She retired earlier this year and I took over a portion of her
patient list. You're here for your fortnightly check-up, right?" He
typed on his computer and squinted at the screen. "I'm qualified
to be your registered GP, but you can ask for someone else, if you'd
prefer not to see me every other week?"

My first instinct was to say that I indeed wanted to be transferred
to another GP, but a sixth sense, a niggling feeling at the back of my
mind, persuaded me that Marcus might be a good person to have in
my life. I didn't like him. I hated that he'd slept with Nina. I wanted
to make him suffer for leaving her at the Guildberry that night, but
for some inexplicable reason I did feel like I wanted access to him.
He loved Grace. Perhaps he would know something about my connection with Nina? "No. Just get on with it."

"All right. Like I said, this is a fortnightly check-up we ask you
to attend. We check normal vital signs like blood pressure, oxygen
levels, weight, muscle responses and any other minor concerns you
might have, like pressure sores."

After he went through the whole spiel and was satisfied that I
was operating as well as could be expected, he asked, "Are there any
concerns from your side?"

"What do you know about neurological linking?"

His eyes widened and it took him a couple of beats to start talking. "Do you mean the molecular and genetic basis of neurological diseases?"

"No. Much more abstract than that. More in the sense of subconsciously connecting with another person. Perhaps through dreams?"

"Mmm." He nodded a couple of times. "That sounds more like a psychological occurrence. I did take psychology as a subject at university, but I would by no means be able to answer any specialised questions. Your mum was Professor Watson, though?"

"How did you know that?"

"I attended her exchange programme in Australia in my second year. I remember you bringing her lunch every day. You must have been, what, fifteen, sixteen?"

"Fifteen." I nodded, almost choking on the memories of my mum's last months. "What about her?"

"She wrote a couple of textbooks on subconscious linking. I'm not sure if she did any research about subconsciously connecting with other people, but she was the expert in creating neurological pathways in the brain. I can ask the university for copies of her textbooks, you might find something useful in them?"

"Thank you." I let out a shaking breath. I wanted to discover what the connection between me and Nina meant as much as I wanted to pretend that it didn't exist and that we were just normal people. My mind was pulling me in opposite directions, but it was the first time I'd taken an active step to try and find more information.

In the weeks that followed Nina and I fell into an easy routine, and even though I never allowed myself to completely forget about our weird circumstances or the devastation that had brought us together, our relationship felt fresh and innocent. It filled me with a sense of hope for the future and I clung to those feelings more than anything.

I was still clueless about how our lives were connected. After I saw Marcus, I did several more useless searches on the Internet and I tried to forage for my mum's next journal from 1990. But rummaging through high bookshelves and heavy boxes was a nearly impossible task from the confines of a wheelchair without asking anyone for help, and I didn't know how to articulate myself without raising questions about why I was looking for those specific journals. I had a few unsuccessful rifles through the boxes I was able to reach by myself, but then decided to put it to the back of my mind for the time being. At least until I saw Marcus again and he provided me with my mum's textbooks.

To be honest, I sometimes still questioned whether it was real. Perhaps our magic had dissipated as it got submerged in day-to-day life? Maybe my new appreciation for the ordinary encouraged me to make a conscious effort to stay away from these thoughts and questions? I just wanted us to be regular people. I hoped that it reduced the risk of the truth ever coming out, and as the days ticked by it became easier to rationalise everything. To just get on with life.

Nina started working more hours at Harritech, while I worked hard in physio and at the gym. I mastered getting myself in and out of my wheelchair by the end of my second week at home, and by the end of the following week I managed to do some of my toileting routines without Stuart's help. He was still present to supervise, but it made a massive difference to the way I felt about myself, and it was good to get some independence and personal space back.

I often went into the garage and practised transferring myself in and out of my dad's classic car. I was never going to drive it again, but more than anything, I used the time to think. It felt like my life was going in the right direction, but I couldn't deny the fact that I was unsure about my future with the band. I would never do anything other than music, but I didn't know if I would be able to perform again.

Apart from general well wishes, I'd not heard from Jack. I expected that Kellan had asked him to give me time, but I knew that he was going to talk to me about my plans for the future at the earliest opportunity he got. No matter how much he liked me, he was still a businessman; he was always going to establish the most lucrative future for the band and for his label.

It was constantly weighing on my mind and I didn't know what I was going to do. The idea of being the crippled lead singer of a rock band didn't fill me with any level of enthusiasm. Teaching music was the most probable and appealing prospect I could come up with, but I didn't know how to tell anyone. I knew that the guys would have a fit if I suggested quitting, so I kept practising with them while I hoped that the perfect plan would reveal itself at some point. I finished a song I'd begun working on while I was still in hospital, and I started fiddling around with lyrics for the new tune I'd composed on that first Sunday morning back home. Even in my uncertainty it felt good to have a sense of focus again.

Nina and I hung out with Sophie and the guys on some evenings, and other evenings we just spent hours in bed, shutting out the world around us. Those were my favourite moments. She stayed over at my house every night and I wanted to ask her to officially move in with me, but I was cautious about putting too much pressure on her, so I decided to wait. I tried to keep my hormones under control, but Nina was intoxicating. I was a junkie and she was my high.

We were both sprawled face down on my bed, basking in the shameless afterglow of one of these debauched fixes for my Nina addiction, when my phone rang and challenged me into the next stage of recovery.

I turned on my side, ignoring the shrill noise. It was early on a Wednesday evening, almost four weeks after I'd been released from hospital.

"You are heavenly." I traced my finger along Nina's spine and her lips curved lazily. Her skin glistened in the evening sun and her hair pooled on the bed in a molten chocolate puddle.

"And you are depraved." She opened one eye to peek at me.

"Are you complaining?" I stroked my hand over the roundness of her bottom and up her back.

"Never. Are you going to get that?" She nodded towards the

still-ringing phone on my bedside table.

"No." I rolled her on her side and pulled her against me, capturing her mouth once more.

"What if it's important?" she said between kisses and I lifted my eyes to glare at the phone, willing it to stop.

"They can call Stuart." I bent my head back to her again, landing fluttery kisses on the side of her mouth and along her jaw, when the ringing finally stopped. "See? Not important." I nipped her earlobe and she sighed again, tangling her fingers into my hair and dropping her head back. My hand caressed her hip and curled around her waist as I licked a trail across her collarbone and up her throat, when the phone started ringing again.

"Just answer it, Ollie." She laughed and I groaned as I reached over to grab it from the bedside table.

"It's Charlie," I huffed, showing her his name flashing on the screen. I briefly considered chucking it across the room, but I knew that Stuart wasn't going to be impressed if he had to go and get another replacement so soon. "What is it, Charlton?"

"Howzit, Olive?" His voice chirped on the other side.

"I'm busy, brother." I pulled a face at Nina, making her giggle. "What do you want?"

"Aweh, bra." He chuckled. "Can I come over?"

"Can it wait till tomorrow?" I frowned, running my fingers through Nina's hair as she snuggled against my chest.

"No, sorry."

"Give me half an hour," I agreed as my fingers played over Nina's neck. I loved how soft her skin was. She stretched against me and a contented purring noise escaped her lips. "Make that an hour." I ended the call and pushed her on her back again.

About forty-five minutes later, Nina and I were having coffee outside on the living room patio while we waited for Charlie. We'd had a quick shower after our afternoon sexcapades and she was looking gorgeously fresh-faced in one of my Lawless T-shirts over a pair of jogging bottoms; her hair was tied up in some messy knot business on the top of her head.

"What?" Her lips curled up when she caught me staring at her.

"I'm happy." I reached over and stroked her cheek.

"Me too." She leaned her face into my hand. "You're incredible."

"Well, I do aim to please."

"I think it's fair to say that you've definitely overachieved this afternoon. Several times." A slight blush coloured her cheeks. "But I'm not just talking about that."

"Yeah?" I asked and she crawled into my lap.

"Thank you for letting me help you." She kissed my cheek.

"Shouldn't I be thanking you for that?" My arm snaked around her waist. I'd been struggling with some pressure sores on my thigh and she'd helped me to change the dressings after we had a shower.

"It means a lot that you're starting to trust me enough to do more for you."

"It's never, ever about me not trusting you." I cupped her neck. "It's about me being self-conscious and coming to terms with the fact that I'm not the king of the jungle any more."

"Definitely the king of my jungle," she mumbled, but instantly blushed and dropped her head on my shoulder as she burst out laughing.

"You're bloody adorable." I squeezed her waist and kissed the top of her head. She lifted her head and I captured her lips in a long, sloppy kiss just as the doorbell rang. "Saved by the bell," I whispered against her mouth and she hopped off my lap to open the door.

"Looking good, Olive." Charlie sauntered in and clapped me on the shoulder.

"Thanks." I squeezed his arm. "How are you?"

"Lekker, bra, lekker." He grinned as he sat down and helped himself to my cigarettes.

"Ta." I smiled, taking two out when he offered the packet to me. Cheeky sod.

"Good day?" he asked, dragging on his smoke.

"Ja." I nodded, lighting both of mine and handing one to Nina when she sat down on the other side. She smiled and I winked at her before returning my gaze to Charlie. "So, what's up?"

"You know it's our birthday on Friday?" He quirked his mouth, shifting forward in his chair.

"Oh, yeah." I widened my eyes. "I actually forgot."

We'd decided to form Lawless just over five years ago and we'd played our first gig a couple of months later at a back-to-school festival for our college. We'd signed a contract with Jack the very next day and we'd celebrated the band's birthday on that day every year since.

"So"—he shifted in his chair—"I was hoping you were up for a short set at the Guildberry on Friday night?"

"I don't think so." I knew I had to start going out in public again, but I didn't know if I was ready to perform yet. Perhaps not ever again.

"Please, Olive." Charlie leaned forward in his chair. "Ian wanted to have a party at the house, but Kellan said that you wouldn't come." Kellan was right. I absolutely would not go to any party. "We agreed to come here. But"—he took a breath—"I arranged with Jack to give us a slot on stage at ten and I thought it would be magical if you could surprise everyone."

I rubbed my hair around my head as I puffed on my cigarette, looking at his expectant face.

"Please, Oliver." He frowned, instantly making my resistance crumble when he used my name. Charlie had only ever called me Olive, or very rarely Ols, but he'd never called me Oliver, not once since the day I'd met him over a decade ago. Sometimes Ian was Ina, and Kellan was Kelly, but I was always Olive. Kellan and Ian ignored Charlie's nicknames, but everything Charlie did made me smile.

"All right." I nodded and scratched my jaw.

"Woohoo!" He jumped up, hugging me tight. "Awesome. You know you're the best one, Olive." He sat down again. "Always been my favourite."

"Okay." I laughed, shaking my head. "How are we going to do

this? Kellan won't agree to go to the club without me, but I want to surprise them too."

"Yeah." He took another cigarette from my packet and shuffled forward. "Tomorrow, when we're over here for practice, I'll tell the boys about it, and when Kel starts saying that we can't do it, you have to say that you want us to go. I'll pretend to agree with him, but you can say something about a good opportunity to update people on how well you're doing, blah, blah." He waved his hand in the air. His enthusiasm was rubbing off on me already. "Jack will be well pleased too, I think he's starting to get a bit mislik about you being gone for so long." He turned down his mouth and I nodded.

"I think we should do the new song," I said, not able to keep the grin off my face.

"Ja!" He bobbed his head. "I was gonna say that too."

CHAPTER 22

When the boys came over for practice the next day, I very much enjoyed the show Charlie and I were putting on and it made me feel even more excited.

"So, Jack asked if we could play at the club tomorrow night," Charlie mentioned as he fiddled around with some notes on the piano. "Because it's our birthday."

"Not without Oliver," Kellan stated without looking up from his guitar.

"That's what I told him," Charlie agreed.

"Uh-huh." Ian nodded, spinning a drumstick on his finger.

"I think you should do it," I piped up, drawing surprised looks from Kellan and Ian.

"No way, Olive." Charlie shook his head.

"Forget it. Right, Ian?" Kellan looked to his brother for affirmation.

"Uh-huh." Ian nodded again, flipping the drumstick over and catching it with the other hand.

"Come on," I persisted, struggling to keep my smile in check. "It's a good opportunity to tell everybody I'm still kicking." I laughed at my own wit.

"We're coming here tomorrow night." Kellan put down his guitar. "We should all be together."

"Yeah, but you can go to the club afterwards. What time, Charlton?"

"Ten," he said.

"Plenty of time to come here and get to the club." I raised my eyebrows.

"What do you think?" Kellan looked at Ian again.

"I don't know, maybe." Ian scratched his head. "Charles, what do you say?"

"I don't know." Charlie bit down on his lip, looking quite sincere. "Can't you just come?"

"No." I shook my head. "I'm not ready. I want you to go though. It'll be good for the band, and it'll get Jack off your back for a while too." I raised my eyebrows at Kellan.

"He's got a point, Kel." Ian nudged his head at Kellan.

"Okay." Kellan finally sighed. "But I don't like it. This is a one-time-only, three-piece performance. We'll do it as a tribute to you, but the next time we go on a stage, it will be all four of us. And Jack can go and fuck himself," he grumbled as an afterthought.

I wasn't surprised that he had already caught on to my reluctance to start performing again and it pleased me deeply to know how happy it was going to make him when I showed up the next evening.

"I agree." Ian bobbed his head. "It's pretty fucking useless to perform without our front man, but I'll go with it this once, if we do it as a tribute to you."

"Me too," Charlie concurred.

"For fuck's sake." I rolled my eyes. "I don't need a bloody memorial. I'm just sorting out my shit. And, as your 'front man'"—I made quotation marks with my fingers—"I'm pulling rank and telling you that I want you to do this performance in celebration of our five years and to keep the band in the loop. End of discussion."

"Whatever," Kellan huffed, clearly not in the mood to argue. "What do you want us to sing?"

"I don't know." I smirked. "How many songs, Charlie?"

"Three." Charlie smiled too.

"Okay, you take lead vocal." I pointed at Kellan and he picked up his guitar again, resting it on his knee. "Start off with 'Lawless', everybody likes that. I think you should do 'Strong, Black Coffee' next. It received good reviews when we performed it at the RAM Fest in

155

May." I met their gazes, looking for confirmation, and they all nodded. "And I'd like you to finish with 'I Shall Not Wholly Die'."

"Not a chance, that's your song." Ian shook his head.

"Ian." I groaned. "I want to get it out and if you tell them that I wrote it in the hospital, it can be your tribute song. Okay?" I pinned him with my eyes.

"Good idea." Charlie nodded too energetically.

"Okay, cool. Sounds good," Kellan and Ian said at the same time and then nodded in unison. "Cheers." They grinned and saluted each other.

"Okay, cool. Let's go through it a couple of times." I picked up my guitar. "I'll play along." I tipped my head at Ian to start counting us in and we played all three songs without any screw-ups.

"Right." I put my guitar down. "Go again." I leaned forward in my wheelchair, resting my elbows on my knees. They played 'Lawless' perfectly and Kellan did a good job managing the vocals and guitar.

"Nice." I smiled, twirling my forefinger. "Next one." They did well with 'Strong, Black Coffee' too, but it definitely sounded better when I joined in. It was just one of those songs that needed all four of us.

"Good"—I chewed on my bottom lip—"but you need to work on that riff in the middle, Kel. Switch to Charlie for the vocals, so that you can focus on the strings." I knew it wasn't necessary, but I also knew they expected me to not be entirely happy with the way it had just sounded.

"Yeah," Kellan agreed. "Charlton, pick up the lyrics at the end of the second verse. I'll fade out before the riff starts."

"Yahtsee." Charlie tipped his head and Kellan started strumming the intro.

"Good." I nodded, smiling broadly when they finished. It sounded much better and I was well chuffed. "Last one," I instructed, excited to hear the new song. It started out decently, but halfway through the chorus they messed up the timing.

"Fucking hell." Kellan held up his hand and turned around to scowl at Charlie and Ian.

"Ina needs to slow down half a step." Charlie bulged his eyes at Ian.

"You both need to speed the fuck up." Ian waved a drumstick between Kellan and Charlie.

They started swearing at each other and I sat back and watched them get on with it. It was always like this, I just normally joined in too. We could spend ages blaming each other and wouldn't stop until somebody stormed out for a smoke. The others would follow immediately and we'd stand around smoking in silence for a while. Eventually, we would come back inside and play impeccably. I waited patiently for them to lose momentum while I made bets on who was going to stalk out first. My money was on Ian and right on cue he jumped up, making his stool fall over.

"Fuck this," he spat over his shoulder. Charlie rolled his eyes, stomping out after him.

"Morons," Kellan called, before walking over to me. "Come on, Ols." He pushed me out to where they were sitting on the patio.

True to form, nobody said a word and I had to hide my smile behind my hand as I watched them glaring into space. We finally went back inside after everybody finished their second cigarette. Ian picked up his sticks and started tapping the beat, lifting his eyebrows at me in question. I nodded that the tempo was fine and Kellan and Charlie joined in. They played it flawlessly to the end and I applauded when they all curtsied after the last note.

"Good." I gave them a double thumbs-up. "Again."

Sophie came in when they were about halfway through the last practice run. "New song?" She gestured towards them after she kissed my cheek, and I nodded. "It's beautiful." She sat down next to me. "Why aren't you playing?"

"They're practising for a gig at the club tomorrow night. I'm not going."

"Ah." She trailed off, looking distracted. "Can I come over tomorrow evening? For the band's birthday?"

"Of course. I was expecting you to."

It looked like she wanted to say something else, but she shook her head and turned her eyes back to the boys.

"Right, we're off," Ian said, clapping me on the arm and winking at Sophie.

"See you tomorrow, Olive. Later, Soph," Charlie called, following Ian out.

"Are you staying?" Kellan asked Sophie.

"I think so," she said, flicking her eyes towards me.

"Right." He nodded, seeming a bit unsure.

"Are you staying?" I asked, quite enjoying his discomfort as he shifted his weight from one foot to the other without answering.

"I want to stop at the music shop before they close. I need some strings. I'll tell the boys to get here for four tomorrow," he told me, but still looked a bit undecided about what he wanted to do. He shook his head, just like Sophie had earlier, swung around and walked out without another word. I almost burst out laughing. I was certain they'd agreed to tell me that they were seeing each other, but that Kellan had chickened out for some reason and that Sophie was now upset.

The next day Kellan arrived about twenty minutes early and I think he wanted to try and talk to me about Sophie again, because he seemed deflated when he saw Nina sitting on my lap. He deserved a hard time for hooking up with my sister. Ian and Charlie sauntered in just after four and plonked down to have a smoke and a coffee before we started rehearsing. I could see that Kellan was out of sorts and that their laid-back attitude irritated him, but he didn't say anything. He probably knew he was being unreasonable. We went inside when everybody was ready and they played through the songs a few times. They managed to get through the entire session without having a shouting match and even Kellan cheered up towards the end.

We wrapped up rehearsing and went outside to join Nina and the others on the patio, where they already had a barbecue going.

"Happy birthday, boys." Sophie lifted her beer towards us.

"To the next five years." I grinned.

Around eight thirty I started yawning and making eye contact with Stuart to let him know that it was time to get rid of everybody.

"Right, Ollie." He got up. "We probably need to start doing your stretches if you want to go to the gym in the morning."

"Yeah, I'm knackered." I pretended to stifle another yawn.

"Are you coming with us, Soph?" Ian asked.

"Yes. I'll record it for you." She wiped her hands on her legs as she stood.

I looked at my bandmates. "Try not to fuck it up." I grinned, struggling to contain my excitement. The twins were going to shit themselves when I showed up.

Nina did a silent little shouty dance when they slammed the door behind them and I burst out laughing.

"What's up with you?" Zach frowned and I smiled at Nina to fill him in. "What!" Zach shrieked when Nina told him. "They're going to flip out! How exciting." He clapped his hands together, hopping up and down a couple of times. "Are you going to change your clothes?" Nina nodded, kissing me on the cheek. "I'll do your hair." He smiled and followed her. Stuart and I chuckled when she turned around and wrinkled her nose at us.

"Can you help me change, please?" I asked Stuart. "I'll do my own hair though," I added with a smirk.

CHAPTER 23

I was sitting on the patio outside my bedroom when I heard the door open. I turned around, expecting Stuart, but my breath caught when I found Nina instead. She was wearing a black strappy thing that hung loosely but somehow still managed to accentuate every swell and curve impeccably. She turned around to close the door and I noticed that her back was bare, with just the straps crossing over to hold the dress in place. Her hair tumbled over her shoulders in a velvet waterfall and she had a dark smudgy affair going on around her eyes. I forgot to breathe, just like that night in the Guildberry when I spoke to her for the first time.

"What's wrong?" She pulled her brows together and hurried over to me.

"Nina, you're..." I shook my head. "I don't even have words. Beautiful doesn't do it justice. You're incomparably, breathtakingly, mind-blowingly fucking phwoar." My eyes trailed over her body.

"You like?" She jutted out her hip and lifted her arms.

"Very much." I groaned, pulling her to me.

"Good." She kissed me eagerly. "You look very handsome too. Are you nervous?"

"A little, but more wired really. And I'm looking forward to ripping this wicked little dress off later." I scraped my teeth along her jaw.

"Ollie." Stuart knocked on the door. "We have to go."

"Yeah," I called, straightening Nina's dress and giving her one last kiss.

"Wow, Nina." Stuart widened his eyes.

"Thank you." She smiled and started pushing me to the living room where Zach was waiting.

"Are you seriously wearing those boots?" Zach frowned at Nina's Dr. Martens.

"Yep." She smirked, making his eyebrows coil even tighter.

"Tomboy." He shook his head.

"Princess." She stuck out her tongue and I felt a grin ripple over my cheek.

"It's good to see you, Ollie." Jack hugged me when Stuart wheeled me into the kitchen at the Guildberry.

"Thanks, Jack." I patted him on the back. "Good to be here."

"I'll tell them to go on in a minute and then Charlie will come for you."

"I feel like I'm going to hyperventilate." Zach fanned his face. "It's just too exciting."

"Me too." Nina grabbed his hands and they hopped around on the spot.

"Eek," I shrieked and did a wiggle in my wheelchair. Their heads snapped around to look down at me. "What? I like going on stage." I shrugged, pretending to be nonchalant again.

"Howzit, howzit?" Charlie bounced in. "Nice one, Olive." He bent down to hug me. "You too, boys." He shook hands with Zach and Stuart before doing a double take when he saw Nina. "Eish, Nina, looking fine, sister." He let out a long whistle.

"Thank you." She winked at him with a cheeky smile, making me smile as well.

"Good evening, Guildford," we heard Jack call to the noisy crowd. "Are you having fun?" he asked and the audience roared in response. "I have something special for you. These boys went through hell this summer, and Oliver is still in recovery, but the rest of the guys agreed to pop in tonight to say hello. So, I'm not going to keep you waiting any longer. Lawless!"

The cheering stretched out for a few moments and I knew that Kellan was scanning the floor, wondering what the hell had hap-

161

pened to Charlie. Eventually the clapping and whistling eased down and I heard the microphone crackle again.

"Hello," Kellan drawled and the shrieking started up again.

"I bet Kellan is planning my brutal murder right now." Charlie laughed.

"Yeah." I grinned.

"Like Jack said," Kellan started, and it quieted down a bit, "it's been a messed-up summer, but Oliver's doing well and we want to thank all of you. You've helped us through a horrible time and it means the world to us. So, thank you." Everybody clapped and cheered once again. "We're celebrating our band's birthday today. Lawless came to life five years ago when Oliver convinced the rest of us that we could work as a band. He's sorry for not being able to be here this evening, but he's getting better every day and he's looking forward to being back on stage again soon. We're dedicating our performance to him tonight—for being the strongest and most talented guy we know, and for giving us the best five years of our lives. We love you, Ols," he finished and my face cracked into a huge smile.

When the cheering calmed down, Kellan spoke again. "I'd love to start, but we seem to be missing somebody. Charlie!" Kellan called and then whistled, like you would for a dog that had run off. The audience erupted in laughter and chanted Charlie's name.

"Ready, Olive?"

"Yeah."

"You're going to be great." Nina kissed me and I squeezed her hand as Charlie wheeled me out of the kitchen door.

"Good luck," Stuart and Zach called and I turned my head to smile at them.

"Charlie," Kellan called over the microphone again. "Come out, come out, wherever you are." He tried to sound like he was having a laugh, but I didn't miss the nasty tone to his voice.

"He's actually giving me the creeps," Charlie whispered and I nodded.

162

We walked on from the back and Jack gave us a thumbs-up as we went past him. Kellan and Ian were standing in the middle of the stage, craning their necks to look for Charlie. Kellan's whole demeanour was tense and Ian was running his hand through his hair.

Charlie pushed me across the stage towards them. Some of the people in the front noticed us and started screaming and pointing. Kellan and Ian both swung around at the same time and I will never, for as long as I live, forget how their faces changed when they saw me. As soon as they turned away from the crowd they lost their game faces and gave Charlie the look of death. This made both Charlie and me chuckle, which made them drop their gazes to where I sat in front of Charlie. Their eyes widened and their hands shot up to cover their mouths before they fell to their knees in front of me and pulled me into a bone-crushing hug.

"Surprise," I whispered, cupping the back of their necks and shaking their heads a little. They pulled back to look at me and I saw tears brimming in two sets of green eyes. It made me choke up a little too. Charlie bent down and wrapped his arms around all three of us.

"I love you guys." I patted their backs before I sat up and cleared my throat. Charlie went up to the mic and tried to get the attention of the out-of-control audience.

"Sorry, guys," he called. "We have a slight change of plan, but I have a feeling you won't mind." He pushed me forward before he lowered the microphone and moved to stand next to me, squeezing my shoulder. Kellan came to stand next to me on the other side and Ian stood behind me, both of them also holding on to me.

"Hey." I leaned forward with a smile and the screaming sounded like thunder through the club. "Kellan's said it all. But I also just wanted to thank you. You're all amazing!" They clapped, and whistled, and howled until I held up my hand, asking them to be quiet. "And to my three brothers here"—I nodded up at the guys—"you are everything." I rubbed my fist over my heart, making the floor go insane. "And lastly," I called when the noise eased off, "let's rock!" I pumped my fist in the air and they went wild again.

Jack walked over to hand me my guitar and I noticed Nina, Zach and Stuart coming around the side to stand right at the front. Sophie pushed through the crowd to get to them and I smiled in surprise when Jeffrey and Ingrid joined them as well. I blew a kiss at them. I didn't think it could get any better than this. I was in my element. I settled my guitar in my lap and the guys took their places.

Ian tapped the beat to 'Lawless' and Charlie followed him on the keyboard. Kellan and I fell into place with our guitars a few beats later. The whole club jumped up and down in a wave of bodies. Goosebumps flared on my arms and I just couldn't believe how lucky I was. I looked over to where Nina and the rest of our group were standing and my mouth curved into a mushy smile. Even Sophie was dancing with her arm wrapped around Stuart's waist. Nina and Zach were dancing together like two pros, and Jeffrey and Ingrid had their arms hooked together while they bopped their heads along to the beat. I caught Nina's eye and her face lit up with the most beautiful smile, making my own face crumple into a grin as well. I almost didn't want to admit it, but this was even better than the first night I'd met her. I remembered feeling moody and awkward that night, and yeah, my body was pretty useless now, but I felt good. I was happy. Perhaps being a cripple wasn't going to be so excruciating after all.

Everyone whistled and clapped when the song finished and I put my guitar down against my wheelchair. I wrapped my hand around the microphone and leaned forward a little.

"We've only performed the next song a couple of times and we were hoping to debut it at the Isle of Wight this summer, but I got hurt the night before the festival, so we decided to give it to you guys tonight. It's called 'Strong, Black Coffee' and we hope you like it." I winked at Kellan to play the intro.

This song had a lot of power chords and it really showed off Kellan's talent. It was a bit more punky than our usual stuff, maybe somewhere between the Kinks and the Ramones, and we all loved it. By the second verse, the crowd caught on to the lyrics and the whole floor sang along to the chorus. Jack was sure it was going to be a breakthrough song for us. When it finished, everybody cheered and clapped again and we beamed at each other while we waited for them to calm down.

"Okay." I took a deep breath as I leaned into the microphone again. "Our last song for the evening is brand new. I started working on it while I was in hospital and we finished it over the past few weeks. It's called 'I Shall Not Wholly Die' and, well, we'll let it speak for itself." I sat back and picked up my guitar, settling it in my lap again.

I was obviously biased, but I thought it might have been the best piece of music I had ever created. The melody was slow and powerful, accentuating the emotional lyrics. I was proud of it. The tune started with a slow picking routine that Kellan pulled off splendidly. The verses were poetic and it worked up into a compelling chorus. Ian and Charlie added a percussion routine that gave the song a nostalgic edge and emphasised the haunting ending.

Oh, non omnis moriar
I shall not wholly pass
Can leave this cage at last
If only in my heart

You live in dreams and... um
No words around my tongue
Memories of where I'm from
I'll still be here when I'm gone

Blood flowing from your veins
Your scent forever remains
My life is yours to claim
Survival not my sole aim

Turn my head into the sun
You say this should be fun

My strength wants to hide and run
Oh, no, what have I become?

Talk about gratitude and love
My broken heart is not enough
I try to find answers from above
It all becomes clear... sort of

When will it be my true turn?
No easy lesson to learn
I try to touch, I just burn
To you I will ever return

Not sure where I've come from
Don't want to feel my soul numb
You promised you'd let me come
Please just let me come along

I got lost in the moment and I must have had my eyes closed through most of it, because I didn't notice the audience's reaction until the song finished and I looked across the room. For a few seconds it was quiet enough to hear a pin drop. People had their hands clamped over their mouths or on their hearts. Nina had tears running down her cheeks and slowly shook her head with a small smile curling around her mouth. She buried her head in Zach's chest and he lifted his hand to salute me. Sophie was crying too. And so was Ingrid, and Stuart. Bloody hell.

Jeffrey clapped his hands together, calling my name in slow staccato. "O-li-ver. O-li-ver. O-li-ver," he chanted.

The whole club joined in and it felt like they were going to blow the roof off. Kellan, Ian and Charlie kneeled down beside me so that we were all the same height and we gripped each other's shoulders, grinning at the spectacle in front of us. It was, without a doubt, one of the most extraordinary moments of my life.

Jack appeared on stage and announced that the next band would be ready in fifteen minutes. We waved one last time and Kellan turned me around to push me out of the back again. I beamed when I saw four copper-haired girls huddled behind the screens. They were an all-girl folk-rock band who each played a different string instrument. They appropriately called themselves the Strings. We frequently performed at the same gigs and festivals. All four of them were petite with elfin features and they kept their hair cropped and coloured in similar shades of auburn. It made them look like sisters, even though they weren't. We'd all hooked up with each other over the years and we were very lucky that things had never got weird.

"Good to have you back Ollie." Thea, the lead vocalist, bent down to kiss me.

"Thanks, sweetheart. It's good to be back." I grinned, still buzzed from our performance.

The other three girls also hugged and kissed us, saying the same thing, before they went on stage and started setting up their stuff. Kellan pushed me into the kitchen and dropped to his knees in front of me, grabbing both my arms.

CHAPTER 24

"I can't believe you just did that." Kellan shook me forcefully. "I nearly shat myself."

"Ha." I gripped his arms as well. "I was counting on that."

"You're fucking insane, man. I've been in a panic because I thought you didn't want to perform anymore and then you do that." He gestured towards the stage.

"A-fucking-mazing, Ols." Ian exploded into the kitchen, grabbed my cheeks and kissed me right on the mouth. "I peed in my pants a little." He wiggled around.

"Nice." I laughed. "It was Charlie who convinced me though." I bobbed my head towards Charlie, who was standing behind Kellan with a huge grin on his face.

"Very impressive, Charlton." Ian swirled around. "You're a conniving little fucker, aren't you?" He brushed his knuckles on Charlie's head before he pulled him in for a hug.

"Yeah, good work, little brother." Kellan dragged Charlie from Ian for a one-armed hug around his neck before he kissed the top of his head.

"Are you ready to face the crowd in there?" Ian nudged his head towards the club floor. "Or do you want to go home?"

"Nah." I beamed. "I want to stay."

"Sweet." Charlie nodded. "Jack reserved a booth at the front. The others are waiting there."

"Cool. Let's go." I gestured at the door and Ian twirled my wheelchair around in a circle a couple of times before he pushed me out of the kitchen. "Idiot." I shook my head, cracking up again.

It took us a while to get over to the other side of the club. People kept stopping us to tap us on the shoulder and have a chat as we pushed our way through. It was nearly quarter to eleven when we finally made it to our booth.

"You were wonderful." Nina flung herself at me and kissed me deeply.

"Thank you." I smiled into her mouth, wrapping my arm around her waist.

"Get a room," Ian sniggered and Nina blew him a kiss.

Jack came over with a tray of drinks that he set down on the low table in the middle of the booth before he flung his arms around Kellan and Ian's shoulders. "Big surprise, eh, boys?" He looked from one brother to the other and they both grinned. "Congratulations to you." Jack smiled at me as well. "Great to have you back on stage again. And excellent for business." He clapped me on the shoulder before he went back to the bar.

Everybody scooted into the couches around the table and Nina pushed me to sit on the end before she settled in my lap again. "How are you feeling?" she whispered against my cheek, laying a soft kiss below my ear.

"Amazing." I turned my head to capture her mouth.

"Was it as good as you hoped it would be?" She pulled away and searched my face.

"Yeah. Better."

"I'm so happy for you, Ollie." She planted another kiss on the side of my face.

"Thank you. Me too." I squeezed her waist as she nuzzled my neck.

"Who are these girls, Ollie?" Ingrid asked. "Do you know them?"

I looked up to see who she was referring to and she nudged her head towards the stage where the Strings were playing. "Yeah. They're called the Strings."

"They're very good."

"They are," I agreed.

"And don't we know it," Ian guffawed, wiggling his eyebrows. I shot him a murderous look. "Especially Kel." He snorted, without noticing my death stare.

"What?" Nina frowned.

"Nothing. He's being a dick." I scowled at Ian again.

"Have you been with one of them?" Nina fired straight away. I sighed and tried not to react, but stupidly tipped my head in the smallest, barely-there nod. "Which one?" Her body stiffened and she leaned away from me.

"It doesn't matter." I shook my head, but she raised an eyebrow and kept staring at me. "Can we not talk about this now, please?"

"Which one, Ollie?"

"All of them," I mumbled, hating that she was forcing me to do this in front of her family. I pinned her with my eyes, silently begging her to stop, but remembering how she'd done the same thing a few weeks ago when she wanted to talk about my teetotalism in front of her parents.

"When?" She kept interrogating me.

"I don't know. Not for a long time, maybe last year." I struggled to keep the annoyance from my voice.

"Don't worry about it, Nina," Ian piped up again. "We all hook up with them. All. The. Time. They're our best girls." He sniggered. I swore I would have throttled him if I was able to get up.

"Shut up, Ian," Kellan growled.

"What? I'm just trying to help." He shrugged.

"Nice," Nina bit out and walked off towards the bar, leaving me feeling like an idiot.

"Thanks, arsehole." I glowered at Ian.

"What did I do?" Ian pulled his eyebrows together.

"Think before you open your mouth." Kellan smacked him on the back of his head and flicked his eyes towards Sophie, who looked quite amused.

"What the fuck," Ian muttered, rubbing his head as he got up. "I'm going for a fag." He walked off. Charlie followed him, shaking his head with a huge grin on his face.

"Sorry." I sighed, looking at Ingrid and Jeffrey. "That was…" I pulled on the ends of my hair, pissed off that we'd had another tiff in front of her parents.

Jeffrey shrugged, waving his hand with a slightly bored look on his face.

"It's in the past." Ingrid offered a small smile, albeit looking embarrassed.

"I'll go and check on Nina." Sophie got up.

Kellan grabbed for her hand and she winked at him as she squeezed his fingers. He visibly relaxed and brought her fingertips to his lips, placing a lingering kiss on them before he sagged back against the couch, letting out a long breath. But he immediately sat up again when he realised we were all watching them.

"Thanks, Soph." I smiled when she squeezed my shoulder as she walked past me. "Can we go out for a smoke?" I asked Kellan.

It was time to get some fresh air and to put him out of his misery. He unfolded himself with a sigh and came to stand behind me without a word.

"We'll be right back." I offered half a smile to the rest of the table as Kellan turned me around and pushed me towards the door.

"Sorry, Ols," Ian said as soon as we joined them outside. "I forget chicks get weird in the brain about ex-shags." He waved his hands around his head.

"Yeah." I shrugged, catching Charlie grinning and shaking his head again.

"We're going back in," Ian said as he stepped on his bud.

"We'll be there in a bit," I called after them.

Kellan fished two cigarettes from his pack and lit both before holding one out to me. I nodded my thanks and dragged on it as I watched Kellan kicking at the dirt and avoiding my gaze.

"So," he said eventually. "I suppose I let the cat out of the bag in there. I wanted to tell you."

"I know," I said and smiled when his head snapped up.

"Yeah?"

"Yeah, man. For a while now."

"Why didn't you say anything?" He rubbed his jaw. "And why aren't you pissed?"

"I was, but Stuart convinced me that you care about her, so I decided to wait until you were ready to tell me." I shrugged.

"I love her, Ollie. Like I've never loved anything in my life."

"Does she feel the same?"

"I do." Sophie spoke quietly from behind us.

I turned to look at her and noticed Nina standing next to her, a soft smile playing around her lips.

"We're going to head off, Ols." Kellan cleared his throat.

"Okay." I nodded with an awkward smile. "See you tomorrow."

"Thank you." He leaned in and hugged me tight for a moment. "Night, Nina." He hugged her as well.

"I'm sorry," Nina said as she sat down in my lap.

"You're the only one for me. Don't ever doubt that." I pulled her closer.

"I know," she said against my mouth and I recoiled at the smell of booze on her breath, but I recovered and kissed her on the lips. "I just didn't like coming face to face with your past," she admitted and leaned back to meet my eyes.

"I understand. But you are my present and my future and the only girl I'll ever love."

"I know," she said again, dropping her eyes. "I really am sorry. I feel a bit stupid."

"Forget about it." I placed a soft kiss on the side of her mouth. "We're together and that's all that matters." I tangled my hand into her hair and deepened our kiss, trying to block out the alcohol I was tasting.

"That's right." She kissed my cheek and hopped off, but lost her balance and stumbled back. "Oops," she giggled. "Let's go back inside."

"Let's." I struggled to keep the irritation from my voice. Surely she couldn't be drunk so quickly? I'd only been gone for a few minutes, hadn't I?

When we got back inside Zach had just delivered another round of drinks to the table and Nina almost tackled him to grab hers.

"There you go, Ollie." Stuart handed me a soda from the tray and I tipped my glass towards him.

"Where's Kellan and Sophie?" Charlie asked, glugging down his beer.

"They went home," I said.

"Oooh," Ian whistled and Charlie shoved him with his elbow, widening his eyes. "Argh." Ian rubbed his arm.

"It's okay." I chuckled. "I've known for quite some time."

"Phew." Ian pretended to wipe sweat from his forehead and everybody broke out in laughter.

The Strings finished on stage and Ian jumped up. "Right, I'm gonna grab me some ginger love. You coming, Charlton?" He wiggled his eyebrows at Charlie.

"Okay." Charlie shrugged. "Bye, everybody." They saluted us and sauntered off towards the girls. Nina shook her head before she drained her drink and went to stand at the bar without a word.

I watched her have two shots of amber liquor at the counter before she came back with another beer and two more shots. I looked around the table to see if anybody else noticed, but they were talking amongst themselves.

I was so upset with her that it took all my self-control to not say anything. This was supposed to be a special night for me and she'd just ruined it. I bit down so hard on the inside of my cheek that my mouth filled with the metallic taste of blood.

Jeffrey and Ingrid stayed and chatted for a few minutes, but left after they finished their drinks.

"You guys ready to go?" I asked, looking at Stuart.

"Whenever you are." He smiled. Zach also nodded and stood up, stifling a yawn.

"No, thank you," Nina mumbled, knocking back another drink,

and Stuart looked at her in surprise. Zach frowned and closed his eyes with a heavy sigh.

"What's that?" Zach picked up the glass and sniffed it. "How many have you had?" He lifted his eyebrows, but she ignored him and glugged the last one before reaching for her beer.

The muscles in my jaw twitched and I gripped the sides of my wheelchair so tight my hands cramped.

"Are you kidding me?" Zach grabbed the bottle from her.

"Piss off." She scowled at him and swung around, to go back to the bar, I presumed, but she lost her balance again and fell against Stuart. "Sorry, Stuey," she slurred.

How the hell had she got that hammered, that quickly?

"I've got you." Stuart wrapped his arm around her shoulders and steadied her. "Come on, darling."

"No, thank you. I'm staying." She squared her shoulders as she stepped away from him.

I could feel my temper pulsing through my veins. "You are coming home with us. Now," I snarled almost too quietly.

She sniggered and turned her head down to say something to me, but swallowed her words when her eyes met mine. She stared me down for a few seconds before she shook her head and lifted her eyebrows.

"Now," I repeated even more quietly.

"Make me," she said and started to turn away, but I grabbed her arm.

"Bring her, Zach," I commanded and held up her arm to him.

Zach put his arm around Nina's shoulders and pulled her against his side as he walked her out of the club. Miraculously, she didn't try to resist, but she did tell both of us to go and fuck ourselves on the way out.

Stuart loaded me into the van while Zach helped Nina in and buckled her seatbelt. We drove home in silence. Nina was leaning her head against the window, keeping her eyes closed while I kept looking at her, trying to find the girl I loved. I really struggled to see past her obnoxious, self-absorbed behaviour and I think I was even angrier by the time we arrived home.

"I'll keep an eye on her while Stuart helps you to bed?" Zach said when we walked through the front door and I nodded with a tight smile as he put his arm around Nina again. The car ride home had done little to sober her up, but she looked quite sheepish when her eyes flicked down to meet mine. I didn't trust myself to speak to her yet.

"I'm sorry, Ollie," Stuart said when we were in the en suite.

"It's not your fault." I pushed my fingers into my hair and pulled on the ends.

"I know. But I'm sorry your special evening got ruined."

"Thanks." I pursed my lips together. "Me too."

"Do you want Zach to take her home?" he asked when he helped me into bed.

I nearly said yes, but I didn't want to send her away. Especially not after our first fight. Although it wasn't even a fight, was it? All I knew was that I was furious. Drinking was going to be a hard limit for me and we were going to have to talk about it in the morning.

"No," I finally answered.

"She can sleep in my room. I'll sleep on the sofa," he offered.

"Thanks, but that's not necessary." No matter how angry I was, I still needed to have her next to me.

"All right. We'll sober her up before she comes to bed though."

"Thank you." I closed my eyes with another sigh and Stuart patted my shoulder as he left.

I felt myself slipping into a dream moments after I started falling asleep and even in my half-aware state I knew that it wasn't going to be good.

CHAPTER 25

I strolled across the stage and took my place behind the micro-phone, letting my eyes glide over the floor. My mouth pulled into a satisfied side smirk. A ridiculously exaggerated, stadium-like version of the Guildberry was chock-a-block with crazed fans. They were chanting our name in slow litany, like it was a prayer that could make all the world's troubles disappear. Perhaps it was. I certainly felt like I had been infused with a mythical burst of zeal.

My body hummed with energy and strength. My bandmates were luxuriating in the same euphoric delight. I sent them a huge grin and turned back to the crowd, curling my fingers around the microphone as I leaned forward.

"Hey," I drawled, waiting for the shrieking to calm down. "Thanks for having us back. It's great to be here." The supersonic squealing and whistling followed again.

I scanned the crowd one last time before I signalled Ian to start tapping us in. My eyes landed on Nina right at the front. I didn't know if it was the strange lighting in the club, or my imagination, but for the briefest moment it seemed like her eyes flashed yellow. It sent an eerie shiver down my spine, but I couldn't remember why it seemed so familiar and when I blinked, it was gone. She was gorgeous, and delicious, and all mine. I couldn't wait to ravish her after the show.

I dropped my head, tapping my foot to the beat of Ian's drum-ming. Kellan and Charlie fell into step with the guitar and the key-board. The crowd was hopping around the floor, singing along to the chorus as I held the microphone out to them. It made me heedless with excitement and my eyes found their way back to where Nina writhed in the ocean of hyped-up bodies. She was magnificent. Her delectable curves; her hair; those beautiful, spectral eyes. I wanted to run my tongue over every line of ink that covered her silken skin.

Wait! What? Nina doesn't have any tattoos. Does she?

I closed my eyes for a moment, bringing the microphone back to my mouth to sing the next verse, and when I opened them again, Nina's skin was pale and flawless like it was supposed to be.

What the hell? I frowned, but Nina's devilish smile chased all the doubt from my mind and the rest of the set continued on the same trend. Me bursting with swagger, but failing to recall basic details from my memory. Nina smiling at me from the crowd, beautiful and utterly delectable, but with slithering tattoos and glowing eyes. I started to feel more and more confused, yet I didn't once question the authenticity of the moment. I didn't once doubt my arrogance, or my sudden ability to walk, or the band's accelerated fame. Something was niggling at the back of my mind and Nina's peculiarities baffled me, but not for a moment did I consider that I might be dreaming.

After we finished the last song, we curtsied in our customary comical way and went out around the back. We were standing around the kitchen courtyard having a cigarette when Nina found us.

"You were wonderful." She jumped on me and wrapped her legs around my waist.

"Thanks, baby." I kissed her senseless as I squeezed her arse.

"I'm going in. I still need to pick a little plaything for the night." Ian flicked his cigarette across the patio. "You coming, Kel?"

"Mmm." Kellan produced a cocky side smirk and followed Ian back inside. Something about it bothered me, but I wasn't sure what. "Charlton?" Kellan called at the door.

"Yeah, okay." Charlie flicked his cigarette and followed them in.

"Slutty boys." Nina laughed.

"Whatever." I backed her up against the outside wall.

"Ollie," she moaned, tightening her legs around my waist and grinding against me.

I growled into her mouth and ripped her underwear off from underneath her flimsy dress, stroking my fingers between her legs. She bit down on my shoulder as I kept her anchored between me and the wall. I brought her higher and higher until she fell apart, shaking against me and gasping my name.

"Let's go home," I ground out.

"Not yet." She shook her head, making me look up at her in surprise.

Her eyes were flaming amber pools and it shocked me so much that I almost dropped her. I took a deep breath and set her down on the ground. I blinked before I placed my finger under her chin and tilted her head up.

"Let's dance." Her mouth curved suggestively on one side, making all my bewilderment evaporate.

"Minx." I tangled one hand into her hair before pushing the wet fingers from the other hand into her mouth.

"Mmm." She smiled as I pulled my fingers from her mouth before she fused her lips against mine, slowly tangling her tongue with mine.

"You're making me crazy," I groaned in her ear.

"Come on." She grinned and started pulling me towards the door, but stopped to retrieve her shredded underwear from the ground. "These are for you." She winked.

"You are an evil, evil little fairy." I shoved the knickers into my pocket.

I didn't normally dance at all, but the atmosphere was electric and my body was on fire for her. I probably would have performed a pirouette in a pink tutu if she instructed me to at that point. Nina gyrated her back against my front and I wrapped my arm tightly around her waist as we swayed with the music. She dropped her head back on my shoulder and draped her arm around my neck. I trailed my hand across her arm and over her body, groaning at the notion that she wasn't wearing anything underneath her dress. I clenched the thin material on her waist and spun her around so that she was facing me.

"I need you," I rasped against her ear, biting lightly on the lobe. "Now."

"Come with me." She pulled away and led me through the crowd again. She steered us into the dressing room below the stage and locked the door once we were inside.

I pushed her against the mirrored wall and she yanked my T-shirt over my head and unbuttoned my jeans in two seconds flat. I lifted her with one arm and she wrapped her legs around my waist as I shoved her dress over her hips with the other hand. I stroked my hand over her body and interlaced our fingers above her head as I slammed into her.

"Oliver," she moaned, throwing her head back against the mirror, and I licked a path from her breast back up to her mouth, forcing my heavy eyes to connect with hers. My body jerked as searing gold jewels glowed back at me. Thin black lines and curves appeared all over her smooth skin.

I touched the markings as they moved over her skin. She was mesmerising. I felt like an untamed animal. I pulled out and swung her around, pressing her back against my chest so that we both faced the mirror. "You are bewitching," I whispered against her ear and tore the dress off before I placed both her palms against the mirror and buried myself in her again. Dark inkings slowly etched their way over her skin and I couldn't pull my eyes away from her.

I looked up to meet her gaze in the mirror, but a heinous sneer pulled at her lips and the blood froze in my veins. I opened my mouth to scream, but the air left my lungs. I watched the drawings on Nina's skin turn into blood. Sticky red lines rolled slowly across her body and over my hands, splattering crimson drops on the white tiles. She linked her fingers through mine and smeared the blood over her naked body.

"No, baby." I pulled my hands away from underneath hers and grasped her shoulders, gently turning her around to look at me. Her irises were swirling amber pools and her sinister scorn burned holes into my soul. This wasn't my Nina.

"Come back to me, beautiful," I pleaded, cupping her face.

"Help me, Ollie," she gasped, grabbing my arms as her legs buckled. I caught her and sagged down onto the floor, cradling her in my lap. "Please don't leave me," she cried, clutching my face as her eyes continued to flicker. Bloody tears streaked her cheeks.

"Never." I dropped my lips against her forehead, tightening my arms around her.

My head snapped up when somebody started banging on the door. I moved to get up, but Nina dug her nails into my skin, shaking her head.

"Please. It hurts," she sobbed, blood gurgling from her mouth. "Don't leave me."

"Oliver!" my mother's voice called from the other side of the door, followed by more banging. "Ollie, you need to wake up now!"

"No, don't." Nina clutched my face, demanding my attention.

"Oliver!" my mother shouted. "Come on!"

I struggled up and stumbled over to the door with Nina still in my arms. I unlocked it with a trembling hand before I slid down the wall, gripping Nina against me as my body shook with raw emotion. My mother immediately pushed into the room and kneeled down beside me, wrapping her arms around both of us.

"Wake up, Oliver. Nina, wake up, sweetheart," she begged. "Open your eyes now."

"What's happening?" I sobbed. "Why didn't I realise I was dreaming?"

"Now, Oliver." My mother shook my shoulders. "Wake up, dammit!"

"Nina!" I cried just before I felt myself slipping away.

CHAPTER 26

I jerked awake as my heart tried to butcher its way out of my body. For a moment I was confused about where I was, but Nina shuddered next to me and I realised that we were in my bed.

"Ollie!" she gasped. "Don't go!"

What the hell was going on?

"Oliver," she sobbed quietly. "No, no, no."

"Shh." I pulled her into my arms, holding her against my chest. "Shh, it's okay." I stroked her hair as she clutched fistfuls of my T-shirt.

I continued to soothe her while I tried to get my own emotions under control. What the fuck had just happened? Had both of us just woken up from the same nightmare? I struggled to piece it together as I held her in my arms. After a few moments her breathing calmed down and I shifted to try and look at her.

"Please don't leave me, Ollie." Her eyes flicked up to meet mine before she buried her face in my chest and started crying again.

"Nina." I kissed her forehead and cupped her face, tilting her head to look at me. "I'm not leaving you. It was a bad dream. You're fine. See? We're in bed. It was just a dream." I stroked my thumb on her cheek.

"It felt so real." She crumbled in my arms again. "Please don't leave me. You can't leave me."

I'd never seen her like that. I hated it. I craved Nina's happiness. I wanted to take her pain away. My anger and disappointment from the night before diminished into a faint memory. All I cared about was making Nina feel safe.

"You're my world, Nina," I promised. "That will never change."

"You don't know that," she whispered, slowly moving her head from side to side.

"I do." I turned her face up again and stared into her confused eyes for a long moment. "I do know that. Nothing can ever change what you mean to me," I breathed and the frown deepened between her eyebrows. "I promise." I stroked the crease away. "I am yours."

She sighed heavily and closed her eyes, hiding her face in my neck again.

I tightened my arms around her and we lay like that in silence for a long while. My emotions were pumping through my body in a torturous rhythm. "Do you want to tell me about your nightmare?" I asked.

"Yeah. But I think we need to talk about last night first." She chewed on her bottom lip as she searched my face.

"Okay." I sighed, pushing my hands through my hair.

She was right. We did have to talk about it, but I wasn't looking forward to it. I sat up and leaned over to pull my wheelchair closer.

"I'll go and get some coffee." She forced a small smile. I could see, now that she had woken up properly and the fog from her dream had disappeared, reality was crashing down on her. And reality was a harsh bitch. I groaned as I dragged my useless body into the wheel-chair.

As soon as I made it outside, I lit a cigarette and stared into the grey skies, exhaling a long stream of smoke. I wanted to cry at the recollection of the last time I'd sat smoking on that patio. The memory of my excited anticipation of the night before stabbed into my heart. It was unbelievable how quickly everything had gone from promising to uncertain in one short evening. Was it really only twelve hours ago I'd thought that things were finally falling into place and that the world was starting to make sense again? Now I had no idea how we were going to move forward. The secrets I was keeping and all the weird issues between us made me question the authenticity of our relationship. I finished my cigarette in a trance.

A few minutes later Nina came out and placed a cup of coffee in front of me. I lit another cigarette and passed her the pack before I took a sip. I dragged on my cigarette while I studied her. She was pale with dark circles under dim eyes. I wasn't sure whether it was because she was hungover, or just tired from having bad dreams. Probably both.

"How are you feeling?" I asked.

"Not great." She shook her head without meeting my gaze.

"Sorry."

"It's my own fault." She shrugged as she flicked some ash into the ashtray. "Are you still angry with me?"

"I'm confused. And disappointed."

"That's worse."

"Probably," I agreed. "I just don't understand how the night got so fucked up."

"I don't know." Her nonchalance instantly revved my temper.

"I want to understand. Help me understand why you decided to ruin a night that was supposed to be special."

"It wasn't a conscious decision, Oliver. You know that."

"Do I?" Frustration bubbled through my gut. "I know that you knew how important last night was to me. I also know that you know I don't like it when people drink. I just don't know why you didn't care enough to take any of that into consideration. So please explain it to me, because I really do want to understand."

"I didn't do it on purpose." She grabbed my hand and squeezed it tightly. "I was upset and insecure and I didn't want to feel like that."

"Why?" I pulled my hand out from her grip and held her chin, forcing her to look at me. "What made you feel insecure? Were you still upset because I used to hook up with the girls from the other band?"

I knew that she'd been annoyed when Ian joked about the girls from the Strings, but I hadn't realised that it had affected her that much. She nodded and a tear slipped down her cheek.

"Why?" I wiped it away with my thumb. "You said that you were okay."

"I know. But I'd already had a few drinks by then and when we went back inside and Ian and Charlie went after them again, it made me feel vulnerable."

"Did I do something to make you doubt me?"

"No." She slowly moved her head from side to side. "I just didn't like seeing them there and knowing that they'd been with you. It felt like I was keeping you from having fun and I freaked out."

"Nina." I exhaled heavily. "I don't give a shit about having fun with anybody who isn't you. They have been with me in the past, yes, but I'm sorry, so have many other girls." It sounded harsher than I intended. She closed her eyes and more tears slipped down her cheeks.

"Look at me." I tilted her chin up and she opened her eyes. "Nobody has ever known me like you do. You are the only one I have ever loved." I moved both of my hands up to cup her cheeks and rested my forehead against hers.

"I know." She finally nodded. "I'm sorry."

"Come here." I pulled her onto my lap and wrapped my arms around her.

"It scares me that I can love you so much in such a short time." She started crying again. "I don't know how to deal with it." She buried her head in my neck and moulded her body around mine.

I kissed her face and ran my fingers through her hair. "I feel the same."

"Tell me about your dream," I said when she started sitting up after a while.

"Okay." She reached for the cigarettes again. "It was insane," she mumbled as she lit a cigarette and passed the pack over to me.

"In what way?" I asked, feeling my heart rate speed up.

"Well, we were at the Guildberry and you were performing with the band, which was suddenly very famous, by the way. But anyway…" She continued to tell me about a dream that was pretty much identical to the one I'd woken up from earlier.

She couldn't remember all the specifics like I could, but it was clear that it was the same dream. I couldn't stop the goosebumps that peppered my skin as I listened. An unsolicited shiver crawled up my spine when she finished and I absent-mindedly tightened my grip on her waist.

"Ollie." She winced and twisted in my arms.

"Sorry." I forced my fingers to relax and rubbed her side. "Shit."

"I know, right? It's wacky, isn't it?"

"Yeah." I inhaled slowly, bracing myself for what I was about to tell her. This was the moment of truth. Well, some of the truth. "But that's not what I mean. I'm going to tell you something, but try not to freak out before I'm finished." I framed her face with my hands, stroking my thumbs in small circles on her cheekbones, and she nodded, confusion pulling at her eyebrows again. "I think—no, I *know*—we, erm, we had the same dream last night. And I think we shared dreams in the hospital too."

"I don't understand."

"The dream you just explained to me"—I brushed my thumb over her lips before running my fingers through her hair—"I had exactly the same one last night."

"What do you mean?" She started chewing on the inside of her cheek.

"We're having the same dreams, Nina." I held her head still with my hands, pinning her with my eyes as I recalled the dream, making a point to acknowledge several details she hadn't mentioned earlier but I knew she would remember. I kept staring at her, giving her time to digest what I'd just said, but I could see that she already believed me even if her brain hadn't quite worked it out yet.

"But how's that possible?"

"I'm not sure. I think we've somehow formed a connection that enables us to get into each other's minds and share our dreams or something."

"That's crazy." She laughed nervously. "Isn't it?"

"Well, yeah, but you told me a few weeks ago that you dreamt

185

about me while you were unconscious. I was going to tell you then that I dreamt about you too, but we got interrupted before we finished the conversation. I know you said that you can't remember the details of your dreams, but I wonder if telling you what happened in my dreams would help you remember."

She pulled in a breath and I stroked my hands up and down her arms.

"Do you want to give it a go?" I asked and she nodded jerkily.

I started telling her about the dreams I'd had while we were in hospital. She listened for a while, but I could see the recognition on her face and I slowed down, leaving out certain details. Without realising what she was doing, she started filling in the blanks. She got more excited when I talked about the dream in Ericeira and eventually she couldn't contain herself any longer. She jumped up and grabbed my shoulders, flawlessly divulging every detail about our encounter on that Portuguese beach.

"Yeah." I smiled, squeezing her arm. "That was a good part."

"Ollie, this is amazing!" She sat down in my lap again. "I can't believe it! I wonder if we can dream together whenever we want?"

"I'm pretty sure that you have to reach a certain level of… oblivion before you dream." I was surprised by how weary my voice came out and she frowned. "I haven't had a single dream with you since you woke up from the coma until last night."

"And I was drunk," she said slowly and I concurred with a nod.

"Yes. And none of our dreams have been good, Nina."

"Perhaps we could change things if we tried it with more control."

"No. Absolutely not."

"Why not?"

"Because it's clearly not safe!" I started getting upset too. "There is no way I would let you get trollied just so that we can dream together. And do you remember what it felt like when you woke up this morning? It's bloody traumatic. I. Will. Not. Do. It."

"What if I could see Grace?" She raised her voice and I could see tears forming in her eyes.

186

"I don't think it works like that, my love." I softened my tone. "Has she been in any of your dreams?"

"Yes!"

"Like these lucid dreams we have together, like my parents who show up?" I frowned, tightening my arms around her again. My heart ached for her and I wanted to make her feel better, but if there was one thing I knew for certain, it was that whatever happened between us to cause us to dream together wasn't something good. It wasn't safe. "Like this? Like our dreams?"

"No, not like this," she mumbled and dropped her head on my shoulder. "Please, Ollie, I want to try."

"I'm sorry." I held her against me.

"So why did you tell me then?" she snapped, leaning away from me.

"Because I want you to realise that our connection runs deeper than we think. I want you to know that you have nothing to be insecure about." I cupped her face with both of my hands before I said the next bit. "And I want you to agree that drinking, or taking drugs, is not something you can do again. Ever."

"What's wrong with you?" She pulled her head away and got off my lap. "We can do something unbelievable! I might be able to see Grace! And you won't help me!"

"I can understand how you feel. But I'm not going to do it!"

"I want to try! Please, Oliver!"

"I said no!"

"Who do you think you are?" she shouted, throwing her hands in the air. "You are not going to tell me what I can and cannot do!"

"I am the man who loves you!" I grabbed her arm and pulled her towards me. "And if it concerns your safety and your sanity, and my own bloody well-being, I absolutely will tell you what to do!"

She tried to pull away from me, but I tightened my grip. "Let go!" She twisted her arm and pulled harder.

"No, calm down." I held on and she swung around and pushed at my shoulder with her other hand, but I grabbed that too and pulled her onto my lap, restraining her in my embrace.

She thrashed around on my lap, but I kept my arms firmly locked around her. "I said let go!" she yelled into my face.

"Stop behaving like a lunatic," I snarled, hoping to get the upper hand. But one look into those lucent pools of turquoise told me that she was wild with rage. "Come on, my love." I changed my strategy. I moved one hand into her hair and rubbed her back with the other one. She kept her body tense, but I continued to lull her until I thought I could feel her soften. "Shhh." I ran my fingers through her hair and relaxed my grip around her.

I pulled away to look at her face, but she jumped off my lap and shoved my chest with both hands before she slapped my cheek hard. I could hear her swearing as she stormed through the house, banging things around.

"Nina! Get back here!" I launched my coffee cup at the wall, shattering it.

"Piss off!" she shouted from somewhere in the living room before she slammed the front door, making all the windows rattle.

"Argh!" I roared and tipped over the table.

Stuart and Zach barged into my bedroom as the heavy iron table clanged on the patio floor.

"Ollie?" Stuart walked up to me, frowning in concern.

"Fuck!" I punched my fists into the air.

"I'll go after her." Zach swung around and ran out through my bedroom door again.

"Are you okay?" Stuart sat down next to me.

"No."

"Do you want to talk about it?"

"No," I spat, but immediately realised that I was being rude to him for no reason. "Sorry." I shook my head, taking in a deep breath. "She thinks I'm controlling and I think she's reckless."

"Can you compromise?"

"No. Not on this."

"Do you think she'll come around?" A less than hopeful expression crossed his face. He'd obviously noticed her bloody-minded streak.

"No." I sighed, rubbing my hair around on my head. "But she doesn't have a choice."

"Mmm." Stuart blew out a breath, but Zach came back before he could respond.

"Sorry, Ollie, she told me to piss off too. She started walking home. I called my mum. She'll meet her on the way." He shook his head.

"Fuck." I groaned as I scrubbed my hands over my face.

"Let her be." Zach bent down to put the table back up again. He retrieved my cigarettes and the ashtray from where they were scattered across the patio before he sat down on the other side of Stuart. "She's unreasonable when she gets like this anyway. It's best to leave her to it. She'll come to her senses again." He reached into his pocket for his cigarettes and placed one between his lips. I was always surprised when I saw him with a cigarette—he didn't often smoke—but he was the only person who didn't just help himself to my fags. I liked that.

"Yeah, okay." I nodded, fishing a cigarette from my own packet. We smoked in silence for a few moments until Stuart pushed his chair back and got up.

"I'm going to have a shower and then I'll make some French toast," he said and Zach and I both nodded.

"Ollie, I don't really want to get involved, but I think there are some things you should understand." Zach held my gaze. "The way she behaved last night and this morning is nothing new. She used to get off her face and create havoc all the time. She's always been wild. She got much, much worse after Grace died, but she's always been unpredictable. She was out of control last year in New York. She went to therapy for a while and she got a little better, but she was still more erratic than most people. Last night was a picnic compared to New York. In fact, I've never known her to be as calm as the past couple of months with you." He pressed his lips together and shrugged apologetically. "Not since before Grace died, maybe not ever. I guess Grace grounded her. And maybe you do too."

189

"I know." I nodded, blowing out another long breath. "Kellan and Ian told me when I first met her, that night of the accident. They both said she was... troubled. She told me some of the stuff too. I guess I just thought that she seemed more content with me, or something."

"I think she is." He gave me a small smile. "But I also think that her volatility is so ingrained in who she is she'll probably always revert to it in certain situations. Do you know what I mean? I'm sorry, Ollie. You'll have to accept this part of her if you want to be with her." He walked back inside.

"Yeah," I sighed.

The seconds stretched out endlessly and the minutes ticked by without any word from Nina. I called her mobile a couple of times, but it went straight to voicemail. I called her house after half an hour and Ingrid assured me that she was safe.

I sat staring out over the woodlands as I tried to convince myself that everything was going to be okay, but I wanted to crawl out of my own skin by the time Stuart brought out the French toast.

"Do you want some company?" He smiled as Zach followed him out and pulled up a chair.

"Sure." I nodded with what I hoped didn't resemble any hostility. I cleared my throat. "Can you take me to see Nina after breakfast, please?"

"Of course." Stuart nodded with a smile and I tried to make my unwilling lips curve upwards as well.

CHAPTER 27

We turned up at their house just over an hour later and Jeffrey opened the door before we even got out of the car.

"Boys." He patted me on the shoulder before he smiled at Stuart and hugged Zach.

"Hello." I tried to smile. "Can I see Nina, please?"

"She's in her room." Jeffrey moved to stand behind the wheelchair. "I'll take you." He started pushing me through the entrance hall towards the corridor.

When we were out of earshot he stopped and hunched down in front of me. "Is everything all right?" Concern lined his forehead.

I looked down without answering, feeling uncomfortable with the unexpected intrusion.

"What happened?" he persisted. "Did you argue?"

I lifted my eyes and noticed that something about his manner seemed off, desperate. It triggered an unsolicited panic in my gut. I didn't want to be rude, but I sure as fuck didn't want to discuss our issues with him.

"Yeah. I'm not sure; it's difficult." I rubbed my hair around on my head. "I don't want Nina to drink anymore. She disagrees. It's hard to explain."

Jeffrey pinched his chin as he studied my face and a few brief expressions swept across his own face before he asked, "Are you sharing dreams?"

"What?" Overwhelm choked me with an iron fist.

"Have you been having the same dreams?"

I nodded almost involuntarily as my heart thrashed in my chest.

"It's okay, Ollie." He squeezed my shoulder. "How long?"

"Since the accident," I croaked, the back of my eyeballs burning.

"I need to talk to you before you see her."

"Okay." I closed my eyes and tried to inhale. I didn't understand what was happening. I felt raw and exposed. I fucking hated this.

"It's okay," he whispered before he got up and silently pushed me past Nina's room, toward his study, at the far end of the corridor.

He locked the door as soon as we were inside. "I apologise," he said when my head snapped up. "We can't risk Nina walking in." He pulled his mobile phone from his pocket. "It's best she doesn't know you're here." He started typing and nodded briefly to himself when his phone pinged a few moments later. "Ingrid just checked. Nina's asleep. She'll take her out when she wakes up. She's told the guys to go for now. We'll let them know when you're ready to be picked up. We need some time to talk in private."

"Okay." My brain was incapable of processing whatever the fuck was happening. How and what did Jeffrey know about this?

He parked me in front of his desk before he walked around to the other side to get a key from a drawer, which he used to unlock a closet behind him. Inside the closet, he used a retina scan to open a safe that was mounted against the wall. He took out a metal box, which he unlocked with his fingerprint, after he set it on the table in front of me. *What the actual motherfucking fuck?* He walked back around to the front of the desk again and pulled up a chair right next to me.

"What I'm about to tell you will be hard to hear, but please give me time to explain."

"All right," I said, my ears buzzing and my chest heating with tension. He rubbed both hands over his face and also took in a deep breath before he stood and opened the box on the table. He reached inside to rummage around for something. Eventually he pulled out an A4 piece of cardboard and handed it over to me. It was a blocked photograph and as I studied it everything I thought I knew about my life swirled out of proportion.

192

It was a photo of my mum, in her early twenties. Next to her were twenty-something versions of Jeffrey and my dad and somebody who looked very much like Marcus bloody Bentley, along with a girl I didn't know and a guy who looked familiar, but whom I couldn't place.

My mum was on the far left. Behind my mum was my dad. His arm was folded across her chest and his chin rested on her head. My dad's other arm was slung around Jeffrey's shoulders, and Jeffrey was leaning his head against my dad's. On Jeffrey's right was the girl I didn't know. He had her pulled into his side with his arm around her waist. On her right was the Marcus Bentley lookalike and his arm was draped around her shoulders. Her head was thrown back in laughter as Whoever Bentley beamed at her. Behind them was the guy I didn't know. He really did seem very familiar, though. They all looked like they had no care in the world.

"I don't understand." I looked up at Jeffrey where he was leaning against the edge of his desk.

"John…" He touched my dad's face. "He"—his voice broke and he swallowed—"he was my best friend. We grew up together. We were like brothers."

"How?" I whispered without looking away from the picture. My brain just could not compute my parents' beautiful, young, tragically happy faces, staring back at me from next to this youthful carefree version of Jeffrey.

"Once upon a time we were very close. The best of friends."

"Why haven't you said anything before?" I finally looked up at him.

"It's complicated, Oliver. I'll explain as best I can, but it's difficult."

"Okay." I guessed I understood. I also had secrets that wouldn't make sense without all the details. "I'll listen."

"Thank you." He rubbed his forehead before he sat down in the chair next to me again.

"Your dad and I grew up together. We lived around the corner from each other, for our entire childhood." He stopped for a beat.

"I'm sorry, I've not talked about this for a long time, we really were like brothers.

"At the start of our first year at university, I started going out with Cynthia." He pointed at the girl I didn't know. "Cynthia is Marcus' mum. Cynthia was good friends with your mum, and they were both friends with James Bentley. James is Marcus' dad." He pointed at the guy who looked like Marcus. "Your mum and dad started dating and we formed an easy group."

My brain felt like it was going to explode.

"That picture was taken at the start of our summer holidays after our third year. We'd all been together for a couple of years by then."

"Who's this other guy next to you?" I studied the photo again. "Wait a second, is it David? My mum's brother?"

Jeffrey sighed and closed his eyes for a moment before he answered, "Yes, your mum's brother. I'll get back to him later." He inhaled. "Your mum, Cynthia and James all studied psychology."

"I thought Marcus' dad was the chief constable of Surrey Police?"

"He did a degree in psychology before he joined the police. The three of them had all their classes together and they shared a particular interest in neurology. At some point during their third year, they started experimenting with a theory that our subconscious minds could connect to each other through lucid dreaming, by using a combination of certain narcotics and sedatives and suggestive therapy."

"What?" I swallowed, even more confused and nervous than before.

"At first it was juvenile curiosity, but some of the experiments they did had remarkable results, even on a molecular level."

"How did they experiment?"

"Well, a few of us participated at the beginning. But your dad was very much against it, and to be honest I didn't feel comfortable with it either, so neither of us joined in after the first couple of times. Your mum and James were determined to learn how it affected our brain chemistry, but things started going wrong. As their experiments became more complicated, the after-effects became more severe. Your dad despised everything about what they were doing. He tried to convince your mum to stop. It was a real challenge in their relationship and they argued often."

It was surreal to hear him talk about my parents like that. I couldn't imagine them fighting—they always just got along—but I did understand how much it would have upset my dad if my mum was putting herself and their friends at risk.

"Anyway." Jeffrey cleared his throat again. "David, your mum's brother, was a microbiologist, and that summer, in the photo, he was visiting from South Africa, where he was living. Your mum convinced him to join the study as well." He paused briefly. "Cynthia and I were still a couple, but because I didn't participate, Cynthia and David were paired for the experiments. They instantly connected on a much deeper level and it was obvious that they fell in love. Everything became very intense after that. Your mum and James were fixated on finding an explanation for their connection. But one night Cynthia and David both got hurt. Cerebral haemorrhage. James somehow managed to save Cynthia's life. David didn't make it."

"No," I whispered. "Mum told us that he passed away when she was in her twenties, but I think Sophie and I assumed he became ill. I just always thought he had cancer. Mum's parents were both gone by the time I was born, so I suppose we didn't talk about her side of the family much."

"Mmm." Jeffrey nodded and stayed quiet for a few moments before he carried on. "Our group fell apart after that. Your mum was devastated. Cynthia was crushed. It was like she died with David. I blamed myself for not trying harder to get her to stop participating in the experiments. We got back together and got married later that same year, but Cynthia was broken without David. We split up after less than a year of marriage. Your mum couldn't forgive herself. After a few months, your dad convinced her to move abroad with him and we never saw each other again."

I couldn't put my thoughts in order enough to respond. I stared at him as I tried to form a sentence, but a million questions swirled together in my gut to form an incoherent concoction of emotions and I dropped my head on my chest with a heavy sigh.

"Oliver," he almost pleaded with me and I lifted my head when he clamped his hand down on my shoulder, "this is a lot to take in. I know you have many questions, but the most important thing now is for you and Nina to be careful."

"What do I tell her?"

"You can't tell her anything. She won't understand what I've just told you. She's too fragile."

"But we argued this morning because I realised that we were sharing dreams. She's furious that I don't want to try again. I don't know how to comfort her."

"You will have to find a way." His eyes pinned me. "Her mental health is not stable enough. Your relationship is far too uncertain."

"What?" I snapped. "There's nothing uncertain about it! I have never been more sure of anything in my life! Why are you telling me any of this if you think our relationship is uncertain? What do you want me to do?"

"I want you to reflect on yourself and think about how committed you really are to my daughter! I want you to realise that you will never be able to keep her safe, or to make her happy, if you are not completely devoted to her!"

"Of course I am!" I shouted.

"Are you willing to give your life for her, Oliver?" He leaned in to my face and rested his hands on the armrests of my wheelchair.

"Yes!" I growled without giving it a second thought.

"Good." He nodded, patting my arm. "Very good."

CHAPTER 28

He removed himself from my space and we sat in silence for a while. I struggled to catch my breath and to keep my chaotic thoughts from overwhelming me. It was too much to understand. None of it made sense. Jeffrey was the only person who seemed to have some comprehension of what we were going through, but for some reason it didn't make me feel comfortable. I knew he just wanted to keep his daughter safe, but he was making me feel unworthy and incompetent.

I nearly blurted out that I had already given her my life. But, as much as he'd upset me, I didn't want him to be more concerned about Nina than he already was. He was a good father. He wanted what was best for her. He didn't know that I'd chosen to fall because I'd believed that was what I had to do to save Nina's life, and I didn't want to tell him, at least not yet, perhaps not ever. Everything was too confusing. I had to figure out why he'd told me and what he expected me to do. But, more than anything, I had to figure out what it all meant for Nina and me.

Eventually he cleared his throat and looked at his watch before taking his mobile phone from his pocket. "I'd better check in with Ingrid."

"Does she know about any of this? The dreams? My parents?"

He shook his head without looking up as he typed on his mobile. "No, we met after Cynthia and I split up. I don't want her to know. I don't want to worry her."

"What does she think about you having me locked in your office without telling Nina, then?"

"She's concerned about Nina's mental health. Nina hasn't been well since Grace passed away. When Nina came home upset this morning I told her I would speak to you about how we could all support Nina."

"Right." I sighed. "So what about Grace and Marcus? Did they share dreams?"

"No," he started, but his phone pinged before he elaborated and I didn't have the energy to ask for more anyway, so I just nodded. "Good. Ingrid took Nina out to lunch. They won't be home for another hour. The boys are back at your house."

"Okay." I rubbed my hair around on my head.

He moved to put his phone back down on the desk, but it beeped and he looked at it again. "Stuart asked that you check your phone. He's sent you a message." He stood and stretched his back. "I'll go and get us something to eat. The loo is through there if you need it." He pointed to an en suite bathroom to the side of his desk.

"Thank you." I reached into my pocket and pulled my phone out. There were two messages from Stuart asking if everything was all right and I fired off a quick text to say that I was fine. I wheeled myself into the bathroom and catheterised on autopilot. I heard Jeffrey come back into the study just as I finished up. I wheeled myself back to the end of his desk and we ate our sandwiches in silence. After I guzzled down some water, I picked up my coffee and turned to look at him.

"Okay?" he asked as he pushed his own plate away and took a sip from his cup.

"Thank you." I picked up the picture again. I studied every expression for a long while. "Why did my parents leave? Why didn't you stick together?"

"We were all devastated and traumatised, Oliver. Your mum suffered the most. It destroyed her. We never really understood what they did, or what exactly went wrong." His throat bobbed as he struggled to swallow and I thought he wasn't going to elaborate, but he carried on after a moment. "Your dad received a job offer in

America and convinced your mum to go with him. He wanted a fresh start. We all did." His voice cracked again and he screwed his eyes shut for a moment. "I still miss him every day. I always thought they would come back eventually. I still can't believe they're gone."

"Yeah, me neither." My own voice quivered. "How did you and Ingrid get together? And James Bentley and Cynthia?"

"About a year after Cynthia and I split up, Ingrid and I met when I travelled to South Africa. David loved South Africa and kept going on about how he'd found himself in Mossel Bay, and I think I was looking for myself, or something like that, too. I needed to find a new perspective after everything we'd gone through."

"Anyway, while I was there, Ingrid and I struck up a friendship, which quickly turned into love. She agreed to move to England and we got married. And James always had a soft spot for Cynthia, even before everything happened. Their relationship slowly progressed after we split up. But Cynthia deteriorated over the years. By the time Marcus was born, she was hardly recognisable. She killed herself when Marcus was two." He screwed his eyes shut again. "James and I remained friends, but we agreed to never talk about what they did. He couldn't forgive himself. He wanted to pretend that it never happened. And, honestly, so did I." He let out a long breath before scrubbing both hands over his face a few more times. "So much loss, so much pain."

"It's okay." I let out a sigh of my own. "We can talk again another time."

"Thank you." He nodded and closed his eyes as he leaned his head back against his chair.

We sat in silence again while Jeffrey composed himself. Eventually he got up to put the photograph back in the box and locked the closet again. "Shall we sit outside?" He started pushing me towards the door. "Ingrid and Nina will be back soon. Perhaps you should let Stuart know to come back now too. I don't want Nina to be confused about why you're here on your own."

"Okay." I nodded as we made our way out.

He parked me at the patio table and went back inside without a word. I sent a text to Stuart and then sat staring at the lake, my mind still void of logical thought.

"Here you go." Jeffrey placed another cup of coffee and an ashtray in front of me.

"Thank you." I briefly saluted him with my cup and took a sip before I pulled my cigarettes from my pocket.

We continued to sit in silence until Stuart and Zach arrived about ten minutes later. They joined us outside and Jeffrey chatted with them. I had no words available to dispose of and just smoked and stared at the lake. Stuart asked once if I was okay, but accepted without further question when I nodded and said that I was tired.

Ingrid and Nina came back half an hour later and a strange sense of calm washed over me the moment my eyes connected with Nina's. Relief passed over her face as well, but she frowned and quickly put her stubborn expression back on again. It didn't bother me though. I was just relieved to be with her. She said hello to everyone and kissed me on the cheek before she moved behind my chair and pushed me to her room without a word. She stopped at the end of her bed and sat on the edge, so that we faced each other.

CHAPTER 29

"You okay?" I tilted her chin up with my forefinger and she shrugged, pursing her lips together.

"I don't want to fight with you." Her voice wobbled.

"Me neither." I pulled her into my lap. "But please accept that I'm not going to change my mind on this." She opened her mouth to protest, but I silenced her by placing my finger on her lips. "I won't ever agree to anything that could put either of us in danger. I love you too much. I understand how much you miss Grace and that you will do anything to see her again. Really, I do. But you know that it's too dangerous. You know she's not there. Those dreams are just you and me, Nina. It's our connection. It's not her. You must feel it inside yourself?" I paused and she closed her eyes before she nodded with a sigh.

I sighed as well before I carried on. "We have so much to figure out and get used to in our day-to-day lives. Everything is so new and so tricky for us. I just don't even want to consider experimenting with this, whatever it is—these dreams, which we don't understand—while we have so many other things to adjust to. We can spend all day, every day, getting to know each other, in real life. Isn't that better than a weird and disfigured dream?" I didn't miss the desperation in my voice.

"I guess so." She blew out a soft breath.

"Nina." I turned her face up to mine. "Every day with you is better than any dream I have ever had, and every night with you is beyond my wildest fantasies. Nothing makes me happier than having you in my arms. Safe, and soft, and real. I don't want to worry about going into some insane dream where you always get hurt, or go crazy, or both. Please, my love, I beg you. It kills me every time I see you like that." I laid a kiss on her mouth. "We don't know what the repercussions of these dreams are. We have enough to focus on here, in reality."

"It's just overwhelming. I miss Grace so much." A tear slipped down her cheek and she wiped it away before she opened her eyes again. "But I know you're right. She's not there. I know she's not." She sighed, but seemed like she wanted to say something else, so I waited for her to carry on. "I can feel how dangerous it is. It gets worse every time." She lifted her head to look at me.

"Yeah." I nodded, searching her face this time.

"I don't want to put you at risk either."

"Thank you." I kissed both her eyes before I placed a kiss on her mouth. I felt marginally better, but my insides quivered with the premonition that it was only temporary.

We sat outside with the others again for a while, but I was physically and mentally depleted. I didn't know how I was going to carry the weight of everything I had just discovered, along with everything I felt obliged to dig into, while keeping it all from her. All while trying to rebuild my own life. I didn't know how I was going to do it. I didn't think I had it in me. I could feel the overwhelm coiling into a ferocious snake in the pit of my stomach, slowly-slowly injecting its poison through my intestines and up to my throat. It took my last bit of energy to keep myself from having a panic attack in front of everyone.

We hardly left my room the next day and the inferno of worry and stress that was blazing through my veins shrank down to a smoulder. The reality of tomorrow faded into a dim concern that could be dealt with later. As long as we were wrapped in our own corrupt heaven, nothing outside the four corners of my bed mattered in that moment.

In the days that followed, Nina worked longer hours at Harritech. I went to physio. I went to the gym. I studied the textbooks Marcus gave me at my next appointment. It contained a well of information about how powerful the subconscious mind was, but there was nothing about subconscious linking with other people. I found a journal from 1994—it would have been nearly four years since my uncle David passed away and since my mum and dad left the UK. I could see that her life was more intense and her mind more focussed. She didn't specifically mention human experiments, but I found a few vague references to what seemed like research on a similar topic. One entry appeared relevant, but I couldn't be certain.

With regards to the theory of assisted neural manipulation, it seems subjects with a brain-derived neurotrophic factor below 6.83pg/ml show remarkable promise in subconscious molecular evolution.

I was probably one of the least sciency people on the planet, but with the help of the Internet and some creative guesswork, I assumed that it meant that people with a specific congenital marker were more susceptible to subconscious manipulation. It was excruciating trying to decipher her writing, and I didn't feel comfortable reading about my mum's thoughts and emotions any longer. It unsettled me to read about any problems between her and my dad. It showed me a side to them I never knew existed. The few notes she did make about her 'theories and research' used medical terms that were very hard to understand. So really, her journals made me more confused and upset than anything else.

I didn't understand what it meant for me and Nina. I didn't understand how to protect us from having dreams. And I had no idea how, or even if, our lives were linked. So I tried to stick my head in the sand.

I practised with the band. Nina came home. We had dinner. Sometimes we made love. Sometimes we fucked. Often both. We went to sleep. Repeat. Repeat. Repeat. Repeat.

For a couple of weeks it seemed like it was going to be okay and I convinced myself that we had fallen into our own version of normal. I arranged our days so that we always had something to do, mostly screwing each other's brains out. On the surface we were besotted with each other, but I sensed a volatility inside her and it scared the shit out of me. I knew it was only going to be a matter of time until she went off the rails and crashed headfirst into a pile of cocaine. There was no way she was going to just let the dreams go, no matter how much she loved me. It would have been unreasonable for me to expect her to forget about it.

I wanted to tell her what I knew. I didn't want to keep secrets from her anymore. I wanted to make everything right. But I didn't know how to do that and she wasn't stable enough. Not mentally, and certainly not emotionally.

I felt more committed to her than ever. She drifted further away from me. Every. Single. Day.

CHAPTER 38

I came home from the gym early one Thursday evening and found Nina lying on the sofa, reading a book and eating a bag of crisps. "Hey, beautiful." I stopped next to her, a twinge of alarm pinging through my brain. "You're back early?" I made a point of never leaving her on her own. She was either with her folks, or with Zach, or with me. Never alone.

"Hello." She smiled lazily, instantly erasing my anxiety. "Did you have a good workout?"

"Yeah." I pulled off my sweaty T-shirt and bounced my pecs, eliciting another smile from her. "Do you want to have a shower?" My mouth curled up on one side as well.

"Yes, please." She discarded her book and pushed me towards my bedroom. "I'm just going to get some more towels," she called over her shoulder.

"Okay." I shimmied my shorts off and launched them at the basket. "Hurry back," I called.

I turned on the water and waited for the temperature to stabilise before I turned my face up into the warm spray. A long sigh escaped my chest and turned into a deep groan when I felt Nina's fingers working on the aching muscles in my shoulders.

"I didn't hear you come in." I smiled up at her, my eyes widening in appreciation when I found her gloriously naked.

"Lean back." She ran her hands through my wet hair and nudged my head to face forward again. I dropped my head back against her stomach as she moved her hands around and down the front of my chest.

"Come here." I caught her hand and pulled her around me. She swung her leg over my lap and hooked her fingers behind my neck. "You are just… I can't even find a word."

"Ollie." She moved her hands into my hair.

"You overwhelm me." I kissed her neck. "You make me feel completely invincible and utterly defenceless at the same time." I pushed her down on me.

My hands travelled up her back and into her wet hair as I kissed a trail along her scar, making her moan as I sucked on the sensitive spot where the scar ended at the bottom of her neck. She lifted her head and opened her pale eyes, holding my gaze as we brought each other higher and higher until we came together.

All my concerns about our relationship disappeared whenever we were together like this. The way our souls connected made me feel like nothing would ever be able to sever our bond.

"Where did you just go?" She pushed her fingers into my hair.

"I was thinking about how relentless you are."

"That I am." She laughed before she kissed me with a loud smack.

"You smell divine." I wrapped a towel around her shoulders. The freshness of the soap was mixing with her delicious Nina scent and it was more than a little intoxicating.

"It's your shower gel." She bobbed her head towards the soap dispenser. "That's how you smell to me all the time."

"No, it's not that." I inhaled, running my nose up the side of her neck and into her hair. "You have your own unique flavour. Sweet roses, blended with wild fire and smooth honey. It's positively exquisite." I pressed a kiss below her ear.

"Only you can make me sound like a delicacy, Ollie."

"That's because you are. A sweet delight. A naughty indulgence. An extravagant banquet to feast on." I nibbled on her ear, making her squirm and giggle on my lap.

"You are so full of shit." She hopped off, fastened a towel around her and threw one at me.

"And you love it." I caught the towel and bent down to start drying my legs.

"If you say so." She smirked as she squeezed the water from her hair.

"Yes, I do. You pretend that you're not bothered by my flattery, but really, it makes you feel goo-ood, doesn't it?"

"Not really," she mocked me.

"Come on, sweetheart." I flicked my towel towards her. "Just admit it."

"Ow," she squeaked as it whipped against her thigh. "You're such a mushy brute."

"Perhaps." I grinned, lashing the towel at her again, but she caught it before it touched her legs. "Feisty little thing, aren't you?" I laughed, pulling her towards me.

"And you love it." She giggled as she fell into my arms.

"More than you'll ever know." I kissed her ferociously.

"Savage," she murmured, before she pushed herself down on me again.

"Thank goodness you're all right," Stuart teased when Nina wheeled me into the living room. "I was worried you might have drowned in there."

"Yeah." I grinned, pleased with myself. "We got a bit distracted."

"Uh-huh." He cocked an eyebrow. "Stir fry okay for dinner?"

"Actually"—I scratched my jaw, a conniving smile curving my mouth again—"perhaps you could take the night off while I take Nina out on a date."

Earlier at the gym, I'd thought about the idea of going on a date. Admittedly, it was an attempt to do something nice for Nina—to distract her from our isolated routine and the burning questions she must have had as well, even if it was just for one night—but it really excited me.

"That sounds great. Would you like me to drop you off anywhere?"

"No, thank you. Nina can drive us."

The van had gone back to the rental company the week before and Stuart had been driving us around in his car for the last few days. I figured since I was confident enough to transfer myself in and out of his car, I should be fine with Nina's new car too. "What do you think?" I turned my head to her.

"Yeah, I'd love to." Her lips curved up.

"Great. I made a reservation at a restaurant in Godalming." I smirked, very chuffed with myself. Well, the physio at the gym had told me about the restaurant, so I'd only had to ring them up and explain my special needs, but still, it was nice to be more like a normal guy.

"Nice." Nina beamed. "A proper date."

"Well done." Stuart patted me on the shoulder and walked off in the direction of his room.

"What time is the reservation?" She looked at the kitchen clock.

"Eight." I shot it a glance as well. It was just before seven.

"I'm gonna nip home quickly. I have to change." She pulled on her trainers and started looking for something on the kitchen counter.

"You look gorgeous." I reached for her hand and pulled her closer.

"Thanks, but I'm not exactly dressed for dinner." She gestured at her ripped jeans and Ramones T-shirt before she extended her search to the living room. "Where the hell are my keys?"

"Zach dropped you off, sweetheart." Stuart popped his head around the corner and I realised that was why I hadn't seen her car in the drive when I came home earlier.

"Shit, shit, shit." She ran her hand through her hair. "I forgot."

"Is he coming back?" I smiled at her scattiness.

"No. He's in rehearsals until nine."

"I'll take you." Stuart strolled back into the living area, putting his phone into his jeans pocket. "I'm going to pop out to see my mum anyway."

"Thank you." Nina sighed. "I'm such an airhead."

"No worries. I'll help you to get sorted before we go," he said to me.

"Hang on a second." I held up my forefinger. "I have a different idea. Let's go in my dad's car." I felt my cheek twitch on one side.

"You mean the million-pound vintage car that's too sentimental to drive?" Nina hauled in her own eyebrows and I grinned as I nodded. "Noooo. Nuh-uh, I'm not driving that."

"Please." I reached for her hand again. "I would really like us to get there by ourselves. Please." I batted my eyelashes for good measure.

"Idiot." She laughed, shaking her head. "You know I'll do anything for you when you flutter those lashes for me."

"Good girl." I pulled her towards me. "I'll make it worth your while." I smirked against her mouth before I nipped at her bottom lip.

"You'd better."

We left my house in the Aston at quarter past seven and although Nina was nervous at first, she quickly got the hang of the car and relaxed into it. When we arrived at her house she ran off to change, calling to her parents as she barged through the door.

"Bloody hell, lad." Jeffrey whistled from the front door as he spotted me in my dad's classic car. It made me smile. The 1960 DB4 really was the elusive Godfather of Aston Martin and this one was pristine. "Ingrid! Come and see!" he called into the house and Ingrid appeared a few seconds later.

"Gosh, Ollie." She laughed as she walked around the car, peering inside. "Are you sure you want Miss Gone-with-the-Fairies in there to drive this jewel?" She nudged her head towards the front door Nina had just disappeared through.

"Yeah, she's fine." I reached behind the seat. "You're welcome to take it for a spin next time. We're in a bit of a rush this evening."

"Lovely," they both muttered and continued ogling my dad's gleaming pride and joy, while I assembled my wheelchair and transferred back into it again.

"You're doing very well, Oliver," Ingrid commented as she started pushing me into the house, Jeffrey trailing behind us.

"It feels good to be a bit more independent." I smiled.

We went into the kitchen and Jeffrey started the coffee machine as Ingrid parked me at the table.

"Thanks." She kissed him on the cheek. "I'm going to chat with Nina while she gets ready." She took her coffee and left the kitchen.

"Did you get my message?" I asked in a low voice when she was gone. As hard as I'd tried to keep my head in the sand, it was impossible to do nothing at all. Especially when I could feel Nina's frustration. I'd run out of ideas on where to look for answers, so I'd sent Jeffrey a text to ask if he thought it might be okay to speak to Marcus and tell him about our dreams and about our parents' experiments. I was hopeful that Marcus might know something. It was a long shot, but it was something.

"I got your message." Jeffrey nodded as he started unpacking the dishwasher. "I'm off to New York early tomorrow morning, I'm just getting everything ready for the trip, but I was going to reply before I go. Please don't speak to Marcus."

"Why not?" I frowned.

"He doesn't know anything. Of that I'm certain. It would crush him to discover that his mother committed suicide. And I don't want to upset James." Jeffrey stopped what he was doing and leaned down on the table to look me square in the eyes. "I'm serious, Oliver. James is my oldest living friend and we've not talked about this for over thirty years. None of us ever understood what really happened. The only reason I told you is to keep Nina safe. Keep her away from drugs and alcohol. Just do not experiment with these dreams. I don't understand what more you want to know."

"Can you understand that it's unsettling to share dreams? To not have any comprehension of what it means, or how it's even possible? Can you understand that I want some answers? Nina definitely wants answers. She deserves an explanation." My eyebrows knitted together. More than anything, I was terrified by the way I thought our lives were really linked. By the fact that I believed I had to be paralysed for Nina to be alive. I'd not told Jeffrey anything about that and I didn't want to before I understood how it was all connected.

"Of course, but…" He trailed off and my temper flared.

"I don't know what to do, Jeffrey," I interrupted him, shaking my head. "I don't know how to keep her safe. I can't police her twenty-four hours a day. Nina is not as happy as she seems. I won't be able to placate her much longer. I want to be honest with her." I dragged my hand through my hair. "Marcus loved Grace! What if they were the same? What if he can help me?"

"No." Jeffrey shook his head. "Marcus and Grace were not the same. I would have noticed. She would have told us."

"Then what do I do?" I threw my hands in the air. "I can't lose Nina!"

"Keep her happy! Protect her!" He leaned into my face.

We stared at each other for a few long moments, our chests rising and falling in synchrony. I was about to open my mouth again when I heard Nina and Ingrid's voices coming into the kitchen.

"How's that for timing?" Nina grinned as she walked up to me. She was wearing a black knee-length dress. It was plain with a high neckline and long sleeves, but it moulded perfectly around her body.

"Wow," I breathed, running my eyes over her. Her hair was tied into a twisted knot thing at the bottom of her neck and she had the smeared eye business going on again.

"Thank you." She tipped her head as her mouth curved into a cheeky smile.

"Bye, sweetheart." Jeffrey got up and stepped towards her.

"Have fun in New York." She kissed him on the cheek.

"I'll bring you back some bagels."

"See you tomorrow?" Ingrid held Nina close for a moment.

"Yeah." Nina kissed her cheek. "Shall we go?" She moved behind me and I nodded. I sent a glance towards Jeffrey on the way out and he returned it with raised eyebrows. I took a deep breath and let the frustration leave my body. I wasn't going to let my exasperation with him and our situation ruin my date with Nina.

CHAPTER 31

W e drove the ten miles to Godalming in comfortable silence, periodically smiling at each other, while I rested my hand on her thigh. I couldn't stop looking at her. She was glowing with an ease that sedated my nerves. I loved it when she was this comfortable, and I'd not seen it in a while. I loved every version of her, but when she was calm and at peace with herself, it quieted my brain.

She parked in front of the restaurant just before eight and we were seated at our table by five past. I still felt nervous every time I had to go out in public, but nobody ever paid me any unnecessary attention. It was liberating to be surrounded by ordinary people who were not attached to me or my paralysis in some way. We were almost like any other regular couple having a nice meal out and our conversation flowed throughout all three courses.

"So"—I reached across the table to take her hand—"I've been thinking," I started as she took a bite of her chocolate mousse and closed her eyes. "And I wanted to talk to you about something."

"Oh, no." She licked her lips and it distracted me somewhat. "Are you breaking up with me?" she asked, pulling a comical face.

"What? Ha." I snorted as I brought her hand up to my lips before I rested it back on the table.

"Mmm." She grinned as she pulled her hand out. "Are you asking me to marry you?" She caressed her fingers around my wrist and under my palm, distracting me again.

"Eh? No." I laughed, shaking my head. "Not yet."

"Phew." She made a sweeping motion across her forehead. "I think my parents would have a few reservations."

"Probably, but shush and let me talk."

"Okay, sorry." She put on a serious face, but only for a second. "I know." She clicked her fingers. "I'm pregnant. No? Okay, you'll have to tell me then."

I rolled my eyes before taking her hand in mine again. "I want you to live with me. Permanently. With all of your stuff there, and not just staying over every night, sleeping in my T-shirts and using my toothbrush."

"Really?"

"Yeah. If you want to."

"Of course I do." She beamed. "I would love to."

"Great." My smile expanded into a full-blown grin. "That's great."

"Were you expecting me to say no?" She frowned, her dimple winking playfully.

"No. Not really. I guess I was just nervous about overwhelming you or something."

"I love you, Ollie." She leaned over to cup my cheek. "I want to be with you. Always." She stroked her thumb over my lips.

"Me too." I smiled before turning my head to kiss her palm.

"Shall we go home?" She sat back in her chair again.

"Yeah," My lip curled up slowly as I lifted my hand to signal the waiter for our bill. "I'm ready for my Nina feast." I wiggled my eyebrows and she widened her eyes as a mischievous little smirk played around her lips.

I was just putting my card back in my wallet and Nina was pushing her chair back in when the innocence of the evening evaporated as a tall, middle-aged version of Marcus Bentley walked up to us. The grim reality of the dishonesty in our relationship got exposed like an infected wound under a bandage.

"Mr. Bentley." Nina smiled and moved to stand next to me. "Nice to see you. This is Oliver," she introduced me and then said to me, "This is James Bentley, Marcus's dad."

"Pleased to meet you, sir." I nodded.

"Hello, Nina." He offered her a small smile before nodding at me. "Likewise, Oliver."

"Oh, hello." Nina's smile broadened when Marcus appeared next to his father. "How have you been?" She leaned in to give him a hug.

"Nina." He patted her on the back before giving me a stiff handshake. "Oliver." He nodded without making eye contact.

"Marcus." I tipped my head and tried to catch his eye, but he didn't quite meet mine. Something was a bit off about him.

"How are you?" Nina asked again, seemingly not noticing anything strange.

His eyes flicked back to her. "Well, thank you." He drifted off again into a slightly uncomfortable silence.

"Well, we need to get to our table," Mr. Bentley said and offered me a firm handshake before turning to Nina. "I'm pleased to see you're being more responsible, Nina. Second chances don't often come along." He walked off.

"Good night." Marcus blinked in our general direction and followed his dad.

I felt like I was having a small heart attack and brain haemorrhage simultaneously. I instantly knew Nina was going to put two and two together and realise that she'd caused the accident because she'd been irresponsible. Nina was many, many things, but she wasn't stupid. I had no idea how to react and wordlessly started wheeling myself towards the door.

Nina fell into step behind me and pushed me the rest of the way to the car. My heart was marching up my throat to a hysterical beat. Nina was deadly quiet.

"It was my fault, wasn't it?" She searched my face when we were in the car.

"What?" I tried to feign ignorance.

"The accident. That must be what he was referring to." She turned her head to stare out of the windscreen.

"Who knows." My voice came out gravelly and I had to clear my throat to try and get control over myself. "It was a pretty weird thing to say."

"But what do you think he meant?"

"I don't know." I scratched my jaw and felt the muscle twitch anxiously.

She stared out of the front window again, but I could almost see the cogs turning in her head. "Don't you want to know if I was responsible?" She raised her eyebrows and I started rubbing my hair around on my head.

"No." I reached for her hand and laced my fingers through hers. "I don't." I realised that it was the truth. I really wished that I didn't know.

She let out a heavy breath, brought my fingers to her lips and placed a soft kiss on my knuckles without saying anything more.

"Forget about him." I pushed my hand into her hair and kissed her slowly. "Let's go home." I tried to smile and she nodded without responding.

The drive home was despairingly uncomfortable in comparison to the trip we'd made there a couple of hours earlier. I was so nervous that it made me feel quite unwell. There was no way that she was going to let it go. It was going to be catastrophic for our relationship when she realised that the accident was indeed her fault, and, more importantly, that I had known all along. How was she going to feel when she discovered how deep our connection really went? What would the price be for keeping all of this from her?

By the time we'd parked the car and made our way back into the house the silence was choking me to the point where I was physically struggling to breathe. I went to the bathroom and changed out of my clothes with shaky hands. I kept taking deep breaths to try and calm myself, but it took all my effort not to fall apart.

When I returned to the bedroom, Nina was sitting in bed with her legs pulled up against her chest. I moved myself to sit next to her and twisted my body so that I was facing her. She turned towards me before she straightened her back and crossed her legs.

"Please let this go, Nina," I whispered, framing her face with my hands.

She closed her eyes and took a slow breath. "Do you know that it never even occurred to me that I was probably off my face that night?" She lifted her eyes to meet mine. I rubbed my hands down her arms and wrapped them around both of her hands where they were lying in her lap. "When I woke up, everybody was so happy. Nobody talked about that night. I asked Marcus about it when he came to see me, but he said that he had an early flight and we left separately. I just accepted it." She dropped her eyes before she carried on. "It didn't cross my mind to ask him, or anyone, how much I had to drink. I guess I got an involuntary detox while I was in hospital and I've not really thought about drinking or drugs that much the past few months. But the thing is..." She sighed as she moved her eyes back up to mine. "I was permanently hammered before I met you. I really can't remember how much I had to drink, or if I took anything else, but I can't imagine why I would have been sober. I have not been sober for two years."

She screwed her eyes shut and forced a line of tears to roll down her cheeks. I wiped it away with my thumbs, but she carried on before I could say anything. "It didn't bother me that I hadn't heard from Marcus. I've been so infatuated with you, I've not even noticed. We weren't close, but we did talk sometimes. Do you think he's been avoiding me?"

She looked completely lost and I wanted to take her confusion away. I wanted to make it better for her. But I knew that ultimately, I would only make it worse. Much, much worse. Time was running out for us.

"Nina, let it go," I begged her. "It doesn't matter. All that matters is that we have each other." My voice sounded raw. The built-up guilt of the lies I'd told over the past few months suddenly came bubbling up to the surface and I crashed my lips down on hers with more intensity than ever before.

She gasped into my mouth and tangled her fingers into my hair as she moulded her body around mine. I pushed her down on the mattress and framed her face with my hands as I rolled on top of her. Our lovemaking was frenzied and desperate and I hid my face in her neck as I felt tears of overwhelming love and profound shame burn a scorching line down my own face.

CHAPTER 32

I felt like I'd been run over by a lorry when I woke up the next morning. My insides vibrated with pain and my body was drenched in sweat. I rolled over and reached for my phone on my bedside table to press the button to call for Stuart, but my shaking hand dropped it on the floor. A groan forced its way out of my lungs as I slumped back against my pillows again.

"Ollie," Nina mumbled sleepily as she turned into me and flung her arm across my chest.

"Stuart, please." My voice strained under the pressure of trying to keep another groan from escaping.

"What?" She forced her eyes to open and the colour drained from her face when she saw the state I was in. "Shit." She jumped off the bed and rushed over to the door, pulling on her knickers and my T-shirt on the way.

"Ollie?" Stuart appeared in the doorway a few seconds later.

"I'll be right outside," Nina said and I pushed up on my elbows in an attempt to send her a smile, but I only just managed a faint whimper before I collapsed again.

"Bugger." Stuart scurried over and held his hand against my forehead. "When was the last time you went to the toilet?" He pressed on the glands in my throat and I frowned as I struggled to swallow.

"Last night when we came back," I rasped.

"Did you feel okay then?" he asked and I nodded as he helped me to sit up, but I pulled in a sharp breath when my stomach churned.

"Are you feeling sick?" He pulled my wheelchair closer and I grunted my response as I screwed my eyes shut, trying to contain the nausea.

"Hold on." He rushed into the bathroom. "We need to catheterise, but the movement will make you feel worse." He came back with a bucket. "Right." He positioned the wheelchair next to the bed and pulled the covers off. "One, two, three." He helped me to transfer into my chair and handed me the bucket just in time.

"Sorry," I mumbled after I threw up four, five, ten times. Stuart squeezed my shoulder as he pushed me into the en suite. He cleaned out the sick and flushed the toilet.

"This is going to hurt, Ollie, I'm sorry." He parked my chair next to the toilet and started getting the tubes ready. I clenched my jaw and gripped the armrests tightly while he went through the routine. I kept taking long breaths, in through my nose, out through my mouth. I managed to get through it without puking on Stuart, or crying like the little bitch I was.

"Okay, finished." He removed the tube, patted my arm and turned around to open the bath tap. "The shower will feel like bullets on your skin." He felt the water temperature. "The bath is better. Right, one, two, three." He helped me to transfer into the lukewarm water and handed me the bucket again.

"Thanks," I mumbled, after throwing up a few more times.

"Lie back and try to relax. I'm going to get some painkillers and antibiotics." He returned within moments, carrying an IV stand, drip bag and several other medical supplies. "It will be much more effective than tablets, okay?"

I gave him my arm. He set up the IV and inserted the needle into my vein before he injected several different vials into the tube.

"That should start working soon." He took off his latex gloves.

"Thanks." I leaned my head back and closed my eyes, taking more deep breaths as I tried to control the sickness that was threatening to overcome me again. After a long while of lying like that, shivering silently in the tepid water, my body started to relax and my breathing evened out a little. I opened my eyes and looked at Stuart where he was perched on the toilet seat.

"Better?"

"Yeah. Fucking hell." I ran my hand through my hair.

"Acute kidney infection. Takes you down like the plague. You've been lucky so far, but urinary infections are common after a spinal cord injury, and although they're usually mild, it can get severe, like it did this morning. We acted fast, so you should be better in a few days. Anyway, I think your temperature is down," he said as he stuck a thermometer in my ear. "Yep. Almost back to normal. Do you want to have a quick wash while I change your bed?"

I pulled myself up and reached for a washcloth and a bar of soap.

"I'm giving you some more pain relief." Stuart pumped another little container of something into my IV tube after he'd helped me to get back into bed. "It's a heavy dose of codeine, so it'll make you feel sleepy. I'll come and check on you again in a little while, and you'll need another dose of antibiotics in a few hours."

"Thanks." I slumped into my pillows. "Can you ask Nina to come back, please?"

"Sure." He walked out, but Nina came in even before he closed the door. She was dressed in jeans and a white T-shirt and it looked like she'd had a shower.

"Are you all right?" She folded herself around my chest, making me flinch.

"I'm fine." I wrapped my arm around her shoulders, discreetly pulling her away from my stomach and into the crook of my arm. I didn't want her to know how uncomfortable I really was. "It's just a urinary infection."

"You look terrible." She frowned.

"I'm okay." I kissed her forehead and she lifted her mouth to my lips. "Are you working today?" I changed the subject, running my fingers through her hair.

"No, I'm off until next week. I told Mum I'd pop in at the shop and then I thought I'd go home to start packing," she said as she stroked her fingers over my chest. "Although I could stay." She looked up at me, concern pulling her eyebrows together.

220

"No." I yawned. "You should go."

"Are you sure?"

"Yeah. Can't wait for you to live here."

"All right, see you later." She got off the bed and gave me one last kiss. "I love you."

"You too," I mumbled groggily.

Some time later the aroma of something delicious swirled around my nostrils. I squinted through one eye and found Stuart fiddling with the IV, and a plate of steaming food and cup of tea on a tray at the foot of my bed.

"Smells nice."

"Ham and mushroom omelette." He smiled and I also managed half a smile as my stomach grumbled. "How are you feeling? Are you uncomfortable again?" He helped me to sit up, and propped some pillows behind my back.

"A little," I admitted without trying to be macho. He would know if I was playing it down anyway and then he would just tell me off for it.

"You're a bit dehydrated, so I've attached a bag of fluids." He gestured at the second pouch on my drip stand and I nodded. "I'll give you your next shot of antibiotics and another dose of codeine after you've eaten." He moved the tray closer. "You also need to drink lots of water." He pointed to a jug on the side table.

"Okay." I stuffed some omelette into my mouth.

"It's only just gone eleven and all the drugs will make you feel drowsy again, so you should sleep for as long as you can. I'll bring some more food later."

I scoffed down the last bit of egg and drained my tea. "How long do I have to stay in bed?"

"The rest of the day. Probably tomorrow too." He got up and lifted my tray. "We'll see how you feel in the morning." He smiled and I sighed, thinking that it was not what I'd had in mind for my weekend.

It was after four the next time I looked at the time. "Have you heard from Nina?" I asked, realising I hadn't checked my phone all day. I didn't even know if it had been picked up off the floor where I'd dropped it that morning.

"She called a couple of hours ago to check on you and to say that she'll be back around dinnertime." He pulled my phone from his pocket and showed it to me, "I'll keep it with me until you feel better." He put it back in his pocket. "Also, Kellan and the lads are coming at seven. Sophie is up in London today. She expects to get here around the same time."

"'Kay," I muttered as he straightened my covers and removed one pillow from under my head.

It was getting dark when I opened my eyes again and I lay staring at the rain splattering against the bedroom window. I let my mind drift back to the night before. The consequences of Mr. Bentley's comment were going to be tragic. The thought was making me feel sick again. Why would he say something like that to Nina? Did he know she was responsible? Or was he just referring to the fact that she was out of control in general before the accident? Regardless, there was no way I would be able to hide the truth from her any longer. I didn't want to, anyway. I had a moral issue with dishonesty, yet I'd told more lies the past few months than ever before in my life. It made me feel awful to know that I was lying to the person I was supposed to love the most. She deserved to know the truth.

"Can I sit in the lounge for a while?" I asked Stuart when he came in. "I'm a bit fed up with the bed."

"All right." He nodded, but I shifted uncomfortably. "I'll give you some more pain relief. It's paracetamol, so it won't make you drowsy. I'll leave the strong stuff for later." Stuart pumped a couple of vials into my IV. "You don't need another dose of antibiotics until after dinner and they're definitely the ones that make you feel grotty. So you should be okay for a while."

"Thanks." I nodded as he pushed me towards the living room and settled me on the sofa just as the bell rang.

"What's up?" Kellan sauntered in and reclined next to me, kicking his feet up on the coffee table as he draped one arm behind his head. "You look like shit."

"Thanks." I scratched my stubbled cheek.

He opened his mouth to talk again, but his mobile started buzzing. He took it out of his pocket and looked at the display. "Sophie," he said to me before he swiped the screen.

"Hey," he drawled at the receiver, making me pull a face. "Yeah, I'm here now. He's fine. Okay, sure. See you later. Hurry back." He flicked his eyes to me. "So, what are you wearing, gorgeous?" He grinned and I whacked the back of his head, growling to get the fuck out of my house. I definitely didn't have to listen to that bollocks.

"Ha, I'm taking the piss, Ols. She's gone." He wiggled his mobile in front of my face. "She would kick my arse if I spoke to her like that."

"Good," I grumbled.

"Anyway, she's running late." He rested one foot on the other knee.

"Where's Ian and Charlie?"

"They went to sort out our shifts. They'll be down in a bit." He looked at me and I nodded, thinking that working at the Guildberry seemed like a different lifetime to me. "Where's Nina?"

"She went home to pack. I asked her to move in with me." I sighed.

"And you're having second thoughts why?" He studied my face.

"No, it's not that." I shook my head. "We ran into Marcus and his dad last night. His dad made a comment and Nina realised she caused the accident."

"What did she say?" He started bouncing his foot up and down, making me feel sick with the movement.

"She was upset. Confused. I tried to play it down, but she's not going to let it go. It's really bothering her. I woke up sick this morning and we didn't talk about it again." I cleared my throat. "I'm going to have to tell her the truth. Before she speaks to Marcus." I wiped my hand across my face.

Kellan nodded slowly. "Bit of a cock-up."

"She's going to be gutted."

"Yeah." He twisted his mouth, shaking his head slightly. "It'll be worse if she hears it from Marcus though." He unfolded his limbs and patted down his pockets as he stood. "Do you want to come out for a fag?"

"I can't face it." I shook my head.

"How are you feeling, Ollie?" Stuart asked as he walked into the living room at the same time Kellan came back inside.

"Huh-uh." I shook my head, glancing sideways at Kellan, not wanting to seem like a wuss, but also wanting Stuart to know that I wasn't feeling well.

"Let's get you back in bed." He dipped his head as he pulled up my wheelchair. I couldn't stop the groan that escaped my chest as Stuart helped me transfer from the sofa to the chair.

"Will you order some pizza?" I tried to distract Kellan when I saw him frown as he looked me over properly for the first time.

"Sure." He nodded and walked off towards the kitchen to get the menu. "Is Zach coming?"

"Yes," Stuart said as he pulled me back to move me around the coffee table. "He'll be here shortly."

"Ah, here are the guys now." Kellan nudged his head out of the window towards the driveway and I saw Ian's van coming through the gate. "Oh, and Nina." He continued to smile, but it turned into a deep frown. "Charlton?"

Nina's car followed Ian's van up the driveway. I craned my neck to see what Kellan was frowning about. The rain was making it hard to see, but it clearly wasn't Nina driving. It was Charlie. I held my breath as I watched them park under the carport in front of the garage.

224

I couldn't see if Nina was in the van with Ian. Kellan silently squeezed my shoulder, but I didn't react. I couldn't move. There could only be a few possible explanations for the situation and none of them were good. Charlie got out of Nina's car and walked towards the front door, which Stuart had already opened.

"Sorry, Olive," he said, eyes downcast as he handed Nina's keys to Stuart. I continued to stare out of the window.

Ian emerged from his van, nodded at us and walked around to the passenger door. I held my breath as I waited for him to come back into view. He appeared long seconds later, cradling Nina in his arms.

"She won't talk to us." Ian shook his head apologetically as he joined us in the living room. "We found her on the Brook Road. She's on something." He pursed his lips together and glanced down at Nina, who didn't look entirely conscious.

"Let's get you to bed, Ollie." Stuart spoke next to me as an unexpected groan escaped my throat.

"Sorry." I cleared my throat after I'd puked into the sick bucket several times just as we made it into the bathroom.

"Is your temperature up again?" Stuart stuck the thermometer in my ear. "Yes, it's quite high." He fastened the blood pressure monitor around my arm and clipped the oximeter onto my middle finger. "Your BP and pulse are through the roof, Ollie. Try to calm down." He handed me a glass of water and squeezed my shoulder. "Come on, deep breaths."

I gulped down the water before I closed my eyes and focussed on the air flowing in through my nose and out through my mouth, my heart rate fighting to return to normal. Stuart talked to me in a soft voice while he went through the catheterising. He helped me to have a quick wash before I brushed my teeth and changed into some clean clothes. When I was back in bed, he took my blood pressure and pulse again and nodded. "That's a bit better. Keep taking slow breaths."

"I have to talk to Nina." I rubbed my forehead.

225

"How is the pain?"

"I'll manage." I sighed and Stuart lifted his eyebrows.

"I'm giving you another good dose of paracetamol. It should get your temperature down and it's effective pain relief when taken intravenously, so it might take the edge off." He swapped the vial he was holding for something else. I slumped back against the headboard. "I'll go see how Nina is doing." He adjusted the IV and locked his medicine case. I closed my eyes, still struggling to calm down.

"Ollie." My eyes shot open when Stuart spoke next to me again.

"Where's Nina?" I swiped my hand over my face. I hadn't realised I had fallen asleep.

"In my room with Zach." He sighed and sat down on the chair next to my bed.

"I want to talk to her." I pushed away from the headboard, flinching a little.

"She's not coherent, Ollie. Charlie said she was smoking something in her car when they found her. She also had a bag of cocaine on her lap."

"Is she okay?" I shifted, trying to ease the pressure in my lower back. I was starting to feel really uncomfortable.

"She's not in any danger, Ollie. It's going to take a few hours for the drugs to wear off, but she's all right. You have to get some rest. The guys went home to give you privacy. Zach and I are keeping an eye on Nina."

"Bollocks." I groaned and closed my eyes again as he stood up and started fiddling with the IV.

CHAPTER 33

I vaguely registered that I was feeling a little better. It was past two in the morning and the rain was still falling steadily against my window. I turned on the bedside lamp before I dragged my wheelchair closer and removed my IV bag from the stand next to my bed, clipping it onto the smaller peg Stuart had attached to my wheelchair earlier. After I wheeled myself to the bathroom, I brushed my teeth again and went into the living room, where I heard quiet conversation.

"You have a bit more colour," Stuart said when I came through the door.

"Thanks." I looked over to Nina where she was curled up in a tight ball on the sofa, on the opposite side of Zach.

Zach sent a tired smile my way, but Nina only made brief eye contact before getting up and going outside onto the patio. She moved a chair under the shelter of the awning, wiping the water off and pulling her legs up to her chest as she sat down. I followed her out and shut the door behind us.

"What happened?" I stroked the side of her face and tilted it towards me, but she dropped her gaze and turned her head away.

"The comment from Mr. Bentley bothered me. I got hold of Marcus this afternoon and asked him if I was sober that night. He didn't want to talk to me. He said I had to speak to you. That you were both trying to protect me." She sighed and I tipped my head once. There was no point in denying it anymore.

"Where did you get the drugs you took today?" I clenched my jaw tightly.

"I found them in my room when I was packing. I was going to throw them out. But I didn't. I went back to the place where the crash happened and just sat there." A few tears crept down her cheeks. "I don't know how long I was there before Ian and Charlie found me."

I dragged my hand through my hair as I tried to process the situation. "Nina." I reached over to take her hand. She looked back at me with tired eyes. "I didn't want to tell you because I didn't want you to feel responsible for this." I gestured at myself in the wheelchair with my other hand.

She screwed her eyelids closed, allowing a few more tears to escape and roll down her cheeks. I wiped her eyes with my thumbs and moved my hands to cradle the back of her head. "Look at me," I whispered and she peeled her lids open. "I shouldn't have kept the truth from you, but I really did want to protect you."

"Everything is so messed up."

"We can make it right." I swallowed hard, struggling to keep the darkness from overwhelming me.

"I don't think we can."

"No, my love." I pulled her closer. She crawled onto my lap and cried against my shoulder, her body shaking silently. I wrapped my arms around her and buried my face in her hair.

"How can I watch you struggle every day, knowing that it's my fault?" Her voice came out raw. "How can we be together if our relationship is built on a lie?"

"Nina, the way I love you is real. Nothing has ever made more sense to me."

"I don't know how to get through this guilt. This resentment." She rubbed her hand over her heart. "I don't trust you anymore."

"We'll get through it together." I cradled her head, forcing her to look at me.

"Ollie, I'm the reason you're in that wheelchair. You're going to wake up one of these days and hate me."

"I've known this whole time." I rested my forehead against hers. "I have never lied about my feelings for you. I never will. You are everything to me." I wanted to be honest. I wanted to tell her everything. But I couldn't. How could I explain to her that our lives were connected in ways she couldn't even imagine, that I'd chosen to be paralysed to save her? I didn't even know if it was really true. I hadn't even told Jeffrey. I couldn't tell anyone else until I understood what our link was and how it worked. But who was going to explain it to me? "I will always, always choose you above everything. No matter what."

I felt her body stiffen in my arms. She dropped her face in her hands, letting out a soft scream. "That's insane, Oliver!"

"Nina, please." I tightened my arms around her, but she got off my lap and started pacing backwards and forwards, getting soaked in the process.

"It's too much. I don't want this." She let out a sob.

"Please, listen to me." I moved my chair forward and finally got hold of her arm. "This doesn't have to change anything."

"Are you demented?" She yanked her arm away and took a step back. "It changes everything, Oliver! Everything I thought we had was bullshit!"

"No." I dragged my shaking hand through my hair. "Seeing you like this is ripping me apart. What I feel for you is as real as the air we breathe. And you know it!"

"No! I don't!" She shook her head and started pacing again. "And neither do you! Your inexplicable need to be with me—no matter what the cost—is not normal!"

"Nothing makes me feel more worthy than being with you!" I screamed.

"I can't do it." She stopped and stared at me.

"No." It felt like somebody had pulled my intestines out. "Listen to me." I wheeled myself closer to her.

"I can't do it, Ollie. It's too much." She held her hand to her stomach like she was going to be sick. "The weight of this guilt and the intensity of"—she waved her other hand in the air—"everything, it's too much. You're too much."

"Nina." I moved forward again.

"Please." She held her hand up and took a step backward. "I have to go. I can't be with you."

"Nina," I gasped, still reaching for her.

"I can't. You deserve more. You deserve to walk. You deserve to be happy." She kept holding her hand up as she moved towards the door.

"Don't do this!" A sob ripped through my chest.

"I'm sorry." Her face contorted before she swung around, slipped inside and flipped the lock before I could reach her.

It felt like I was having an out-of-body experience. I was floating somewhere in space, looking down at a pathetic guy, sitting in a wheelchair, getting soaked in the pouring rain as he thumped on a door, screaming in agony.

"Open the door." I rattled the glass as I pounded my fists against it. "Open the motherfucking door!"

Stuart's head shot up as he realised that I was shut out. He rushed over and unlocked the door, standing to the side as I wheeled myself inside.

"Nina!" I howled and she stopped at the front door.

She looked me straight in the eyes as she said, "It's over, Oliver."

"No!" I screamed. "Stop her! Stuart! Zach!"

"It's okay, Ollie." Stuart hunched down next to me and Zach went after Nina. "It's going to be okay." Stuart hugged me tightly.

I wailed like an animal. "No!" I pushed him away and flung myself forward, tearing the IV from my arm in the process. I tumbled out of my wheelchair and smacked my face against the coffee table with a thud.

"Oliver," Stuart gasped as I hit the floor. I started seeing spots and then everything went black. I really hoped that I was fucking dead this time.

CHAPTER 34

04:00 A.M.

Faint voices were babbling and I wanted to ask them to be quiet, but my lips were too lazy and my eyes were too heavy. I tuned them out and went back into the darkness.

04:45 A.M.

The all-too-familiar smell of antiseptic assaulted my nostrils and made my throat burn. I turned my head away, but a dull ache on that side of my face made me frown. I turned to the other side again and welcomed the nothingness.

05:00 A.M.

The voices were disturbing me again. They were clearer this time, but I only caught a word here and there. They weren't making sense and they were giving me a fucking headache.

"Shut up," I tried to say, but it came out like a drunken mumble.

"He's waking up," one of the voices said and I turned my head away from it, forgetting that it wasn't a good side to lie on.

I groaned and lifted my fingers to touch the hurt, but my arm didn't want to come all the way to my face. "Whah dufck?" I frowned.

"Oliver," a voice close to me said. "Can you hear me?"

I grunted, forcing my eyelids to lift, but only managing to peel them apart briefly before they dropped again.

"You're okay, Ollie," the voice soothed, but the numbness was too overwhelming to figure out who it was.

05:58 A.M.

The weights on my lids finally eased and I dragged my eyes across the room with effort. My vision was blurred and my head hurt like a motherfucker.

"Oliver," the voice next to me said again and it took me a moment to recognise that it was Stuart. I turned my head towards him and blinked slowly. Gradually, his face came into focus.

"Where am I?"

"In hospital."

"What?" I frowned, my brain not able to form proper thoughts. "Why?"

"You had a bad fall," he said, but it still didn't make sense.

"What?" I lifted my hand to run it through my hair, but it was wrapped in a bandage. I tried to push up on my elbows, but my arms were too wobbly and I collapsed back on my pillows. My mind was murky with deformed sentences.

"What happened?" I searched Stuart's face, forcing myself to stay focussed. "Where's Nina?" My eyes widened and I tried to sit up again.

"Take it easy, Ollie." He gently pushed me back down against the pillows. "You have a concussion, so you have got to take it easy. Stay calm, okay?"

"Where's Nina?"

"She's not here," he said and I drew in a sharp breath as the images started to seep back into my head.

"Where is she?" I persisted, struggling to keep my voice steady.

"She's fine. Zach took her home. You have to stay calm, okay? You fell out of your wheelchair."

My insides contracted painfully at the glimpse of the memory that entered my brain just then.

"You banged your head pretty hard and lost consciousness, so I had to call an ambulance."

"Is it bad?" I groaned.

"No, you're okay." He shook his head, giving me another gentle smile, but not managing to calm my nerves. Not even a little. "You were only unconscious for a couple of minutes, but you were very confused when you came to and since we couldn't check your neurological functions, you needed to have a CT scan to make sure the concussion wasn't serious. But everything came up normal.

"Your shoulder dislocated when you hit the floor, so it had to be put back and X-rayed. But again, there was no other damage, so it will be fine in a day or so. You cut your cheek on the corner of the coffee table and it needed a few stitches. And the IV needle got ripped from your hand when you fell, but the wound wasn't deep, so they just taped it up," he finished with a small smile.

I tried to keep my eyes on him while I took a few deep breaths in another attempt to stay calm and clear my foggy mind.

"I know you're feeling uncomfortable, but your injuries aren't serious and you'll be fine in a couple of days."

I continued to stare at him as I tried to process it all, but the synapses in my brain weren't firing at full speed.

"Does Nina know?" I finally convinced my mouth to ask.

"I don't think so. I told Zach when he called me a few hours ago, but Nina was asleep when I spoke to him. I expect he'll tell her when she wakes up."

"And Sophie?" I puffed out an exasperated breath. My head was still not willing to cooperate.

"Yes. She's here with Kellan. They just went downstairs to get coffee."

"Okay. Thank you." I cleared my throat. "I'm sorry," I whispered.

"Don't worry. Everything will be okay."

I closed my eyes with another heavy sigh. I didn't agree with him at all. Everything was very, very far from okay and I couldn't see how it was ever going to be okay again. Not without Nina.

"When can I go home?" I asked after a while. "What time is it?"

"They want to observe you for a few hours. So probably around breakfast time. It's just before six now."

233

"Okay." I bobbed my head once and closed my eyes.

"Ollie," he said and I peeled my lids open again. "Don't worry if you're struggling to remember everything. It's normal to feel disoriented after a concussion. It won't last long. Your mind will clear."

I tried to concentrate on his face, but I was too tired and dropped my gaze after a few seconds.

"Get some rest." His voice lulled me. "I'll be right here."

06:30 A.M.

I opened my eyes again after what felt like two seconds, but could have been two hours, or two days. There was no way to know. I stared at the ceiling for a while, but the murmuring of conversation pulled at my attention. I rolled my head towards the droning and found Sophie and Kellan chatting to Stuart.

"Hey, Ols," Kellan whispered when my weary eyes met his bright green ones.

"Hey," I rasped.

"How are you feeling?" Sophie asked, stroking the side of my face.

"Okay."

"Do you want to sit up?" Stuart stood and started fiddling with the controls on my bed.

"No," I croaked and cleared my throat, but he ignored me and raised my bed. He propped some pillows behind my back and handed me a glass of water.

"How's that?" He searched my face. "Are you feeling dizzy?"

"No." I shook my head and drained the glass.

"Good. How is your head now? Are you feeling confused?"

"I'm fine."

"Can you remember why you're here?"

"I hit my head when I fell." I let out a heavy sigh.

"That's right. Can you say the months of the year in reverse for me, Ollie?" he asked and I pulled my brows together before rambling them off.

234

"Good. Can you touch my finger, please?" He held his forefinger in front of my face and I tapped it with mine. "Now, touch your nose," he instructed and I rested my finger on my nose. "Good. Now do it a few times. Quick as you can."

My jaw clenched in irritation as I moved my finger between his finger and my nose until he was satisfied.

"That's good. You're fine."

"Wonderful." I sighed sarcastically and closed my eyes again.

I wished he would stop saying that I was fine. Everything annoyed me. I wanted to close my eyes and disappear into nothing.

For the first time ever, I had completely lost the will to fight.

CHAPTER 35

As Stuart expected, I was discharged a few hours later when they were satisfied that I was eating, drinking and reacting like a normal person. I went through the motions like a robot, ignoring Kellan's worried glances and avoiding any attempts Sophie made to talk to me. Thankfully Stuart managed to convince them to go to their own house instead of coming home with us, and when we finally got to the bungalow he helped me to have an uncomfortable wash before he hooked me back up to the IV, using my good arm. I still had to finish the antibiotics for the kidney infection and I was back on the strong painkillers, so he pumped me full of drugs and I zonked out, welcoming the dullness like never before.

I woke up some time later and just lay there, staring at the rain that was still tapping on my window. I didn't bother to look at the clock. I didn't care about the time. It was just a reminder of how long I'd been without Nina. Stuart came in to check on me at some point, but I hardly acknowledged him.

"I brought some food." He unfolded a wheelie tray and placed it next to my bed.

"I'm not hungry." I turned my head away.

"You can't have any more painkillers if you don't eat."

I rolled my eyes as I sat up with an exaggerated grunt.

The narcosis the painkillers brought was my only salvation at that moment. Without them the intensity of my emotions would hit me with full force and I would have to deal with the pain of being without Nina. I couldn't do that.

"Have you heard from Nina?" I pulled my tray closer and slurped at my soup.

"I spoke to Zach…" He paused, looking uncertain whether he should go on.

"And?"

"She doesn't want to speak to you. I'm sorry, Ollie." He sighed and it took all of my strength to stay in control.

The beast in me wanted to throw the bowl of scalding soup at him and tell him to fuck off, but the shred of sanity that was floating around in my head reminded me that none of this had anything to do with Stuart. So I broke off a chunk of bread, dipped it in my soup and brought it to my mouth with so much restraint that it made my whole body shake. I didn't ask about Nina after that.

I didn't experience any symptoms from the concussion after Saturday. The fever and most of the pain from the kidney infection were better by Sunday night. Three days had been all it took for my entire life to fall apart, and the world carried on as if nothing happened. Again.

I tried to convince Stuart to keep giving me the drugs, but he removed the IV and told me I was fine. I had to finish the course of antibiotics by taking tablets twice a day, and apparently I didn't need painkillers at all anymore.

I told him to go fuck himself. He had no idea what fine meant. I was the opposite of fine. My body was mourning the loss of Nina's touch and my heart was raw in the absence of her warmth. My brain could not accept the fact that she had left me just like that. Her name echoed through my mind with every beat of my shredded heart. Remnants of her scent invaded my senses with every breath I took. It was killing me and I revelled in it. I wanted nothing more than the peace of death.

I listlessly complied with the actions I was required to perform. I went to the toilet. I had a bath. I ate my food. And I slept. I kept seeing glimpses of Nina in my sleep and I tried reaching out to her with everything I had in me, but I just couldn't get to her. My thoughts dissolved before they even took shape. It was agonising and it was soul-destroying and I could feel a foreign deep darkness seeping into my spirit.

Sophie and the guys came in to see me on Monday afternoon, but I ignored them. Stuart tried to convince me to go out for some fresh air when the rain finally stopped, but I told him to piss off. By Monday evening, I was once again able to transfer into my wheelchair without any help from him and I only felt a slight stiffness in my shoulder. Yet I still continued to bask in the glory of my self-pity.

I woke up on Tuesday feeling just as miserable as the day before and apart from sticking to a strict toileting routine and having a shower I didn't leave my bed. On Tuesday afternoon, Stuart decided that he'd had enough and orchestrated an intervention. I heard my door open and found him flanked by Sophie, Kellan, Ian and Charlie.

"Bugger off." I turned my head away, but they ignored me and filed into the room, each carrying a dining room chair and seating themselves around my bed. "What the fuck? Get out!"

"Not a chance." Kellan kicked his legs up on my bed and linked his fingers behind his head.

"Nope." Ian copied him. "Not going to happen, Ols."

"Yeah, sorry, Olive." Charlie folded his arms across his chest and leaned back in his chair.

"We'll go after you've talked to us." Sophie raised an eyebrow in an obvious challenge.

"And if you don't talk, I walk." Stuart dipped his head once and widened his eyes to emphasise how serious he was.

"Suit yourself." I gestured at the door and closed my eyes, pretending to ignore them and hoping that they would give up. But of course they didn't.

"What happened, Ollie?" Sophie asked after a long period of silence.

I groaned and turned my head towards her. I didn't want to talk, but it was clear that they weren't going anywhere, so I explained that Nina had found out that she was responsible for causing the accident, but that the hospital somehow messed up the blood test results, which was the only reason she hadn't been charged with drink-driving.

They all stared at me for far too long without responding and it ramped up my irritation another notch. However, it did briefly cross my mind that they had a limited frame of reference. Ian and Charlie knew nothing. I was certain Zach hadn't discussed Nina with Stuart—I certainly hadn't—so even though Stuart would have picked up bits and pieces from conversations he'd overheard, I knew that his professional integrity wouldn't allow him to speculate about anything. Sophie knew I dreamed about Nina and that I believed our lives were connected, although I was certain she was still convinced it was all in my mind. But she hadn't known that Nina had been drink-driving.

Kellan knew much more than the others and I'd told him almost everything about my connection with Nina, the fact that she caused the accident and even about my dreams, but no one knew about our parents' history or about the experiments. I hadn't had the guts to talk to Sophie about it and I wanted to tell her in private, before I told the others. She deserved to know the truth, but she didn't need to hear it with all of us watching her. It was a conversation I wasn't ready to have on that day, especially since Charlie and Ian didn't even know about the dreams yet. So I just focussed on the fact that Nina had caused the accident because she was drunk, but I'd kept it from her because I hadn't wanted her to feel guilty that I was paralysed, but she'd then found out anyway when Marcus' dad made the comment when we ran into them.

"So, she broke up with me," I finished on a sigh and stuck my thumb and forefinger in my eyes as I leaned my head back against the pillows and waited for them to react.

I expected Sophie to talk first, but it was Stuart who broke the silence. "Something's off, Ollie," he said. "I doubt that there could have been a fault with the blood tests from the hospital's side."

"Well, that's just bollocks, isn't it?" I blurted, not caring how intolerable I was. "I know the people in that hospital saved my life and for that I'm grateful, but you are *not* naive enough to think that the bloody NHS doesn't make mistakes like these."

"No." Stuart shook his head without reacting to my tone. "But the police have to follow very specific procedures to request blood from a drink-driving suspect. It will be well documented, NHS or not."

"Yes, and?"

"The police may have taken blood at the scene, which is what they would normally do in serious car accidents. The mistake must have been on their side. But it will also be well documented."

"Stuart's right, Ollie." Sophie nodded.

"Yeah, so what?" I barked. "Doesn't matter where the fuck-up was, though, does it? Not really the point."

"I know, Ollie. But James Bentley is the chief constable, isn't he? Why would he make a comment like that to Nina?"

"I don't know." I turned my head away, refusing to even acknowledge to myself just how out of place James Bentley's comment was. I didn't want to talk any more. Anything I could add from that point onward would only open another can of worms I wasn't ready to face yet.

"If Mr. Bentley was aware that Nina was driving under the influence, it would mean that someone tampered with the blood test results. And that he knows about it. I'm sure you can imagine what the repercussions of that would be. It's a very serious offence, Ollie," Sophie carried on and my irritation flared.

"So what, Soph? It's not going to make any difference to how Nina feels about the fact that she was hammered that night, or that I've been keeping the truth from her all this time. It's not going to bring her back to me."

"Yeah, Ols," Kellan chipped in, "but the whole story is off. Does Zach know anything?"

"Not much." I shook my head. "I told him that Marcus said she wasn't sober, and he admitted that she was definitely drunk and that he suspected they messed up her blood results when she wasn't charged with drink-driving, but I doubt he knows more than that. Zach's not close with Marcus."

"I don't think Zach's seen Marcus since the night of the accident," Stuart said. "He doesn't like talking about it, but Zach blames himself for leaving without Nina that night. He wouldn't have left her if he knew Marcus wasn't going to drive her."

"Really?" Sophie frowned. "So why didn't Marcus drive her?"

"I'm not sure." I sighed. "It bothered me too and I asked Marcus about it, but he said they had a fight and she didn't want to get in the car with him. He said he called them each a taxi. He had to get to the airport and his taxi was the first one to arrive. He assumed that she would wait for hers. He didn't expect her to drive."

"Hang on." Ian jumped up. "That's bullshit!"

"What?" the rest asked in a chorus, but I just stared at him.

"It's bollocks!" he shouted and I bit back a groan. I just wanted everyone to go away, but Ian carried on. "He didn't leave without her. And Nina didn't drive!"

"What are you talking about?" I frowned, sitting up a bit straighter.

"I was outside, getting a"—he gestured at his dick—"from some girl. I was just starting to enjoy myself when Nina stormed out and shouted at someone about something. At first I ignored them and tried to focus on—" He made a cocksucking gesture, proudly smiling at himself.

"Get to the fucking point." I scowled at Kellan, expecting him to whack Ian on the head, but Kellan ignored me.

"So, anyway," Ian waffled on, "I was trying to ignore Nina and focus on what what's-her-name"—he waved his hand—"was doing. But then whoever was with Nina—I didn't care at the time, but thinking about it now, it was Marcus." He paused and closed his eyes as he tapped his forehead a few times. "Yes, definitely Marcus!"

241

"Are you sure, Ian?" Sophie frowned, visibly irritated as well.

"Yeah, Soph. It was him. I'm sure. He jingled some keys in front of Nina's face and my eye caught the Grace tattoo on the inside of his arm. I definitely saw it. He jingled the keys and got in the car without Nina. He started backing out of the parking space and I remember thinking that I hoped he didn't leave her there for us to deal with. So I told Blondie"—he widened his eyes while gesturing at his chest—"to wait a minute and I turned all my attention to Nina. She was having a right strop and kicked the door in as Marcus turned the car around." He shook his head. "I was like, 'Whoa, girl, not cool,' but Marcus stopped, got out and walked around the car. He said something quiet to Nina, which calmed her down, because they hugged and she got into the passenger seat. He walked back around to the driver's side and drove off." He bobbed his head up and down.

"Fuck," I gasped.

"Are you sure, Ian?" Sophie asked again.

"Yes, positive." Ian continued to nod adamantly.

"Why haven't you said anything?" Kellan asked.

"I dunno. I guess what's-her-name finished me off and I forgot."

"And even when you heard that it was Nina who was in the accident with Ollie, it didn't occur to you that the fact that she wasn't driving might have been a useful piece of information?" Kellan's eyes flashed with annoyance and I perked up at the prospect that he might whack Ian on the head after all.

"No, Kel." Ian became agitated too. "I did think about it, actually, but I decided that it would be much more entertaining to keep it to myself until now." He threw his hands in the air. "What do you think, numbnuts? Maybe I thought Marcus was in the accident too? I don't know. I don't keep tabs on him. I hardly know the fucker. Maybe I didn't think I had to analyse every fucking detail of that fucking night other than being fucking grateful that Oliver made it out alive! Maybe I didn't even know that Nina was or wasn't supposed to drive herself? For fuck's sake!" He jumped up, making his chair fall over, and stormed out.

"Actually"—Charlie got up—"I think Ian did mention something about Nina throwing a tantrum just before we all left that night. I guess it wasn't important at the time and then things got crazy after that." He sent Kellan an angry look and followed Ian out. Kellan groaned as he unfolded his limbs and went after them. I sighed, vaguely remembering Ian telling us something like that.

"Shit," I breathed, covering my mouth with both hands. "We have to tell Nina."

"I'll call Zach." Stuart got up and reached for his mobile as he moved away.

"Shit," I said again, rubbing my hair around my head.

"This is serious, Ollie." Sophie stood and started pacing the room. "Something's not right."

"Yeah." I nodded. "Should we call the police?" If Marcus' dad, the chief constable of Surrey police, was corrupt in some way, would the police even be able to help us?

"Not yet." She stopped and tapped her chin with her forefinger. "We have to make sure that we have our facts straight before we make any accusations. I have contacts in the police who I trust, but I need evidence before I get them involved. We have to get Marcus to tell us what happened." She started pacing again.

"We have another problem," Stuart said as he walked back into the room. "I think Nina is in trouble. Zach had to go to rehearsals today, and Nina was going to meet him in Guildford for lunch, but she didn't show up and she's not picking up her phone."

"Maybe she forgot?"

"No, Ollie; Zach and Nina have shared a tracking app since New York. Her phone is at Mr. Bentley's house."

"Fuck." I breathed in and out a few times, feeling like I was going to be sick.

"Zach's been trying to get a hold of Marcus and Mr. Bentley for the past twenty minutes. They're not answering their phones either." He shook his head. "He's on his way back now."

"How about Jeffrey and Ingrid?" I rasped in a shaky voice.

"Jeffrey's in New York until Friday." Stuart pursed his lips together. "Ingrid's at the shop. Zach doesn't want to worry them yet."

"Do they know she broke up with me?" I forced the words out.

"Yes. Ingrid was worried that she might go off the rails and didn't want her to be at home by herself, but Nina convinced her that she was okay and that she just needed some time on her own." He sighed deeply. "Zach said she really seemed okay."

"Fuck." I buried my face in my hands. My first instinct was to have an outburst, but I had to pull myself together and think with a clear head. "Can you get Zach back on the phone, please?"

Stuart got his mobile out again and swiped the screen, handed it to me when Zach picked up.

"Hi, Zach," I said.

"Oliver, something's wrong." He sounded stressed. "I just phoned the health centre and Marcus didn't show up for work today."

"Shit." My breath caught. "What about Mr. Bentley?"

"I can't get hold of him. He's not at work either. I've left rehearsal." His voice disappeared for a moment. "Sorry, bad reception. I'm on my way to Mr. Bentley's house now."

"What's the address?"

"It's The Stables, Meadow Green Lane, in Brook," Zach rambled the address off. I could hear him honking at someone. "I'm about twenty minutes away. I'll meet you there." His voice started breaking up again.

"Thanks." I handed the phone back to Stuart and dragged my wheelchair closer. I threw the covers off and transferred into my chair. Stuart helped me to get out in record time and we were on the road less than ten minutes later.

Kellan, Sophie and Stuart went to the hospital. Stuart still had friends there and they were going to look for Nina's medical records. And Sophie was going to speak to her contacts in the police. Charlie, Ian and I pulled up in front of Mr. Bentley's house exactly thirty-seven seconds before Zach.

CHAPTER 36

Meadow Green Lane was one of those posh, single-track countryside lanes where all the houses had names, the gardens were manicured to perfection, and the front doors were painted in colours with names like duck egg blue and elephant's breath grey. Marcus' dad's house, The Stables, was a converted barn behind a gravelled courtyard. Zach rang the old-school bell and banged on the door a few times before we started trying the knob, but it was locked. We were about to turn around when the door swung open, revealing Marcus Bentley looking dishevelled and sporting a bruised cheek, gaping lip, and blood-soaked sweater.

"What happened to you?" Zach frowned.

"Come on." He cleared his throat and wiped his lip on his shoulder. "We have to go." He shut the door behind him. I was still trying to figure out how to react when Marcus started pushing me towards the street where Charlie was parked.

"Whoa." I held up my hand. "Hang on. Let's talk first."

"I want to help." He continued to move away from the house. "We'll talk in the car."

"All right." We approached Ian and Charlie where they were leaning against Charlie's car. "He's coming with us," I told them when they both pushed away from the car and moved towards Marcus defensively. They frowned and nodded, but didn't relax their postures. I transferred back into the car and Charlie jumped in behind the steering wheel, while Zach and Ian dismantled my wheelchair and stuffed it into the boot before squeezing into the back seat on either side of Marcus.

"Go," Marcus ordered and wiped at his still-bleeding lip again. "Go!" He peered back at the house.

"Where to?" Charlie frowned at him and I also twisted in my seat to face him.

"The hospital."

"Why the hospital?" I asked, my heart rate picking up its pace.

"She's there," Marcus answered. "I'll try to explain on the way. Just go." He rubbed his hand across his eyes and I noticed that his knuckles were bruised and bleeding too.

"What happened to you?" I repeated Zach's question as I gestured at his injuries.

"Listen to me. Nina wasn't driving the car that night. I was."

"We've figured that out, yes." I bobbed my head and raised my eyebrows.

"Why did you make it look like she drove? You don't drink! Why not just take her home like I fucking asked?" Zach grabbed Marcus by his sweater and pulled him over into his space.

"I was drugged up to the eyeballs, Zach." Marcus pushed Zach away from him. "I've been surviving on a diet of cocaine and zolpidem since Grace died." He kept his eyes on Zach, who nodded, but didn't drop his scowl. "I didn't want to compromise Nina, but I wasn't rational either. I rang my dad to ask for help."

"Is your father involved in all of this?" I asked.

"Yes. But he's not working alone and he's definitely not in charge."

"Who else?" Ice splintered in my veins.

"I don't know. But we have to end this today, Ollie." He kept me pinned with his stare until I nodded.

"What are you talking about?" Zach grabbed Marcus and shouted into his face again.

Marcus pushed Zach back again. "You need to let me talk to Oliver before we get to the hospital."

"Zach, please," I urged as well and Zach lifted his hands and sat back into his side of the seat.

"Who else is involved?" I asked again, even though Marcus had already said he didn't know.

"I really don't know. At least two more people. I suspect they might be doctors or medical personnel. But I'm not certain."

"My mum wrote journals," I blurted, but he didn't look surprised. "She mentioned the initials JH, and also an MH. Does that mean anything?"

"No." Marcus frowned.

"What's your dad's involvement?" I asked. "What does he know about me?"

"I'm not entirely sure about that either." He shook his head with a short jerking movement.

"Then what the fuck *do* you know?"

"I have gaps in my memory, Ollie. I've been trying. My mind isn't clear; it's difficult." He blew out another heavy breath and I felt an unwelcome twinge of sympathy for him, but I managed to stop my face from showing any emotion. "Oliver." He pinned me with his eyes again and I immediately knew something terrible was going to leave his mouth next. I closed my eyes and stopped breathing as I waited for him to continue. "I had a microchip implanted at the base of my skull."

I opened my eyes to see him twist his neck to show me the back of his head. He lifted the hair at the bottom of his skull and revealed a deep one-inch cut that was still bleeding heavily through a small piece of surgical tape that looked like it had been flicked on as an afterthought. The back of his sweater was also soaked in blood.

"What the fuck?" I whispered at the same time the others gasped.

"You have one too. And so does Nina. Ollie, they've been tracking you. Hearing everything around you. Probably influencing you in some way. I am certain that I've been sedated and manipulated. So has Nina…" He trailed off and I couldn't help the snarl that escaped my mouth as the reality of the level of intrusion hit me in full force. To know that whoever the fuck they were had been integrated in every aspect of our lives was just hideous.

"Fuck," I whispered again. This was worse than anything I could ever have imagined. "Just give me a second." I closed my eyes and tried to envision the true malice of what we'd been living with. "How did you get it out?"

"I removed it just before you arrived at my father's house. It's not as deep as it seems. I will remove yours and Nina's safely. Mine had to come out in a hurry."

"Is Nina being drugged at the moment?"

"Yes, I think so."

"What?" Zach shouted.

"Wait!" Marcus growled.

"Can they track me now?" I panicked, scratching at my neck.

"No, I don't think so. At least not at the moment. I think my father was the person who monitored us. I found an app on his phone and disabled the microchips, but I don't know how long they'll be offline. That's why we have to hurry."

"Who's in charge of all of this?"

"I don't know! I have not seen anyone else's face, Oliver. The only person I can identify is my father." He pressed the palms of his hands into his eyes. "My father received a call on Thursday night, before we showed up at the restaurant. He made that comment to Nina on an instruction from someone else. I was sedated. I expect they knew that Nina would want to talk to me about it." He shook his head. "When I came to my senses again on Monday, I was concerned about Nina and got hold of her on the phone. She was very unsettled." He inhaled slowly. "I went over to her house this morning, but she wasn't there. When I returned to my father's house, I found him in his study with Nina's phone in his hand. He wasn't himself. He was aggressive and unhinged when I tried to take her phone off him. He said that I wasn't allowed to leave the house. I had to physically restrain him." He rubbed his hand across his eyes again. "It wasn't my intention to hurt him."

"What did you do?" Zach asked.

"I had to get away from him. He was alive when I left him. We need to get to Nina." He looked haunted.

"Where are they?" I asked just as we turned into the hospital's main entrance.

"The app I found on my father's phone located Nina's chip at a laboratory in the basement of the pathology department," Marcus said and the goosebumps on my arms flared up again. It sounded grotesque. "Park around the rear there." He pointed Charlie towards the staff parking.

"Basement of the pathology department." Zach had his phone pressed against his ear. "They've been drugging her," he said into the phone and then listened before he looked at Marcus. "Is it morphine?" he asked and Marcus nodded. "Yes, morphine," he said into the phone again. "Okay. We're going in now. Call the police."

Zach put his phone in his pocket and shot out when Charlie stopped the car. Ian jumped out of the other door and ran around to get my wheelchair, but Marcus put his hand on my shoulder. "I'm sorry, Oliver, about everything. I loved Grace. So much. I would never hurt Nina."

"I know." I held his gaze for a moment before Ian yanked my door open.

"There you go, Ollie." Zach pushed my wheelchair right up to the side and I lifted myself into it. Charlie pushed me across the car park as they ran towards the doors. Marcus and Zach kicked the doors and Ian held them open as Charlie and I barged through.

Zach ran ahead down the dim corridor, slamming into empty rooms and coming back out again. I was getting more worried with every step we took. This wasn't just a couple of students experimenting with drugs, this was proper horror. We stormed through a second corridor and abruptly came to a stop as Zach rammed open the last set of doors.

A whole lifetime of terror manifested itself in the few seconds it took my brain to register what my eyes were looking at.

CHAPTER 37

The room was bigger than I'd expected. There were no windows, but the white tube lights on the ceiling made it look too bright. Sheets of thick, clear plastic enclosed a surgical area on the left, and on the right was a lab area with high-tech equipment and computers. Half a dozen people scurried around, all wearing full surgical uniforms and face masks, just like any hospital ward.

The guys and I all gasped in unison.

Right in front of us, not more than ten feet away, inside the surgical area, Nina lay in a hospital bed attached to many wires and monitors. She wasn't conscious and I could see that her heart rate was struggling to reach forty beats per minute. Even with my limited medical knowledge I knew that was much too slow.

The person leaning over her with a syringe in his hand was familiar to us all.

"Welcome." Dr. Harold turned around with a warm smile that still reminded me a bit of my dad and somehow made me feel an unwarranted sense of reassurance. My eyes landed on his name tag. Dr. Malcolm Harold. MH. "You're right on time. I just administered a third dose of morphine, forty milligrams," he explained conversationally, like he had done so many times while I was in hospital. "She will shortly start experiencing the symptoms of an opioid overdose. In an hour from now, I will administer another forty milligrams, which will be fatal. However, if you cooperate, Oliver, and help us conclude our research, I will administer an adequate dose of naloxone to stabilise her." He stroked Nina's cheek, but the horror of his words didn't quite get time to register with me.

An animalistic sound came from Marcus and he shot off across the room. It took me several long moments to realise that amongst the group of masked medical personnel, there were also two more familiar people in this hellhole with us.

"Grace!" he cried and collapsed on top of an identical girl in the bed next to Nina's.

My brain refused to reconcile what my eyes were looking at. Not the fact that Grace was lying in the bed next to Nina. Not the fact that she was breathing, or that she had a heartbeat. And above all, not the man typing on a computer, at a large white desk, in the corner of the lab area.

Jeffrey looked up from the numerous widescreens in front of him. "Oliver." He nodded at me with a casual smile. Like I'd just rocked up at his house to take his daughter on a date. Jeffrey was JH! Nina's father was involved in all of this!

A few things started happening at the same time and Jeffrey's smile didn't quite get a chance to settle on his lips.

Charlie and Ian flew at Dr. Harold and grabbed him by the arms. Zach gave me a final shove towards Nina.

"Nina!" I clasped her hand in both of mine. "Why are you doing this?" I shouted at Jeffrey.

He opened his mouth to speak, but Zach launched at him before any words left his mouth. Zach grabbed Jeffrey by the throat and started lifting him out of his chair, but a nurse appeared behind Zach and stabbed him in the neck with a needle. Zach collapsed onto the floor and two people moved him to an empty bed, opposite Nina and Grace.

Jeffrey resumed his typing at the same time the nurses stabbed Ian and Charlie in the neck and transferred them to beds next to Zach. Someone wheeled a bed next to Grace's and restrained Marcus to it before Dr. Harold dusted himself off, walked over and attached Marcus' arm to an IV drip.

"Right." He turned to me as if the past eighty-two seconds of chaos hadn't just happened. "Like I was saying, if you cooperate I will make sure Nina is stable. She will live. If you don't, she will die."

"What do you need?" I grasped Nina's hand even tighter.

"It's not that simple, Oliver." Jeffrey got up and walked over to join Dr. Harold next to Nina's bed. "You have an important choice to make." He smiled and the blood froze in my veins.

"Why are you doing this?" I tried to get myself closer to her. "How can you do this to your children?"

"I created these children for this specific purpose, Oliver," he explained calmly. "I am doing exactly what I intended to do. But you're wasting time. Do you want to save Nina or not?"

"Of course I want to save her! What do you want from me?"

"That chip we implanted in your neck controls your paralysis. If you choose to save Nina, we will induce you in a coma and you will live in your dream world, with Nina, much like Grace is now. Nina will be alive." He flitted his eyes to where Grace and Nina were lying. "If you choose to let Nina die, I will remove the chip and you will walk out of here, unharmed."

"Nina!" I screamed. "I choose Nina!"

"Wonderful." Jeffrey walked back to his desk.

"Very well." Dr. Harold nodded at a couple of nurses I didn't notice behind me. They moved me into the empty bed on the other side of Nina and hooked me up to an IV.

"Why? Just tell me! Why?" I shouted to Jeffrey, who was typing on his computer like it was a normal day at work.

"It's a very long and interesting story, Oliver. But I'm afraid it's one you will never hear. Just know that you are changing the way the world works. One tiny anomaly in your DNA was all we needed to create the perfect link. You have the last piece of the puzzle running through your veins. Your mother started an experiment that is going to revolutionise humankind—the way we fight wars, the way society operates—and Harritech is at the heart of it all. Your mother was a pioneer. It's a shame she wasn't brave enough to follow through. I was sad to have them terminated. But as they say, needs must." He shook his head before he turned away and continued typing.

"You killed my parents!" I yanked on my restraints. "You destroyed my family! I hope you burn in hell!"

"He's ready." Dr. Harold interrupted my outburst. "Good luck, lad." He smiled down at me and within seconds I found myself flailing in a dark and relentless ocean. Wave after wave after wave crashed on me.

CHAPTER 38

"**O**llie." Nina's voice sang over the wind. "I'm here, my love."

"Nina!" I screamed.

"I'm here." She suddenly appeared next to me and the storm settled, the water still, the sky clear.

"We have to get out of here." I thrashed around again, trying to grab onto her, but she paddled around me.

"It's lovely, isn't it?" She laughed, frolicking in the water, just out of reach. "Come on, Ollie. Have some fun with me."

"Wake up!" I shouted. "It isn't real!"

"Why can't you just give me what I want?" she snarled and the sky darkened again. "You're such a fucking liar! You say you love me more than anything. I want to stay here. If you love me so fucking much, then stay here!" she howled into the wind as the waves became higher and higher.

"Wake up, Nina!" I screamed and kicked, trying to get closer to her. "Wake up!"

"Ollie!" She gulped and went underwater for a moment. "Help me!" she choked when her head came out again.

"Nina!" I put all my strength into my body to get to her. I clasped my hand around her ankle just as another wave crashed on top of us. Its force slammed all the breath out of my lungs and every muscle in my body was on fire, but I did not let go of Nina. I dug deeper and deeper into the water. Underneath the waves. Like I used to do when I surfed with Claudia and her brothers in Ericeira. I dragged Nina through the water until I could wrap both my arms tightly around her waist.

254

When the next wave rolled over us, I kicked my legs as hard as I could to get us to the surface before the following one crashed on top of us. I filled my lungs with as much air as I could fit into the two seconds I had before the wave broke. I dove us back down just as it started cresting above our heads. I sealed my mouth over Nina's and breathed all my air into her lungs.

CHAPTER 39

When I tried to kick my legs again to get us back up to the surface for the next greedy gulp of air, I realised I was lying on my back, paralysed, in a bed in a bright white room. Reality slammed into me with a force that made a guttural scream explode from my mouth.

I frantically searched the room and my eyes fell on Stuart as he pulled on a pair of surgical gloves and opened a plastic box. He ripped the cover from an enormous needle and extracted the fluid from a glass vial at lightning speed. "Hold her down," he said to Kellan, who I hadn't realised was standing next to him. Kellan pushed Nina's shoulders into the bed. I just lay there, tied to the bed, drugged up, watching like a delirious fool.

"Open her shirt," Stuart ordered and Kellan ripped it open, exposing her chest, before holding her down again. "I'm going to inject two milligrams of naloxone into her heart. It is a pure opioid antagonist and it will counter the effects of the morphine. Time two minutes when I say go," he told Sophie, who was standing next to Kellan.

Where had the three of them suddenly come from? She got her phone out and swiped at the screen.

"Right." Stuart flicked the syringe. "One, two, three." He stabbed the needle into Nina's chest and slowly pushed down the syringe. "Okay, go." He nodded at Sophie and she clicked the phone.

Time slowed to a stagnant pace and stretched out far beyond eternity. My head wasn't right. I felt like I was watching every-thing from a distance. I vaguely noticed that Ian had his back braced against the wall while he gripped Dr. Harold in front of him and restrained both his arms behind his back. Charlie was beating Dr. Harold to a pulp until Ian dropped him on the floor in a bloody heap and started pulling Charlie away from him. Charlie jerked his arm away from Ian and landed his boot in Dr. Harold's face as he walked past him towards us.

Zach had both his hands around Jeffrey's throat and shoved him backwards into his desk before he jumped on top of him and began pummelling his fists into Jeffrey's face. I turned my head back to Nina and saw her back arch away from the bed. Her high-pitched scream vibrated through my soul. Dozens upon dozens of police officers and paramedics swarmed into the room and Stuart called commands at everybody.

My sister nodded at Stuart and moved away from Nina to talk to the officers. They tipped their heads at her and continued to move around the room, arresting some people and talking to other people.

Marcus was back on Grace's bed, entwined with her as he sobbed into her chest until several paramedics surrounded the bed and blocked my view. I looked around the room to try and find someone to explain the situation to me, but a noise came from Nina.

Stuart injected another ampoule into her chest. The seconds decided to take even longer. I heard my heart valves open and then close in slow motion as they struggled to shift the blood through my veins. My muscles tensed as I waited for her to react, but she didn't. She was still. Her arms hung limply from her sides. I felt the trickle of tears as they slithered down my cheeks.

"She's stable. Go!" Stuart called and took a step back from her, lifting both his hands in the air. Four paramedics stepped in and connected her to oxygen, an IV line, and a heart monitor before they lifted her onto a stretcher and left with her.

"Why are they taking her?" I screamed as the fog in my head suddenly cleared a bit. "Nina! Stuart?"

"She needs to get to the hospital, Ollie." Stuart came over to me. He untied my arms and helped me to sit up before he moved my legs so that they were hanging off the side of the bed. "Take some deep breaths and just sit for a minute, all right?"

"Is Nina going to be okay?"

"I don't know." He dragged my wheelchair closer, but two paramedics came up to us before he could elaborate.

"Oliver." One nodded as she attached a blood pressure monitor to my arm. "My name is Sam, and this is Ross." She gestured at her colleague, who was pressing a stethoscope against my chest. "We need to make sure you're okay before we move you, all right?"

"Okay." I nodded, blinking a few times.

"You're good to go." Ross smiled after a little while and helped me to transfer into my wheelchair when Sam removed the blood pressure cuff from my arm. "Take it easy for a couple of days and tell Stuart if you experience any nausea or confusion."

"Drink plenty of water," Sam said as she scrolled through several pages on a tablet. "And make sure to complete the antibiotics you were taking for the kidney infection."

"They're all fine," Ross said to Stuart. "I'm prescribing a mild sedative to help them sleep tonight." He wrote on a form and handed it to Stuart. "Look after yourselves." He smiled again and they walked off.

"What's going on, Stuart?" I asked, my voice hoarse. "What happened?"

"You were all drugged, Ollie," Stuart said and I looked over to Ian, Charlie and Zach, who were all talking to the police. "The boys were only given a very low dose. Just enough to knock them out for a few minutes to restrain them. They were already checked over and are all fine. You were given a bit more, so you might feel drowsy for a few hours, but like the paramedics said, you're all okay."

It was like my ears were incapable of successfully transferring the words to my brain. I was still staring at Stuart when two police officers came over to speak to us.

"Mr Lawrence, Mr Davies, I'm Inspector Thomas." A short, solid man nodded at Stuart and I. "This is my colleague Special Sergeant Khan." He gestured to an equally short, but lean woman.

"Yes," Stuart said, but I didn't respond.

"We won't keep you, but we need you both to sign this declaration before you go." Inspector Thomas held out a clipboard and a pen. I stared up at him in a daze without taking it from him.

"Miss Lawrence appointed herself as your legal counsel," Special Sergeant Khan interjected when I still didn't respond. "This declares that you agree for Miss Lawrence to represent you, and that you will contact us within forty-eight hours to give your formal statements."

I found Sophie near the door talking to two other officers, but I managed to catch her eye and she nodded at me once. I wordlessly took the clipboard from Inspector Thomas and signed where he indicated. Sophie, Kellan, Ian, Charlie and Marcus had already signed the forms. I handed it to Stuart when I was done.

"Thank you." Inspector Thomas took it back after Stuart signed and they both turned around without another word. I tracked them as they walked back towards Sophie. Inspector Thomas shook her hand and left the room.

"Good luck." Special Sergeant Khan leaned over to give Sophie a brief hug.

"Thank you, Rajean." Sophie nodded with a small smile. She said her goodbyes and walked over to me.

"What's going on, Soph?" I managed to ask. "Why do we need legal counsel?"

"Don't worry about it now, Ollie. You're not in trouble. But the police need to know everything you know. They're just doing their job."

"Okay." I looked up when I realised Stuart hadn't said anything since the police gave us the statement to sign. He had moved a few steps away from me and was talking to one of the paramedics before he nodded, took out his phone, made a call, nodded again and came over to me.

"Is Nina okay?" I momentarily snapped out of my trance.

"We don't know yet, Oliver." He hunched down in front of me. "I just spoke to the hospital and she's in the critical care unit."

I closed my eyes and let out a long breath.

"Ollie." Stuart spoke again and I slowly opened my eyes. "I know you're in shock and that you want to get to Nina, but it will be at least ninety minutes before we know anything. We can go to the hospital now, to wait, but I have to insist that you cooperate when we get there. You need to eat something, have a drink of water and go to the loo, okay? Like the paramedics said, you still have to take your antibiotics. The last thing you need is for the kidney infection to flare up."

"Okay." My brain still wasn't firing on all cylinders. I was struggling to understand the ramifications of everything I had just witnessed. Nina! Grace! Dr. Harold! Jeffrey! Marcus! "Is Marcus okay?" I dragged my eyes over to Sophie. "And Grace?"

"Marcus is all right. He needed stitches and he broke his wrist. He'll also have to take some medication to manage opioid withdrawal. He'd been drugged for months. But he's going to be fine. They took him to A&E to be patched up and checked over. The guys just left to go and be with him. They'll look after him, Ollie."

"And Grace?"

"I don't know." Sophie's voice caught. "The paramedics took her away without explaining."

I scanned the room again. I counted at least two dozen police officers in white protective gear and goggles, collecting evidence and dusting surfaces. "Can we go?" I looked at Sophie again and she nodded again. Stuart started pushing me toward the door and Sophie stopped to talk to Special Sergeant Khan, who had come back inside.

When we got outside there were a dozen more police officers, multiple patrol cars, two police vans and one ambulance. We drove around the hospital to the visitors' parking area, went to the cafe by the main entrance, ate something—although I can't remember what—drank water—I assume—and went to the toilet, in silence.

Stuart led us into a waiting area in the critical care unit. When we got there, Ingrid and Zach were sitting near the door, grasping each other's hands. Ingrid's face was pale and her eyes were red and swollen. Zach's face was expressionless. Stuart parked me on the other side of Ingrid and she took one of my hands in her free hand. Stuart and Sophie sat on the other side of Zach.

We continued to sit in silence for an hour and sixteen minutes—that's four thousand, five hundred and sixty seconds—until a doctor entered the room and called Ingrid and Zach outside. I stopped breathing.

After twenty-two minutes—that's another one thousand, three hundred and twenty seconds—Ingrid and Zach came back in and finally broke the silence.

"Nina is going to be okay," Ingrid said softly after she sat down next to me and took my hand in hers again.

"Thank you," I whispered and let out a long breath. "Can I see her?"

"Yes." Ingrid squeezed my hand. "Only for a minute. They had to intubate her, so she's sedated."

"Okay." I nodded and Ingrid got up and pushed me out into the critical care unit. I kept my head down and blocked out the five other patients who were also in there, fighting for their lives.

Nina's bed was in the far right corner. A nurse was sitting next to her. "We have to monitor her closely for the next twenty-four hours," she explained.

Nina was entangled in tubes, wires and monitors. "May I hold her hand?"

"Yes. I can give you a moment." The nurse moved to the side and spoke quietly to Ingrid at the foot of Nina's bed.

I took Nina's hand in my own and placed a soft kiss on the back before I held it against my cheek and closed my eyes for a few breaths, my mind empty.

"It's time to go, Ollie," Ingrid said after one hundred and eighty-two seconds. I pressed a kiss into Nina's palm and put her hand back on the bed.

Ingrid pushed me back to the waiting room, where she sat down next to me and took my hand in hers once again. "Ollie, I know you want to stay here until they wake Nina tomorrow." She screwed her eyes shut for a moment and a tear dripped down her cheek. "But I would be very grateful for some privacy, please."

"Why?" I shook my head.

"Oliver." She sighed. "Did you notice that Grace was in the bed next to Nina's just now?"

"No." I felt my eyes widen and my heart jerk. "Is she going to be okay?"

"No, Ollie. She's brain-dead. She's on life support. She's never going to wake up. We'll have to say goodbye to her again." Ingrid let out a quiet sob and covered her mouth with her hand.

"Did Jeffrey do all of this?" I whispered, feeling my own voice break as glimpses of the horror in that white room started coming back to me.

"Yes." Ingrid nodded and more tears rolled down her cheeks.

"Oh, Ingrid." I put my free hand on top of hers. "Is he in custody?"

"Yes." Ingrid's eyes went hard. "And he will stay there." She took a deep breath and her eyes softened for a moment before she wiped a tear from my cheek. "Ollie, I don't want to force you to go, but I would like to try and process this in private before Nina wakes up tomorrow and I have to tell her."

"Okay." I sighed and felt more tears roll down my cheeks as well. "I understand."

"Thank you." Ingrid leaned in and hugged me tight. I put both arms around her and held her while we both cried quietly. Eventually she pulled away, fished a tissue from her bag and blew her nose. "I'll let you know when she's awake."

"Thank you." I cleared my throat as I wiped my nose on my sleeve.

Stuart stood and held Zach close before he kissed him softly, squeezed Ingrid's hand and pushed me out of the room. I assumed Sophie followed us out.

CHAPTER 48

We drove to my house in silence and I noticed it was only just past eight p.m. as we came through the front door. It felt like an eternity had passed since we'd left the house earlier that afternoon.

"Can I give you something light to help you sleep for a few hours, Ollie?" Stuart said. "The paramedics prescribed it earlier. It's safe to take with your antibiotics. You too, Sophie?"

"Thank you." I nodded. "Will you stay?" I moved my eyes to Sophie, who was also nodding at Stuart.

"Yes." She blinked. "The guys are coming too. Marcus was just discharged from the hospital. They went home to get clothes."

"Will you sleep in my room?" I sounded like a scared child. I didn't care. That was exactly how I felt.

"Yes." Sophie gave me a small smile and I dipped my head in thanks.

Stuart helped me get ready and settled in bed before he gave me my antibiotics, a small pink tablet and a glass of water. I didn't hear the guys come back, or Sophie come in.

When I woke up again it was nearly one a.m. and Sophie was snoring softly with her back turned to me. I saw dim light down the hall and heard muted conversation coming from the living room. I got into my chair and wheeled myself through.

"How are you feeling, Ollie?" Stuart got up when he spotted me.

"Better. Did you get some sleep?"

"Yes. A good four hours."

"Good. And you?" I moved my eyes to Kellan, who was lying across the armchair.

"Not yet." He shook his head and suppressed a yawn. "We were keeping an eye on him while Stuart was asleep." He jerked his chin to where Marcus was passed out under a blanket on the long sofa.

"Where's Charlie and Ian?"

"I just sent them to have a sleep in my bed," Stuart answered as he got his medicine box off the sideboard.

"Go sleep in my bed, Kel," I offered.

"Thanks." Kellan stretched in the chair without making an attempt to get up.

"Please take a sleeping tablet." Stuart held one out to him.

Kellan popped it in his mouth and took a swig from his beer bottle. He stretched one more time and yawned before he unfolded himself. He bent down to hug me tight and slumped off to my room without another word.

"Would you like to sit outside? It's quite mild." Stuart opened the patio door and turned on the outside lights.

"Thank you." I wheeled myself out, grabbing Kellan's cigarettes and lighter off the coffee table on the way.

"I'll get us some food." Stuart closed the door behind me. I sat staring at the darkness as I attempted to process everything that had happened.

Stuart came back with toast, scrambled eggs and coffee after I finished my second cigarette.

"Thanks." I took a sip before I cut into my food. "Have you heard from Zach?"

"I just spoke to him. Nina's still stable."

"How's Ingrid holding up?"

"She's devastated. She didn't suspect anything." He shook his head.

"I don't think anyone did," I agreed. "Is Zach okay?"

"I don't know."

"And Marcus?"

"Not good."

We ate in silence until Stuart spoke again. "Sophie will explain more when she wakes up, but the police found all the proof they need to put everyone responsible away for a very long time. Dr. Harold kept detailed records at that lab. Mr. Bentley is dead. Marcus didn't kill him," he added quickly when I pulled in a sharp breath. "He shot himself."

"Shit." I blew out a heavy breath. "It's like my brain is incapable of accepting that something like this can happen. I can't even begin to understand how it's all connected."

"I know." Stuart rubbed his hand over his face.

"I can't see how Marcus will ever recover. And how will Nina, Ingrid, and Zach ever be able to move on?" My voice broke and my eyes burned. "How could Jeffrey do this to his children? To his wife?"

"I know." Stuart sighed again.

"He told me he had my parents killed," I said and immediately started crying. I dropped my face in my hands and allowed myself to sob for long moments. "I suppose it doesn't make a difference how or why—they died, they're still gone—but it's like the small bit of closure I did have has come undone again."

"I'm sorry, Ollie," Stuart said as the tears continued to roll down my cheeks.

"I'm assuming they kept Grace on life support the past two years to experiment on her? And on Marcus?" I still couldn't get my voice to stay steady and I noticed my hands were shaking too.

"I think so."

"Did Marcus know about Grace?"

"I don't think so. He went to sleep as soon as they came back and the guys said he didn't talk in the car. But I don't think he knew."

I sat in silence for another minute. "Were they going to experiment on Nina as well? I mean keep her there. Like Grace?"

"I think so." Stuart cleared his throat. "And you."

"Shit." I dropped my eyes and rubbed my hair around on my head. "Do you know how they got Nina and I to have the same

265

dreams? I understand how they could have influenced our emotions and beliefs with suggestive therapy, but how did they actually get us to have the same dreams?"

"I don't really understand, but they found evidence to suggest that certain people who share a similar set of congenital markers are more likely to form a deep emotional connection with each other. It seems they manipulated you to be unconditionally committed to Nina, which made you much more susceptible to control."

"So do you think the dreams were all suggestive and manipulated?"

"I don't know. I suspect that you really did have variations or fractions of those dreams, but that they somehow got enhanced and then transmitted to Nina. Whether it was by suggestive mind control alone, or by your subconscious brains really connecting somehow, I do not know."

"Do you think that someone does know?"

"This is an enormous medical misconduct case which has carried on for three decades, Ollie. Some of the world's most esteemed authorities and scientists will get involved to find the necessary answers."

"Will people know about us? Will they experiment on us?" My heartbeat thumped against my skull and I broke out in a cold sweat.

"No, Ollie." Stuart shook his head. "That would still be major misconduct. Human experimentation is strictly against the law. In every country in the world. Your identities will be protected. I meant that the research your parents and Dr. Harold did will be studied. After you talk to the police, you won't have to talk about it again."

"Oh, right. Good." I took another slow breath, noticing my hands were still shaking as I lit another cigarette. "What was Jeffrey's part in it? Why would he do this?"

"I'm not sure. But I do know that Harritech manufactured the microchip you have implanted in your neck. And I think they were going to sell the technology to the government. The police will tell us more when they can."

"Okay." I nodded, but couldn't stop my breath from hitching when I remembered about the microchip in my neck. I cleared my throat, but my chest became tighter and tighter. "Fuck." I tried to get my lungs to expand, but they couldn't cooperate. "The chip," I stuttered as I bent over and tried to force some air into my lungs.

"Ollie, shh. Someone's coming over later today to remove the microchip. It's a small procedure. We can safely perform it at home. It just needs to happen under police supervision with a registered doctor present. You're going to be okay." He reached over to squeeze my shoulder.

"Okay." I finally managed to take a normal breath, although I could still feel my heart thumping against my sternum. "Dr. Harold said something about inducing my paralysis with the microchip. Do you think I'll be able to walk when they remove it?"

"Gosh, really?" Stuart's head shot up, his eyes alarmed. I nodded jerkily. "I didn't know about that, Ollie. I honestly don't know. I suppose anything is possible, but I'm not sure how that will work. Don't get your hopes up, please."

Stuart and I sat outside and talked for a very long time. Although he didn't know much about what exactly they were doing, why they were doing it, or who they were doing it for, he did explain again that every national and international law would protect our identities. Sophie was also going to get a high court injunction to ensure that all necessary precautions were taken before any research would be handed over to anyone for analysis.

I then asked about Nina's recovery from the overdose and Stuart explained that she should come off the ventilator after eighteen hours and that it could then be another six hours until she started waking up, which meant that she would be asleep until the next evening. I wouldn't get to see her until well into the day after that, if I was lucky. Every fibre in my being begged to be with her, but I was grateful that Stuart managed my expectations.

I told him about my mum's journals. About how it all started innocently, but escalated to her brother's death. He told me that James Bentley had left a suicide letter that had made him seem like a victim in his own way. He'd been devastated after Marcus' mum, Cynthia, committed suicide. He'd wanted to understand why and how her brain was so affected by the experiments. He'd never wanted to hurt anyone. I tried to find some sympathy for Mr. Bentley, but I couldn't. I couldn't fathom how Marcus would ever recover. He had nobody left.

Eventually Marcus got up and came to sit outside. Stuart went back in and Marcus and I sat and smoked in silence until Stuart returned with coffee and a plate of pastries.

"Thank you." Marcus swallowed down two croissants with his coffee and lit another cigarette.

"Better?" I asked and he made eye contact with me for the first time.

"Yeah. Thanks."

"I'm sorry about your father. And about Grace."

"Thank you. I'm sorry about everything."

"None of this is your fault, Marcus."

"I suppose." He dropped his eyes for a few beats. "They had me in that room with Grace, I don't know how many times. I kept telling myself I was dreaming, or hallucinating, I don't know, I didn't want to believe it. Yesterday, yesterday was the first time I realised it was really her. I don't know." He dropped his head on his chest, rubbing the back of his head. I didn't know what to say. What could I possibly say?

The next twelve hours passed in a haze. We all slept and talked in intervals. Zach phoned twice to say that Nina was still stable. Nobody asked about Grace. We knew there was no point. Sophie explained the purpose of the statements we were required to provide the police and the way the legal system would protect us. At some point Special Sergeant Khan and Inspector Thomas came to the house with a doctor.

"Mr. Lawrence." Inspector Thomas leaned forward on the sofa. "We have evidence to suggest that your paralysis might be induced by the microchip in your neck and that it will be rectified as soon as the chip is removed. This is Dr. Wesley, and if you agree he can remove the chip now." He nodded at the doctor next to him.

"Oliver." Dr. Wesley offered a small smile. "I realise this must be highly unsettling, but I can assure you it's a simple and safe procedure. If the medical reports I studied are correct, you will experience an immediate recovery."

"And if they're wrong?"

"The procedure for removing the chip is the same. It's implanted at the bottom of your skull, just underneath your skin. It's an artificial neural transmitting system which works by bypassing and imitating biological neurons. If the artificial neural transmitter is removed, normal neurotransmission will resume."

"Was the computer system that controlled our chips shut down?" I asked, my heart thrashing around in my chest cavity.

"Yes." Dr. Wesley nodded.

"Then why am I still paralysed, if the system is disabled?"

"The microchips work on individual and independent operating systems. Communication took place via the software system. But the chips were also preprogrammed with certain parameters. Yours is blocking the neurotransmission between your brain and the L4 and L5 lumbar discs in your spine." He paused, but continued when I didn't respond. "Oliver, I'm certain you will recover when I remove it. In the unlikely event I'm wrong and you don't regain full use of your legs, I can guarantee that there is no other risk to you. Marcus removed his own chip with a kitchen knife and bathroom mirror without any side effects. I removed Nina's chip this morning without any change in her medical profile. In my professional opinion there is no reason to not remove it, but since you're conscious and coherent, I do need your consent. So, if you could sign this"—he held out a tablet and electronic pen—"we could get you walking before the hour is up."

"Okay." I covered my face with shaking hands before I took the tablet, flicked through the form and scribbled my name.

"Thank you." He nodded, went through the form again, signed his own name and handed it to Inspector Thomas.

CHAPTER 41

S tuart pushed me to my en suite, where Dr. Wesley laid out a surgical pack on the bathroom counter. They sanitised their hands, covered our clothes in surgical coats, put a headband and hair net on my head to lift my hair from my neck and cleaned my neck with surgical alcohol.

"Ready, Ollie?" Stuart smiled and I nodded without uttering a word. "Right, sharp scratch coming," he warned before he injected my neck. "Okay, keep still." He gently pushed my head forward to lengthen my neck before he held my head against his stomach with both hands.

I stared at my lap, willing my heart to beat slower. I felt a faint tickle on the back of my neck, a little pull, a couple of tugs and then Stuart said, "All done, Ollie."

I kept my head bowed as I took several slow breaths. At first I wiggled my toes in my trainers without saying anything to Stuart and Dr. Wesley. I did it again and a lump swelled in my throat and my heart beat inside my brain as blood rushed to my ears. I didn't register what Stuart and Dr. Wesley were doing as I first straightened my left leg. I assumed they were cleaning up, discreetly giving me space. I straightened my right leg and then bent over at the waist and hung my head between my legs for several seconds. I pinched both shins right above my socks before putting my feet on the ground, gripping the arms of my wheelchair and pushing myself up.

"Steady, Ollie," Dr. Wesley said as he took my right arm.

"Just stand for a moment." Stuart took my left arm. "Slow steps." He started walking me forward, into my bedroom, out onto the little patio and onwards to the back garden.

I stood outside, turned my head to the sky and took more slow breaths.

"Try on your own," Dr. Wesley said and he and Stuart let go of my arms and walked beside me for a couple of laps around the back garden.

I came to a stop in front of the little gate that led to the fields and the forest and I fell to my knees in front of it. I bent over at the waist and screamed into the damp grass. A raw, savage scream. Like a wild beast. "All this time!" I shouted at the soil. "All this motherfucking time!" I slammed my fists into the lawn. Eventually the rage left my body. I unfolded my foreign limbs and turned around.

Stuart stood behind me, tears rolling down his cheeks. I towered over him. Head and shoulders. I bent down to hug him and he gripped me tight. "I could not be happier, Ollie."

After we walked back into the house and had another emotional episode in the living room, Special Sergeant Khan and Inspector Thomas took our official statements and then spoke to us for a very long time.

Jeffrey and Dr. Harold had been at the helm of an enormous terrorist initiative to manufacture and program the microchips, which they were in the process of selling to a rogue government organisation, which Mr. Bentley worked for. Nina and I had been the last, and only successful, two test subjects in a long list of experiments. Like Jeffrey had said just before they sedated me, I did indeed have an anomaly in my DNA, which enabled a definite and complete link with Nina through the microchip. The microchips were going to be used to control people. To overthrow the government. To create an army. A dystopian society.

The reason I'd been manipulated into believing that I had to be paralysed in order to save Nina's life was because the test subjects proved to be more cooperative, more loyal and much more susceptible to mind control when they had a strong emotional link with each other and believed they were responsible for each other's safety. Everything Nina and I had been through was a test. To test my commitment to Nina. Jeffrey had told me about my mother's involvement, about their early experiments, to make me feel even more responsible for Nina. Every single thing was to reinforce my loyalty to her.

My mother's initial experiments indicated that test subjects with certain biological similarities were more likely to link more effectively. When her brother died, she'd dedicated her life to identifying the exact congenital markers that were responsible for the link. That was why we'd moved so often. She'd studied people all over the world. She'd finally identified the specific genetic variation when I was fourteen and at the same time discovered the gene in my DNA. She then spent the next two years to find a safe way to manipulate the gene in order to protect vulnerable people, like me. Jeffrey had found out about my mum's research and he'd had my parents killed before she discovered a solution.

Even though I had already known Jeffrey was responsible for the accident which killed my parents, I still lost it when Sophie broke down as Special Sergeant Khan told us. As soon as the reality of the malevolence we'd been subjected to manifested in Sophie's mind, she just crumbled. Kellan held her as raw sobs shook her body. I wordlessly got up, walked to my room, shut myself in my bathroom and repeatedly punched my fist through the door until Charlie forced his way in, wrestled me to the floor and kept his arms wrapped around me until Stuart bandaged my bleeding knuckles.

Sophie and I eventually pulled ourselves together again and the police resumed their talk. Grace had a microchip. Her genetic markers weren't a match for Marcus', not like Nina's and mine, which was why Grace had suffered a brain haemorrhage. Like my uncle David. Like all the others before Nina. There had been hundreds of test subjects over the span of thirty years. Over twenty babies had been genetically created or modified, including Grace and Nina. None of the test babies had survived past their twenties, when they were experimented on. Until Nina. They couldn't experiment on us until after we met in real life. Everything after our first meeting at the club was manipulated. The crash was staged in order to test our DNA to confirm our genetic match, to implant the microchips and get initial control over us. Our injuries were all simulated. Superficial wounds like fractures, bruises and cuts were inflicted.

Dr. Harold had not discovered the anomaly in my DNA, or the way it significantly strengthened the link, until I was in hospital. They'd never known about my mum's journals, or that I had the key to create the perfect link in my DNA. The key was always that in addition to being physically attracted and genetically compatible, one of the test subjects in the pair also had to have the DNA anomaly. Nina and I really were attracted to each other and we really had fallen in love. So had Grace and Marcus. But only I had the DNA anomaly. And, as soon as they discovered what the anomaly was, they knew how to produce it artificially and were able to create links between all people who were genetically compatible and attracted to each other.

Grace was never going to wake up. Her brain function was too low to recover, like every other test baby who had undergone experiments before her. They were going to take Grace off life support the next day.

Marcus fell apart when they told him that, even though he already knew. We all knew. He'd still hoped. Of course he had. I'd hoped too. The reason Marcus had survived was because he wasn't a test baby. And neither was I.

After Marcus calmed down, Special Sergeant Khan and Inspector Thomas went on to assure us that nothing like this would ever happen again. Because of Marcus—all the digging he'd done, finding the app on his father's phone, finding the location of the laboratory, realising he was being drugged, and mostly because of the way he'd fought to get away from his father and lead us to the laboratory—an entire terrorist organisation and its members had been identified and dismantled. I knew the price Marcus had paid was far, far too high though. He had nobody left.

Special Sergeant Khan and Inspector Thomas assured us that our identities would be protected. We would never have to talk about anything we'd gone through ever again. It was all over.

At quarter to six that evening Ingrid called to say that Nina had been successfully taken off the ventilator and that she was breathing well on her own. We all sighed in relief and continued to sleep, eat and talk in shifts, while we waited for the call to say that she was awake. At three the next morning Zach called to say that Nina had started waking up for short periods around midnight and was fully awake around two a.m.

"Can I come and see her?" I urged.

"Sorry."

"Can I just talk to her?" I pleaded.

"Ollie." Zach sighed. "Not yet, please. We'll call you when Nina wants to see you, okay? We can't prioritise you. Please give us time."

I wanted to demand that they let me be there. I wanted them to want me to be there for Nina. For all three of them. I didn't want them to go through losing Grace for a second time alone. I didn't want Nina to find out what her dad had done without me being there. But I couldn't force myself on them. I was fully aware of the fact that I was the only one who'd walked out of the situation semi-okay. Of course they couldn't prioritise me. Furthermore, Nina had broken up with me. I knew the only right thing anyone could do was to ask Nina if she wanted to see me. I knew the only right thing I could do was to wait without putting more pressure on them.

"I understand." I finally sighed as well.

"Thank you." He rang off.

The next call eventually came that afternoon. Grace had been put to rest at ten in the morning. They'd brought Nina home at lunchtime and she'd asked to see me at three p.m.

My heart hammered in my throat from the moment I ended the call until I walked into her room and her eyes connected with mine.

274

Her eyes were dead though. Dull and entirely void of emotion. She looked like a breathing corpse. She didn't comment on the fact that I was walking. It didn't surprise me.

"Hi," I breathed and rested my hand on top of hers.

"Hi." She dropped her eyes to my hand and dragged them back up to my face without moving a muscle.

"I'm so sorry, Nina," I whispered.

"Me too." She closed her eyes as tears slowly rolled down her cheeks. "Ollie, I need time."

"Nina…" I blinked, my own eyes burning.

"I can't put myself together while I'm with you. I need to do it on my own."

"I'm not going to stop loving you." My voice broke. "I will wait. As long as you need me to. I will wait until you're whole. I will do whatever it takes to make myself whole. But I'm not going to stop loving you."

She stroked my cheek before she leaned in and kissed me softly on the lips. I cupped her face and tried to draw out the kiss for as long as possible. She threaded her fingers in my hair and our tears melted together as we whispered over and over about our infinite but brutal love.

"Please go, Ollie." She eventually pushed against my shoulder.

I caressed her face one last time and wiped her tears with my thumbs before I laid a final kiss on her beautiful mouth.

I walked out of her room without looking back.

CHAPTER 42

NINA

14 MONTHS LATER

T he Guildberry is packed with crazed fans. The atmosphere is electric. I almost feel a spark of excitement, but I don't allow it to settle in my bones. Not yet. I've been preparing for this moment for a long time. I know I'm ready. I just need to stay calm.

The lights on stage dim and the club goes quiet. I try to take in a shaky breath. The lights come on, the crowd explodes and a smile finally plucks at my lips as my eyes fall on the band. I can't believe we're finally in the same room. For the past six months they've been on tour. Several songs have made it into the charts. They're the next big thing.

Since our microchips were removed, Oliver and I don't share dreams any more. We don't have any forced connections or manipulated feelings. Yet every cell in my body longs for him. My heart whispers his name with every beat it takes. When I close my eyes, I see his face. When I'm awake, I daydream about his touch.

"Hey," Oliver drawls into the mic and a lump forms in my throat. "It's good to be back." He offers a half-smile to no one in particular before he turns his head to nod at Ian.

Ian taps them in and for ninety minutes I stand like a statue in the middle of a storm. I watch in awe as they woo the crowd with song, after song, after song. I don't think I blink. I definitely don't breathe like a normal person. I don't want to miss a second. It's nearly over. What if he doesn't want to see me? I try to force some air into my lungs.

"I want to bring our last song to life here," Oliver announces. "Where it all started."

My heart stops. Oliver wraps his hand around the mic and takes a deep breath before he leans forward. He closes his eyes and I start weaving my way through the crowd. People are mesmerised. They don't notice me. I'm almost at the front when he opens his eyes and starts singing.

Remembering yesterday,
She's crumpled up and so am I.
Brushing dreams and fears away.
When do we laugh, when do we cry?

All too soon, I'm laid bare,
Infatuated with her face,
Feeling lost in my nightmare.
Her eerie song is hard to trace...

Her gaze can set me free,
I burn where she touched me.
I'm the junkie, she's the high,
Lucid illusion, open eyes.

Emotions stagger, what might be
Unfurls in explicit detail.
Severity in my blood screams,
But this harsh love can never fail.

Her gaze can set me free,
I burn where she touched me.

I'm the junkie, she's the high,
Lucid illusion, open eyes.

A painless hell, feeding my rage.
The beast inside me wants to reign.
Release me from this unseen cage.
Her pale blue eyes heal me again.

A thousand waves crash down on me,
A brutal flash and I'm awake.
Hallucination? Am I free?
My real heart is hers to take.

Her gaze can set me free,
I burn where she touched me.
I'm the junkie, she's the high,
Lucid illusion, open eyes.

Her gaze can set me free,
I burn where she touched me.
Is this real, or is this fake?
Am I asleep, or wide awake?
I'm the junkie, she's the high,
Lucid illusion, open eyes.

The song finishes and I'm right at the front. His eyes fall on me. I have tears streaming down my face. I'm still struggling to catch my breath. His face dissolves into something I can't explain.

"Thank you." He smiles into the mic without moving his eyes away from me. The guys flank him to curtsey and they leave the stage.

The crowd is whistling and clapping around me. I'm still frozen on the spot, unable to move. What now? My heart starts hammering. My breath is coming out fast. Too fast. Did I imagine him looking at me? What if he didn't really see me? Worse—what if he did see me, but doesn't want to speak to me? I'm just about to push my way back through the crowd to find Jack and beg him to take me to Oliver—I will plead from my knees if I have to—when a hand folds around my elbow.

"Come with me," someone says in my ear and I look up to find Marcus. I nod frantically and he steers me through the crowd, out of the back and into a dressing room under the stage. He pushes me inside. I swing around to see him leave, closing the door behind him again. I lean my forehead against the door and try to take a breath.

"Hi." Oliver's voice speaks softly behind me. I snap around, lose my balance and almost fall against his chest.

He's so close I can feel his warmth on my skin, his breath on my face. He's tall, at least a head taller than me, and big. So many muscles. My eyes travel from his impossibly wide chest over the spot where his pulse is tapping on the side of his throat, over his cut jaw, his full lips and finally his pale, pale eyes.

"Hi." I straighten and try to remember how to make my heart beat. I close my eyes. Try harder to get some oxygen into my lungs. Open my eyes.

Ollie watches me with a small smile pulling at his lips. "You came."

"I came." I nod multiple times and then hiccup. I can't get myself to be normal.

"Have you had enough time?" He suddenly looks vulnerable.

"I have."

"Thank fuck for that." He laughs and takes my hand, pulling me closer.

I collapse into his rock-hard chest and his arms automatically wrap around me. He holds me so close I can feel his heartbeat against my cheek. For the first time in over a year I really breathe. "Welcome home, my love," he says into my neck and I come undone.

"I'm sorry it took me so long." I start crying. "I never stopped loving you."

"You're here. That's all that matters." He captures my lips and I know that this is it. Every tear. Every moment of pain. The loneliness, the lost hope, the new hope, and every other emotion in between. It was all worth it to get to this moment. I am who I want to be. He is who he wants to be. We are together because we want to be. Not because we need each other. Not because we can't live without each other. Only because we want to be.

Full stop.

ACKNOWLEDGEMENTS

Writing is an easy obsession. Like all art, it's a desire that can comfortably consume every thought. For me it's a dream that lives inside all the fibres of my soul. It's a dream that's perpetually urged on by a combination of uncontrolled imagination, deep admiration for fellow artists, and an undying love for reading, but mostly by an obsessive need to create. It's not difficult to find the drive or courage to write.

But publishing a book is scary and hardcore. Publishing this book required a team of skilled and professional women who I still can not believe I got lucky enough to work with.

To my Editor, Eleanor, you are a wonder and I will always, always appreciate every letter you type, or delete. Your thoughts are golden. To Sam, Design extraordinaire, your creativity, talent and infectious laugh enthralled me from the start. To Laura, Typesetting pro, thank you, and thank you again, for your patience, guidance and insight.

And to the lovely, amazingly clever Marketing Queen, Vickie, without you this book would still be gathering dust on my laptop. You are invaluable!

Ladies, I am so grateful to all of you and I hope I get to work with you for a long, long time!

To Lisl for your time, input and advice on the very first, very rough, draft all those years ago. To my bestie Ben, for your help on the lyrics and spending many, many hours trying to teach me about music. I cherish every moment spent with you. I still don't know how to play my guitar, though.

To my gorgeous Ames, for inspiring me, challenging me, and understanding me like nobody else. You are my heart. To Riaan, for encouraging me, and for sustaining me, but most of all, for believing in me. You are my home.

To every reader – I will never, ever, be able to get over the fact that I can call myself an author and without you it would not be possible. You are everything! Thank you, thank you, thank you! From the bottom of my heart!

9 781738 576111